ENAMORED IN DEATH

A Story of Thanatos and Makaria

MOLLY TULLIS

The Bibliophile Blonde LLC

Copyright © 2022 by Molly Tullis / The Bibliophile Blonde LLC

All rights reserved.

Editing by Damoro Design.

Cover art and design © 2022 by Damoro Design.

No part of this book may be reproduced in any form or by any electronic or mechanical means, including information storage and retrieval systems, without written permission from the author, except for the use of brief quotations in a book review.

For everyone who struggles to love their shadow self.

A NOTE FROM THE AUTHOR

The beauty of mythology is how it transforms as it is retold, from generation to generation. *"Enamored in Death"* tells the story of Thanatos, a god who does not have many stories written about him. This story includes original plot lines and mythological references that do not follow existing accounts to the letter.

"Enamored in Death" is a Greek mythological retelling that contains graphic violence, swearing, and sex scenes.

PROLOGUE

"There will be no resurrection. This death is final. This death will echo through the ends of time." — Malialani Dullanty

People thought death was violent.

It wasn't.

The softest, sweetest embrace of a lover couldn't compare to the kiss of death. It was like slipping into a warm bath or falling asleep after a long day. Death only came after the rage and the anger, once the preludes and trappings of ego had been stripped away. Death came in the darkest hour of the soul, whisking it away—not to nothingness, but to rebirth.

For some, there was penance. For others, there was solitude. For the sweetest souls, there was reunion. There was laughing and kissing and gaiety in the fields of Asphodel, amongst lovers and family members who had made the great journey first; lovers and family members who had whispered to Thanatos the names of their beloveds still living, pleading that he would be kind to them when the time came.

Death was always kind.

Thanatos was always kind.

It was the gods and man who were cruel, who were violent. But pain needed an avenue; grief needed somewhere to go. So the souls of the world looked down on Thanatos with eyes that flickered with fear and with crooked, pointed fingers.

Beware of Thanatos.
Be careful you don't catch Thanatos's eye.
Be cautious of Thanatos.
All good things come to an end...because of Thanatos.

There was no soul on earth that held a greater capacity for love than Death himself—but who could fall in love with the reaper?

※

HERA, queen of the gods, was dead. It hadn't caused the stir amongst the Olympians that one would assume. Zeus appeared relieved, even if he tried to keep his expression stoic when the news broke. The other gods were simply glad to be freed from her schemes. Hecate, the Goddess of witchcraft, had delivered the killing blow in a battle between the goddesses that shook the Underworld. Thanatos had been there, his body expanding and his immortal form taking over as he swept over the fields and whisked away what had remained of Hera.

This meant that it was business as usual for the Pantheon. They kept up appearances and refused to let the news of Hera's death leak to the mortal realm. If the prayers of Hera's worshippers fell on deaf ears, so be it. Hera's capacity for answering prayers and tending to mortals was the same whether she was dead or alive. The world went on, none the wiser.

Thanatos had known that one way or another, Hera would

meet her downfall amongst the gods. She had been too petty and too cruel, which was almost impressive, by a god's standard. Thanatos had not known that she would come to her end by Hecate's hand, although she was one of the most powerful gods among them. He had *really* not known that Hera would come to her end by the hand of Hecate because she was defending the man she loved. Of all the things that had shocked him most in his long life—which was a very short list—Hecate falling in love was near the top. Almost even more so, was the fact that Aeëtes, her new consort, had seen her embody the necromancer and loved her all the more for it.

Thanatos had watched as the power of the dead had overtaken Hecate's features, as it had morphed and twisted her body. He had been sitting next to Aeëtes on the battlefield when it happened, and he had felt a sharp pang of melancholy for Hecate.

Surely no one could love such a creature of death and deconstruction—no one could see this and find tenderness for it.

Thanatos had thought that with no judgement for Hecate. He had said it full of condemnation for himself. When Aeëtes had not only stayed with Hecate after the battle, but loved her even more, parts of Thanatos cracked inexplicably. He thought that he would have to carry off bits of his own soul to the afterlife.

The fundamental truths that he had forced himself to believe, the whispers of man and gods alike that had defined him, started to shake. He had buried those thoughts before they could even become fully formed to spare himself the additional heartache.

The God of death was as stoic as stone, but gentle as the grass. It was the sharpest blade that was the most merciful, that always struck true and struck once.

Thanatos was the God of death and the blade of extinction. There was no immortal soul waiting for him that could learn to peer past the curtain of his eternal mortality and fall head-first into the boundless compassion that awaited the lucky looker. There was no immortal soul that could kiss both sides of Thanatos's coin and discover that his bed was warm, not cold as ice as it was rumored.

There was no immortal soul…yet.

She was about to cheat Death himself, and in doing so, she would run right into his arms.

I

I

The temple smelled of incense and smoke. It always smelled this way, which brought Makaria a sense of peace. There were never any changes to her routine and hardly ever any visitors or other worshippers. Makaria, who had been brought to the temple when she was a child, was the last mortal priestess of Nyx. She now found solace amongst its tiled floors, shining with marble and mother-of-pearl.

As Nyx's temples had fallen around Greece, survivors had flocked to the last one, bringing pieces of the other sanctuaries with them. There were massive, dark wood beams that crisscrossed the ceiling, heavy-laden with ornate tapestries that depicted the moon and stars. The pictures of constellations shown with silver and gold thread, giving the appearance of looking up at a night sky—of Nyx's full power spreading out across the heavens.

A large marble statue of the goddess was in the very center of the hall, with a small altar in front of it that burned with an eternal flame. Makaria spent most of her time tending to the altar and its basin, relighting incense sticks and keeping the dust off of the statuary.

Centuries ago, Makaria's mother had been a child at one of

Nyx's temples when it was attacked by Hera. She escaped and managed to marry Makaria's father, a fisherman. He was a deceitful man, and when he died with many debtors, they had turned their attentions to his widow. Nyx had come up from the Underworld and helped bring Makaria's mother to safety at the last temple dedicated to the goddess.

Makaria had been born inside the temple's stone walls and had held watch over it ever since. The priestesses' numbers had dwindled over the years, until she was the last woman standing. She had wept for days when the last worshipper had died, leaving her alone in the quiet sanctuary. Everything that Makaria had ever known was inside those borders, and when the only other acolyte died, Makaria realized that she didn't know another breathing soul on the planet. It had filled her with an aching, deep sense of loneliness, one that struck her down to her bones.

How many times had she repeated the same routine? Every evening and each morning, waking up alone and going to sleep alone…getting up with the dawn to do it all over again. It had become so familiar to her that she didn't know how to break herself free from the routine even though it filled her with an impenetrable sense of longing. It was as though she was trapped in a maze of her own creation.

Makaria had no regrets when it came to spending time honoring Nyx, but Nyx had no requirements for her worshippers—even if Makaria was the only worshipper left. Regardless, she didn't require vestal virgins like Hestia or Artemis or gifts in poetry and music like Apollo. No, Nyx just seemed… happy that someone was there.

Makaria had only come close to leaving the temple once. She had fallen in love, as all young women are oft to do, with an *aoidos*. It turned out that he was as fickle as the muses he served and left town before Makaria could be entirely convinced to forsake her temple service. She had walked back inside the great hall and swore her eternal allegiance that very evening and became Nyx's last high priestess.

There were no regrets in her heart, but she often found herself looking around the market, seeing the lives of others, and wondering if she had simply watched life happen *around* her instead of *living* it. It was possible for an acolyte of Nyx to have a full life outside of their temple service, but Makaria had refused. Now, as her hair was graying and it took her longer to get warm in the morning, she wondered if she had squandered her time. She would go to Nyx's Tartarus, of this she was almost certain, as though she had lived her entire life waiting for death.

▸▸▸

IT WAS A COLD, crisp morning when Makaria died. She didn't notice the drop in temperature as she slowly stood from her bed, dressed, and went out to the great hall to light fresh incense. She went through her morning routine as if nothing was amiss, not noticing that she had left her body behind. Her shade moved effortlessly throughout the temple, the entire space already primed for the spirits and ghosts of those who belonged to the Underworld. It was Nyx's holy ground, after all.

As Makaria stood up on her tiptoes to brush the dust off the statue of Nyx, her fingertips grazed its shoulder. She recoiled slightly, shocked to find that the stone felt warm to the touch—like skin. It didn't feel cool or solid, and it almost seemed to give under the pressure of her fingers. Makaria took a few steps back, studying the statue, until her mouth dropped open. At the very bottom of the carving, the hem of Nyx's chiton started to turn black. It spread upwards slowly, as if dark water was being poured over it and defying gravity. The gray, veined arms of marble started to take on a more lively, white color, blushing with ichor running beneath the skin. Makaria watched on as the statue slowly came alive, beginning with the feet as they poked out from the garment, up to the shoulders as they shifted.

Ever so slowly, Nyx's face emerged from the cold expression, smiling. She stepped down from the small dais where the statue had stood, her arms extended out towards the last priestess.

"Makaria." Nyx's voice was like the night sky, rich and full of wonder. Makaria was too stunned to speak, her hand coming up to cover her gaping mouth as she blushed furiously. She took a few steps backward, almost overcome with the sight in front of her.

"Goddess!" Makaria gasped slightly, attempting to slide down to one knee. Nyx stopped her, placing her arms on her shoulders and gently helping her stand.

"None of that, now. Let's not pretend that things are formal between us." Makaria's eyes widened at that, having believed that they could only ever be formal between a mortal priestess and the goddess that she served. Nyx seemed to read her mind and shook her head, a soft, chiding look on her face.

"Why…" Makaria trailed off before she could even ask the question, still slightly in shock at having seen Nyx step out of her own statue. The same one that she had tended to and dusted her entire adult life.

Makaria had previously had interactions with Nyx and Erebus, Nyx's consort, but it never felt like this. There was something to Nyx in this expression that made Makaria's heart beat faster—or it felt like it should. Makaria was shocked that she hadn't fainted at all. Nyx, again, seemed to read her mind. The goddess guided them both over to a low bench across the far wall, helping the priestess sit down.

"Makaria…" Nyx said the words very slowly, giving her hands a squeeze. "You're dead."

"I'm *what?*"

Makaria's eyes got even wider as her breath caught in her throat, and she realized…she wasn't breathing at all. She hadn't passed out when Nyx had stepped out of the statue because her heart wasn't beating. The stone had felt warm because she was likely the same temperature as the statue. She tried to steady herself, only to find that after the initial shock, she didn't have a hard time accepting the news. Her whole life had been lived in service of Nyx and the Underworld, and her goddess had shown up to, presumedly, take her there directly.

It called back to the ransacking of Nyx's temple, when the goddess had ensured that the acolytes' strings were cut by the Fates before they could be defiled. Nyx had also come up from the depths to ensure that Makaria's mother made it to safety. The priestess was overwhelmed at Nyx's attentiveness to the women who prayed to her, and she was just one in a long line of those who the goddess tended to personally.

"I'm honored that you would come," Makaria dipped her head in respect, assuming that Nyx had come in place of Thanatos, her son and the God of death. Nyx smirked.

"I would like to talk to you about that." Nyx stood, offering her elbow to Makaria. Makaria took it, and with a wink, Nyx snapped her fingers. Immediately, the temple walls around them began to disintegrate. The only home that Makaria had ever known started to melt around her, the colors, banners, and wisps of incense smoke all running together like dripping paint. It took mere seconds as the temple faded away and they were standing in a rolling field.

Makaria took a deep breath, feeling air return to her lungs as she tried to comprehend the sights around her. They were standing in a small valley, with hills all around them, with fields of narcissus flowers and a river running through the grass. It didn't take long for Makaria to recognize that this was most likely Asphodel, the meadow of souls, and that Nyx had indeed brought her to the Underworld.

"Don't you need to take me to Styx?" Makaria turned, dropping Nyx's elbow and turning to face the goddess. "Isn't that where every soul starts, and then Charon—"

Nyx's smirk hadn't left her face as she chuckled softly. "In a matter of a few minutes, I appeared in your temple, told you that you were dead, and brought you down to the Underworld. Your first question is regarding a technicality?" There was humor and geniality on Nyx's face, but Makaria flushed with embarrassment regardless.

"Well, I... I just thought..."

"Walk with me." Nyx started off in the direction of the riverbank, and Makaria quickly followed.

She didn't know how long they walked in comfortable silence, Makaria taking in the sights of Asphodel around her and the sense of peace that hung in the air. Something did start to pull at her conscience, however... If she was dead, what would she *do?* Makaria had lived her whole life in servitude of Nyx, and while she had love for the other acolytes and her mother, she wasn't exactly rushing off to find the soul of a long-lost lover for a reunion. For the third time that day, Nyx seemed to sense Makaria's thoughts.

"You have done me a great service in your years of watching over my last temple," Nyx smiled at her, "which is why I have a proposition for you."

"Anything!" Makaria exclaimed eagerly, her eyes lighting up as though she were a child again. She did not fear death, but she certainly feared being useless; if her whole life had been in service to the Underworld and of the gods of the dead, what use did she have with an eternity spent just *watching* them in their kingdom?

Nyx stopped on the banks of the river, her hands beginning to glow with dark tendrils of power that wound around her fingers.

"Makaria... I offer you the gift of immortality. It is why Thanatos did not grace your door this morning and why you need not pay Charon a single coin. You watched over my last space in the mortal realm with loyalty, provided sanctuary—and even counsel—to my husband at times," Nyx laughed at the memory, "and there is good in you. I offer you this boon with the title *Goddess of Blessed Death*. Do you accept?"

Makaria felt her whole world come to a standstill. This was something beyond her wildest imaginings. Nothing could have prepared her for an offer of immortality. Words failed her as she shook her head back and forth in utter disbelief.

"I know it's a shock," Nyx cut through her thoughts, "but... I do need to know now. You do not have to say yes. I can easily whisk you to the shores of Styx, coin in hand, if you wish to join the mortals in a peaceful afterlife."

"Isn't...isn't Thanatos the God of death?" Makaria's head tilted to the side as she thought through what she was being offered. Nyx laughed.

"Your only question is, again, on a technicality? Let me worry about my son," she waved a hand in front of her face like she was batting a fly, "and I did say blessed death. It is something that you will, in time, come to understand on your own."

Makaria didn't hesitate, nodding her head once. "I accept."

"Excellent." Nyx's smile widened as she raised her hands and flicked her wrists. The dark clouds of glittering black power wrapped around Makaria, snaking up her arms and legs. She felt her bones shifting under her skin as everything in her was slowly reborn, piece by piece. It wasn't painful, but it was uncomfortable as she felt the mortal coil almost physically pulled from her body.

Her aging, gray hair suddenly grew out down to her waist and turned a shining, brilliant shade of pure white. The lines on her face receded until they were gone entirely, and Makaria blinked her eyes until they were a clear, luminous gray color.

Her body twisted and shifted, undulating with the ribbons of magic that Nyx had wrapped her in, until she realized that she was floating a few feet off the ground.

As Nyx's influence slowly dropped her back towards the earth, Makaria knew that she had been transformed. She now wore a chiton, similar to Nyx's, that looked like tar when she moved. It was pitch black, but whenever she turned, rainbows of milky color seemed to flicker across it. She glowed with a golden aura as the ichor settled into her veins.

When her feet touched the grass, Makaria stumbled, and Nyx was there to steady her. The last priestess had passed away an old woman, but now, she looked no younger than her late twenties.

Nyx was beaming at her with a smile that contained a multitude of starlight, pulling the newly minted goddess into a tight embrace. Makaria couldn't stop herself from crying a little, realization of everything that had just happened crashing down on her all at once. Nyx pulled back and stroked her arms tenderly, like a mother, waiting for Makaria to adjust as much as she could. When Makaria was finally quiet, Nyx spoke.

"I must tell you," Nyx sighed deeply, "while I can grant you immortality, only you can earn it. You are now Makaria, the Goddess of blessed death. You have one mortal year to make it permanent...or your shade will disappear."

2

Thanatos had never liked Delphi. He didn't necessarily have a problem with the city at large or its oracles, but it reeked of human desperation.

The oracles, who were stationed throughout the city, had been blessed by the gods—something Thanatos could confirm—and were, oftentimes, willing to indulge a multitude of questions on behalf of the men who came seeking answers. Yet, as the years went on, he found himself growing impossibly bored with man and their unoriginality. The question the oracles were most often asked was how to cheat death. Thanatos hated going through the city as the prayers of mortals rushed through the air as if they were tripping over themselves to avoid him.

Thanatos cared deeply for humans and their souls; they held a capacity for love and empathy that most of the gods didn't. Every man had the potential for wickedness, and that was why Thanatos had a vengeful side too. He was a double-sided coin, but instead of gambling with split odds, only you could decide which version of the god you would encounter—and you started deciding the day you were born.

Thanatos found that, in Delphi, those who were there to

try and cheat him were the ones who would be due his scythe. He got closer to the city, and the whispers drifted up to him even then.

"How do I cheat death?"

"Do you know when I will die?"

"How can I avoid Thanatos...?"

"What is the best way to hide from the God of death..."

"Will you petition Thanatos to bring back..."

Thanatos scoffed at that request. It wasn't even his decision who died, and he couldn't bring anybody back. That was a prayer better left for Hades, God of the Underworld. The souls reported to him as soon as they stepped out of Charon's boat.

The sun was bright, and the weather was almost unseasonably hot as he rolled through the streets, unseen by mortal eyes. Occasionally, a perceptive or sensitive soul would see an extra shadow or catch a chill, but Thanatos remained out of eyesight to even the most awakened of mortals. Eventually, every human saw Thanatos, so there was no good sense in them greeting him prematurely. The city streets were crowded, too crowded, and Thanatos realized that it must be a festival of some sorts. He had no business keeping up with the pantheon, and they were happy to leave him out of it, so he never kept track of all of their feasts and name days.

There was only one reason that Thanatos was in Delphi today, and it wasn't to honor another immortal. He was moving through the city limits for one soul, Theodosia Galanea. The moment that her name flickered across Thanatos's conscience, he knew her entire life's story, where she lived, and the exact moment that he must bid her to Styx.

If only the city wasn't so goddamned crowded today. Thanatos grumbled. He hated being late. Punctuality was important when it came to someone's death. It would be easy for him to appear in front of Theodosia out of thin air, but next to punctuality, appearances mattered. There was no point in scaring someone half to death right before they died. No, as much as he cared about timeliness, Thanatos cared about the mortals more. Which meant that when he traveled through human cities and collected souls, he did so while exercising as little power as possible.

Even though that put him firmly in the middle of a packed city street, getting held up by human traffic. *How pedestrian.* Thanatos bit back a growl and then immediately chastised himself as he rounded a street corner, disappearing over a fisherman's cart. It wasn't fair to Theodosia to show up in a bad mood. Dying was hardly her fault. She had been a kind soul, always willing to help her neighbor—or anyone who asked, really—so it certainly didn't seem fair that *this* was how her death had to transpire. Thanatos was already in a bad mood over it, even as he continuously reminded himself that it was in Theodosia's best interest to remain calm.

He finally whisked over a cart full of wine, appearing in front of Theodosia's door, which was regretfully hidden out of sight from the main thoroughfare.

Probably one of the reasons that this has been allowed to happen. Thanatos's thoughts were grim as he settled himself in, slowly letting his corporeal form take over. He looked up at the sun and judged its midpoint in the sky.

Three, two, one…

Thanatos watched as two men, unkempt and in torn chitons, snuck around the corner. They were thieves, and rumors of Theodosia's goodwill had finally gone too far, which was impressive in a world where excessive hospitality was expected.

Thanatos felt a heavy weight in his heart as he watched the door get ripped off its hinges and the men disappear inside. For a split second, Thanatos's vision blacked out as time stopped. Two more names were scrawled on his arm, as if in blood, and a smile crossed his face. Thanatos was no longer here to only collect Theodosia, but the thieves as well. It looked like the Fates were going to give him a little bit of justice today, after all.

The god ducked his head and followed inside the modest dwelling, snapping his fingers as time resumed at a slower pace in front of him. The shock of the thieves' entrance had stopped Theodosia's heart where she stood, now collapsing towards the floor in almost slow-motion. She was not without defense, however, and a large dog came barreling in from the kitchen with its jaws spread wide. Thanatos knew that it would take a minute for the hound to do its owner justice, so he turned to the fallen body of Theodosia.

He released his glamor, revealing himself to her for the first time, and her shade responded. It stood up from her body, eyes wide as it looked upon the God of death.

"Thanatos?" Her voice was barely above a whisper, and he nodded in response. He appeared before her without any of his usual regalia, his sword stowed away and his expression warm. He looked almost like any other man in Greece—if mortal men were well over six feet tall, with black hair that was cut shorter than the modern fashion. He held out a hand for her, moving slowly so he wouldn't spook her. He had hidden the mauling of the thieves from Theodosia's view.

"The very same," he winked flirtatiously at the old woman, making her shade blush. "If you've seen anyone else going by that name, I would ask that you tell me immediately. I can promise you that I'm the genuine article." The woman flushed further, an impressive feat for a ghost, and took a step towards him. He gave her a nod of encouragement, and she slid her hand into his.

"Is it going to hurt?" Theodosia chewed on her lip. That was another thing that Thanatos loved about mortals, their physical mannerisms almost remained the same, even when they had left their bodies behind.

"Not at all." His grin spread wider, and he released a pulse of his power down through Theodosia's hand, smelling of charcoal and lavender. It calmed her down and settled her freshly designated spirit.

"Is it as awful in some parts of the Underworld as they say?" Theodosia leaned forward and raised a brow as if she was gossiping with her neighbor and not speaking of Thanatos's home. He chuckled, a low sound that was almost inaudible.

"For some people, it is. Not for you, Theodosia." She fought to keep a smile off her face when Thanatos said her name, a smitten grin lighting up her face. He let go of her hand and offered her his elbow.

"Shall we?"

There was a beat of silence as Theodosia looked around, taking in the sight of her home for the last time. She paused and took a step back, looking afraid.

"Oh! My dog," she bit her lip again, "I don't know where my dog is." Thanatos opened his mouth to speak but stopped himself.

He's currently eating the livers of the men who scared you, but I would really like to keep that visual of your final moments out of your head.

Theodosia continued, "Do…do dogs… Are they allowed?" she trailed off as if she was scared to ask the question. Thanatos smiled, his heart ballooning and filling him with a sense of empathy and warmth. A lot of humans asked this question when they died, and it was his favorite to answer.

"Of course. Hecate would take my soul if they weren't." He extended his arm a little more, and Theodosia took the hint, grabbing hold. Thanatos walked them towards the door. He always found it helped the transition if a soul could depart their home as if they were mortal one last time. He sensed that she got nervous crossing the threshold and continued speaking. "Your dog has a little more business to finish up here, first, but rest assured, Theodosia, I'll bring him straight to you in Asphodel when the time is right."

The woman smiled brighter than he had seen yet, and as soon as they stepped into the sun, she disappeared on the wind. Thanatos sent a push of guiding power after her shade, knowing that it would steer her spirit straight to Charon's dock. He liked to go personally as often as he could, but there were two other souls inside that were now overdue.

Running late, Thanatos growled to himself, only half-heartedly, knowing that he would still choose running late over rushing a job and scaring a mortal soul. Besides...he did love appearing as the face of justice when the situation called for it, and judging by the tender Theodosia that he had just sent off to the arms of Charon, the situation called for it.

He rolled his shoulders as he turned back towards the house, his features shifting as he walked inside. His teeth grew out into pointed fangs as the color drained from his face, and his eyes started glowing an eerie, iridescent blue. His sickle appeared from thin air and strapped itself to his belt. The warm, weathered feeling of his scythe's leather handle materialized in his hand.

Thanatos laughed, a dark, twisted sound, and came face-to-face with the shades of the thieves. He had made them wait a little longer than most souls, letting their anxiety build as they were forced to watch a dog eat their own corpses.

The temperature in the atmosphere dropped, even though no one in the dwelling could feel it, and Thanatos kept laughing. This was the God of death that he was rumored to be. According to his reputation, this was his true face. The gossips disregarded the side of Thanatos that comforted old women and promised to bring their dogs to them in the Underworld, and focused on the angel of death as the avenger.

The thieves knew who stood in front of them, and they screamed. One of the men dropped to his knees and began pleading with Thanatos, begging to give them another chance, to slip their shades into their bodies.

"What bodies?" Thanatos smirked cruelly, pointing behind

them. "Those bodies? You wouldn't make it another minute before you died again." He rolled his eyes, and his broad chest shook with laughter. "No. You, kleptos, deserve to die."

Thanatos raised his scythe and prepared to strike as the thieves began to pray. To *Hermes*. Thanatos dropped his arm and groaned exasperatedly.

"I don't know how many times I have to repeat myself. You pray to Hermes, God of thieves, but I promise you, he is not listening to you now. The violence that you have committed in your crimes has cut the ears off of Hermes, and he is willfully blind to your prayers."

There was another wail from the thieves, and Thanatos rolled his eyes. "Sometimes, I really hate this job." The blade swung, heads rolled, and Thanatos whisked two mutilated shades to the shores of Styx.

He caught his breath for a few moments, letting his glamor hide away the evidence of the vengeful and terrifying god. These jobs were always the most draining, when he appeared as both the gentle angel and the wicked reaper. Thanatos waited until he felt at peace, always careful that he would never frighten anyone who didn't deserve a good scare. As he left the house, the time around him sped up. In actuality, the whole incident with Theodosia and the thieves took no more than a few seconds. The streets were still crowded, and mobs of people began pushing their way down the alleys.

Everything smelled like wine, and that meant only one thing—Dionysus.

For fuck's sake. He grumbled again, knowing now that everyone must have congregated for a feast for the god of wine. For Thanatos, this meant only the most vain and vile of prayers would be spilling about in the ether. He cursed again and looked down at his arm. Luckily, he was always needed elsewhere.

3

Makaria's mind was spinning. She had woken up that morning, a solitary priestess in a temple widely forgotten by man and immortal alike, and before lunchtime, had become a goddess.

"What?" She reeled back from Nyx's grasp, her eyes going wide in shock.

A cold, wretched feeling of betrayal ran through her as she bit back tears. Makaria had always been a friendly, gentle person. The idea that Nyx would keep the terms from Makaria's new immortality from her until it was too late hurt. Nyx sensed this and waited for Makaria to excise the feelings that were building in her chest, emotions that had been growing insurmountably since she learned that she had died. It was an enormous amount of information for anyone to comprehend in a very short amount of time, but they were on a schedule. Makaria was pacing on the riverbank.

"I'm sorry," Nyx said gently after a few minutes. Makaria snapped her gaze to Nyx and nearly growled, the first show of the god's blood that was now running through her veins. Even if she didn't realize it, her immortality ran in line with her emotions, and now that she was on better footing with Nyx—

no one was equal to Nyx—she reacted accordingly. This time, with a threat.

Makaria had always been insecure about her place in the world. If the only place that she belonged was in a temple that the world had forsaken, what did that say about her? Everyone in her life slowly left, from her mother to the other priestesses. Now, it felt like even Nyx was abandoning her.

Makaria's sense of usefulness had always been tied to the service of the goddess, which was something she had chosen. She just didn't know what that meant about *her*. It felt as though there was no corner of the world that was sized perfectly for her and that her strengths had been hidden away, dormant. If she lost her chance at immortality, she might never get the opportunity to discover them.

Nyx motioned for Makaria to follow her and began walking along the river towards the edge of a wood in the distance. Makaria was running through all of the implications of what Nyx told her as she watched her walk away. She was slow to follow. Nyx sensed her hesitation and turned around, a wisp of black power curling around her fingers.

"Come along, child, and I will explain."

"I was owed an explanation before I agreed to this." Makaria intended for her voice to sound threatening, but it only sounded sad. Nyx sighed. She cared for each woman who crossed her path, but there were some things that even she was bound by.

"You were." Makaria was startled by Nyx's simple agreement, and she took a few steps closer to the goddess. "There are contingencies when someone is granted immortality. Those who are born immortal have their own challenges too—not everyone becomes a god. I'll explain everything, but I do think that there's a better setting for it."

Makaria looked around at the rolling hills that they were nestled between, trying to get used to the Underworld. She felt different. *Everything* felt different, but she had to agree that she would rather have this conversation elsewhere. She sighed and nodded her head slowly, trailing after Nyx like a child would their mother.

The goddesses walked in silence across the grass, approaching the tree line until a small home came into view. It had a wide, open courtyard with tall columns and an altar in the very center. The estate had the presence and energy of a temple, which immediately made Makaria feel more relaxed. She could smell the scent of incense from where she stood, even if it was cinnamon and rosemary, and not the jasmine that she was used to.

As they walked towards the courtyard, the ground seemed to shift beneath them, and Makaria nearly tripped when she realized how close they were. She looked down at her feet to see the ground *moving*, like a current under their feet, expediting their walk.

Nyx chuckled softly, "There are many little things that come with being a god. I will admit that some of them are annoying, but most of them are of the utmost convenience."

Makaria could only nod in stunned silence as they stepped onto the tiled floor of the courtyard. As soon as their feet touched the property, two large, black dogs came loping out of the front door. They were massive creatures, but their tails wagged as they recognized Nyx, jumping up and licking the goddess. One of them turned to Makaria and nuzzled at her hand, petitioning for pats.

"Heel!" A warm, male voice rang out through the courtyard. Makaria picked her head up from the dog as a tall, curly-haired man stepped out of the house. He managed to look like he'd come straight from the beach, even though they were firmly in the Underworld. The dogs didn't react to his command whatsoever, which made Nyx laugh and the stranger break into a comical, over-exaggerated frown.

"It seems that the dogs still don't listen to you," Nyx joked good-naturedly, stepping across the courtyard. The man went to greet her, and they embraced, both laughing.

"Boys, down!" A woman with long, auburn hair and wearing a purple peplos emerged from the doorway. The dogs reacted to her instantaneously, getting off Nyx and Makaria and running towards their master. The scene caused the other immortals to break into fresh bouts of laughter. There was warmth in it that Makaria had been looking for all her life and didn't know it. Even amongst the priestesses, she had never felt that sort of relaxed kindred. She shifted unconsciously until the red-haired woman's attention fixed on her. A pleasant, calm sensation spread through Makaria, and she felt a touch of the kinship she'd been searching for.

"Ah, we have a new arrival, I see." Makaria didn't move, unsure of how to respond as all three of the immortal's gazes turned to her. Nyx grinned, sidestepping the man and hugging the other goddess.

"Hecate, this is Makaria," Nyx held her arm out, "Makaria, this is Hecate." Makaria had spent her life in worship of Nyx, which meant that she knew exactly who the Goddess of witchcraft was. Hecate didn't seem to notice Makaria's shocked standstill, and she pulled her into a tight hug.

"Welcome, sweet one." She kissed Makaria's brow. "Come inside. I need to know everything about you if you are to be a new goddess of the Underworld." Makaria nodded, still a little dumbstruck, and Hecate grabbed her hand and pulled her towards the door. She paused in front of the man, giving him a quick kiss on the cheek and nodding her head in the direction of the river they had come from.

"Aeëtes, be a dear and go visit your parents for a while." There was a command in Hecate's voice, but there was softness too, which immediately let Makaria know they were together. He nodded, his expression utterly smitten as he looked at the goddess.

"I'm sure we'll have plenty of time to get introduced later."

Aeëtes turned his attention to Makaria. "Fear not. You're in good company with all of the immortals of the Underworld. An invitation to Hecate's kitchen is a coveted one." He gave her a sly wink and a quick bow in Nyx's direction, then he jogged off.

"Inside, inside, come on now." Hecate was fussing, and Makaria had to admit that it felt nice. Her trust had been slightly shaken in Nyx, and while she was a protector of her acolytes, it was a different kind of affection. Makaria followed Hecate inside with Nyx right behind them. As soon as she entered the kitchen, she knew that it was as sacred a space as any temple.

The kitchen was a massive room, with large workbenches and a heavy table set up in front of one of the largest hearths that Makaria had ever seen. It took up almost an entire wall and was likely only rivaled by Hestia's hearth. There was a low ceiling with exposed rafters, and dried bunches of herbs hung from each beam. It felt like there was an entire garden on the ceiling and had the effect of making the space smell like lavender, rosemary, and cinnamon. There was a large pot that hung over the lit fire and that magically seemed to always be at the point of bubbling over, but never quite spilling. There were sticks of incense that stuck out from cracks in the walls, holes in the rafters, and in clay cups. Makaria felt herself unwind almost completely like she had walked into a spell.

Nyx smiled, poured herself a cup of wine from a heavy-looking amphora, and sat down at the table.

"Hecate has wards set around the kitchen," she answered Makaria's unspoken question, "which is why you feel more relaxed when you step in here." Hecate gently maneuvered Makaria to sit down across from Nyx, grabbed two more cups of wine, and sat next to her.

"Wait," Makaria paused with the cup halfway to her lips, "Is that why you wanted to have this conversation here? So I can't get angry at you?"

"Oh, that's not how magic works." Hecate shook her head, her voice stoic. "It never takes away your free will. It can't control your emotions. I've created the most peaceful atmosphere possible, but if something pisses you off…you'll still feel it." She grimaced as if she was remembering past conversations in her kitchen that hadn't gone well. Makaria nodded, sipping her wine. She gasped quietly, the sweet, almost honey-like taste causing a shock to her senses.

"It's nectar and wine," Nyx smiled softly, raising her cup in a small toast. "Welcome to immortality."

Makaria's mood soured. "Temporarily."

"Let's discuss that." Nyx placed her wine on the table without taking a sip. "If there weren't any…guidelines, let's say, on granting immortality, then the pantheon would be in chaos."

"Think about it." Hecate rolled her eyes dramatically. "Can you imagine what would happen if Zeus were allowed to turn any mortal woman that he fucked into a goddess? Cerberus's balls," she cursed, and Makaria stifled a laugh.

"It's true though." Nyx made a *tsk* sound. "The guidelines for immortality were established long ago by gods and primordials alike. We were bound by the oaths of Styx."

"So…you can't tell someone that becoming an immortal comes with… conditions." Makaria stumbled over the right word choice. Nyx nodded solemnly.

"It's incredibly serious when a decision is made to grant someone immortality. They have one year to prove that they are worthy of it, worthy of whatever dominion they've been given. I was bound not to tell you of this condition until after you have made your decision to accept. If someone wants immortality for the right reasons, they will strive to earn it. If they do not, it will quickly become apparent. Think of it as…a final test. You accepted immortality and bypassed the judgement of Rhadamanthys, Minos, and Aiakos. This ensures that every creature, mortal or immortal, proves themselves capable of their lot."

Makaria stared down into her cup. "I still don't understand why you couldn't tell me that if I *don't* manage to prove my worthiness...my shade will vanish."

Makaria shivered. When mortals died, they went to the Underworld. When gods died, their shades vanished entirely, and no trace of them remained. It was Hecate who answered, her voice soft.

"It would've swayed your answer, would it not have?"

"Of course it would've." Makaria's brow furrowed, but Hecate nodded once.

"Exactly. Now, in the case of someone who was dishonest and wanted immortality for the wrong reasons, it might frighten them off." The goddess sighed and placed her hand on Makaria's shoulder. "But it might frighten off the most timid of souls, and sometimes those are the most worthy." Makaria found herself suddenly fighting back tears. Nyx reached across the table and grabbed her hand.

"Makaria," she pleaded, "the only other person I have ever granted immortality to is Hecate. I would not have done it if I didn't believe that you were worthy of it." The confidence in Nyx's tone broke something in Makaria, and she swallowed thickly as tears fell down her cheeks.

"Oh, child," Hecate cooed, leaning over and pulling Makaria into a hug.

Nyx got up from the other side of the table and joined them, wrapping her arms around both Hecate and Makaria. It was overwhelming for the new goddess, who had become eternally used to being ignored and not fitting in. Now, there were two of the strongest goddesses in existence, creatures of the Underworld, hugging her tightly as they told her how much they believed she was worthy of *immortality*.

Makaria didn't know how much time passed in the kitchen —time was already becoming a funny subject as immortality settled in her bones—before the goddesses released her.

"Well! I think sweets are the answer."

Makaria gasped as Hecate pulled a plate of *teghana* out of thin air, the sweet dough smelling of honey. She didn't hesitate to grab one, one question still running through her mind as she chewed.

"How…" she swallowed, some of the honey sticking to her throat, "How do I prove that I'm worthy? The Goddess of *blessed* death?"

Nyx and Hecate exchanged a look that Makaria couldn't quite interpret. The goddesses reached for sweets themselves, and Nyx licked some of the gooey residue off her fingers as she answered with a grin.

"You'll find a teacher."

4

Makaria was shown to Hecate's guest room after that, both of the goddesses leaving her to some well-deserved peace and quiet. The room was welcoming, and Makaria wouldn't be surprised if she learned there was some spell craft hidden in the walls. She was asleep before her head hit the pillow—discovering that you were immortal had a way of knocking you out. When she finally woke up, Makaria had no idea what time it was, although it looked like it was dusk.

Did I really sleep for a full day?

She made her way slowly down to the kitchen where she heard the voices of Hecate and Aeëtes.

"Oh!" Hecate looked up from where she was working. "I thought you might be asleep for a few days, honestly. It happens when you turn immortal." Hecate smiled as if this was very casual information. "How did you sleep?"

Makaria burst into tears. She was so stressed and overwhelmed about her sudden immortality—she wasn't even close to having fully accepted that yet—and now, she was cracking. Hecate handed the mortar and pestle off to Aeëtes, who momentarily looked confused as to what to do with it, and simply decided his presence was not needed in the kitchen. He quickly exited, and in his haste, ended up taking the mortar with him. Aeëtes struck a funny silhouette as he jogged out of the kitchen, carrying the mortar and pestle with both hands. Makaria would've laughed if she was not overburdened with a crushing weight of her perceived failure.

"Oh, come here." Hecate pulled Makaria close to her and said nothing as she navigated them to the kitchen table. Makaria was buried in Hecate's arms, and she stayed there until her tears ran dry.

Makaria pulled back, sniffling, and scoffed quietly at the stain on Hecate's shawl. "Gods, I'm so sorry. I'm such a mess."

"Hush." Hecate's voice turned stern. "I don't want to hear it. There's no apologizing for crying in my kitchen. What's on your mind?" The goddess tilted her head to the side and waited for Makaria to begin. Makaria took a slow, deep breath as she tried to keep from crying at the thought of everything that was stewing within her.

"Am I interrupting something?" A soft, feminine voice filled the kitchen. Hecate and Makaria turned around, and Makaria was shocked to see another goddess standing in the doorway. She felt her eyes get a bit wider as she tried to temper her surprise, but she still wasn't used to seeing so many immortals appearing at whim around her.

This goddess was undoubtedly a resident of the Underworld, but there was something about her that was filled with joy. She had a duality to her that made Makaria think of a solar eclipse, equal parts darkness and light, balancing each other out in a dance for supremacy. Her long, blonde hair was wrapped in a braid that went down past her waist, and her brown eyes sparkled with a surprising aura of mischief. She clearly knew Hecate, but she turned and smiled at Makaria, giving her a good look at her charming, heart-shaped face.

Makaria couldn't help but feel drawn to her instantly. Here was another person who might know what it was like to be trapped between two worlds.

"Come on in," Hecate smiled, waving the goddess over. "I have a feeling that this conversation could use your input too."

Makaria bristled slightly, not liking the idea of appearing vulnerable to an additional person, but she tried to quell the fear.

"I don't mean to pry," the goddess feigned modesty but sat down across from them while winking at Makaria. The small gesture of familiarity immediately put her at ease, even if they didn't know each other.

"Yes, you do," Hecate ribbed playfully. "You're Hades's eyes and ears all over the Underworld."

Hades!? Makaria tried to keep the shock off her face.

"Ha! Don't confuse me with Minthe. I am a free agent." The goddess scoffed and snapped her fingers, but Hecate shook her head in disbelief. An amphora of wine and three cups appeared on the table, as well as a plate overflowing with pears, cheeses, cured meats, and—

"Pomegranates," Hecate rolled her eyes as she grabbed a few of the seeds, raising a brow. "How cute."

"What?" The goddess feigned ignorance and popped some into her mouth, smirking all the while. Makaria couldn't help but be endeared to the woman's entirely unbothered energy. "We haven't met." The woman grinned, passing Makaria a cup. "I'm Persephone."

"Persephone!" Makaria couldn't hold back the squeaking sound that she made. Her brow furrowed as she tried to rationalize what she was seeing. "As in Persephone, Demeter's daughter? In the…Underworld?" Makaria hadn't been an immortal for very long, but she was fairly certain that the Goddess of the harvest wouldn't like her daughter being in the Underworld.

"Or Persephone, Goddess of spring." She pursed her lips and slathered a piece of bread with honey, and Makaria got the impression that there was no love lost in that mother-daughter relationship. "Yes, in the Underworld—"

"She's here to drive Hades insane," Hecate quipped, wagging her eyebrows in Persephone's direction, who only laughed and toasted Hecate in response.

"He'll be fine," Persephone sing-songed, sipping the nectar and wine. "His subjects are already dead. What's he going to do? Kill someone?" This was apparently hilarious, although Makaria assumed there was some subtext that she was missing.

"You're awful," Hecate grinned approvingly. "But not why we're here. Makaria, darling, what's stewing in that head of yours?"

Makaria took a deep breath, her eyes downcast as she fought a fresh wave of insecurities. She wanted so desperately to be like the two goddesses in front of her, so carefree and confident, assured of their place in the world. Persephone was as far away from her mother's dominion as she could get, and she still sauntered around the Underworld with ease. Makaria knew that she wouldn't get anywhere keeping it bottled up, so she picked her head up and recounted all of her concerns about her new immortality. Hecate helped fill in for Persephone the parts about Makaria's mortal life—which Makaria was not shocked to learn that Hecate knew about—at which time, Persephone reached across the table and gave Makaria's hands a welcoming squeeze.

"Goddesses of the Underworld have to stick together, no?" She smiled and Hecate let out a playful shriek.

"I'm assuming you've told Hades you've accepted his proposal then?"

"Absolutely not!" Persephone grinned wildly, standing up on the bench and pouring fresh cups of wine for the table. "Listen to me, Makaria, always make them sweat it out!" The women broke off into laughter, and Makaria was more than happy to have the conversation diverted away from her, but Hecate gently steered them right back to it.

"I don't even understand how I got here," Makaria moaned, leaning her head on the table. "I mean... I know how. That was Nyx. It just seems so...misplaced."

"You have to be careful with new powers," Hecate sighed, rubbing Makaria's back gently. Makaria leaned into it, all too desperate for the motherly affection. "It's overwhelming, to say the least, and you're going to need to find some sort of an... outlet...for a while."

"Is Thanatos going to be the one teaching her?" Persephone turned towards Hecate with a quizzical look on her face. Makaria's eyes went wide. This was the first she had heard of this.

Hecate hissed, and Persephone's face contorted, realizing that she had revealed that particular piece of information too soon. Hecate answered begrudgingly. "He will be. There's not a better fit and you know it, Seph, so don't give me that face. Don't scare her off."

"I'm not!"

"Scare me off of what?" Makaria perked up, her eyes dancing between the two goddesses.

"Thanatos is... Well, he's not the most welcoming..." Hecate chewed on her words and licked a little bit of honey off her finger, mulling over her response. "He's been through a lot." Makaria was surprised to hear Hecate defend him. Persephone had the same pensive look on her face.

"Thanatos and Hades are close," Persephone offered up, her voice taking on a serious tone that Makaria had not yet heard her take. "Even then, there are things that Thanatos won't tell Hades. He's not known to...open up."

"Eternity is a long time to think that people hate you. To feel like you don't belong," Hecate murmured, waving her fingers over the table and refilling their cups again.

"What?" Makaria looked at both of the goddesses with a stunned expression. Hecate and Persephone exchanged a look, and Hecate nodded, apparently giving Persephone permission to tell whatever story she was sitting on.

"Cumulatively, I've spent more time in Olympus than I have the Underworld. It's not my fate, but that's…a work in progress." Persephone waved her hand. "The gods on Olympus, Makaria, they despise Thanatos. In some ways, more than they hate Nyx or Hades. He's the one thing that every pompous immortal fears."

"Death," Makaria whispered quietly, the ichor draining from her face at the idea of so many powerful beings collectively despising someone.

"Don't be fooled." Persephone's smile turned a little wicked. "All gods fear death. Even more than the mortals."

"I thought he didn't kill anyone?" Makaria interjected, and she surprised herself with the intensity of her objections.

"He doesn't," Persephone shrugged.

"Then why do they have so much resentment for him?"

"They need to blame someone." Hecate gave her a grim smile. "The Fates make the decision who lives and who dies, but the gods won't openly despise the Fates. Then they'd really be asking for it."

"So… Thanatos becomes their scapegoat." Makaria sighed, feeling a heavy weight sink in her chest. What must it be like to work so hard for the mortal realm, only to return home to the pantheon and realize they all hated you? Based on a falsehood? She hadn't even met Thanatos yet, but it sounded like a raw end of the deal.

"He doesn't care terribly about the Olympians' opinion. None of the Underworld gods do." Hecate shrugged. "Even down here, there are some people who bar their doors or look the other way when Thanatos passes. He's the God of death, the sword of Hades…"

"The destroyer of souls." Persephone made a *tsk* sound as though she didn't appreciate that moniker. Makaria felt cold.

"I didn't think that he...killed, though?" Makaria muttered confusedly.

"He doesn't destroy mortal souls, Makaria," Hecate murmured softly. "When it comes time for a god to die, however, that's when..." she stuttered, and Makaria felt faint when she realized what Hecate was saying.

"If I don't prove my worthiness then...then it's Thanatos who..." Makaria trailed off, and neither Persephone nor Hecate said a word in response. "I'm supposed to work with the man who could be my own executioner?"

Persephone gave her a soft smile. "He won't be. You'll be able to prove yourself. I can tell."

"I have to be honest with you." Makaria's voice sharpened a little. "All I've heard for the past day is several goddesses telling me 'not to worry about it' without offering me anything tangible. It's a little anxiety-inducing." Makaria tossed back another sip of her wine.

"It's not our place to tell you everything," Hecate reminded Makaria gently, "especially when it comes to the matters of the dead. It will be Thanatos who does that when the time comes."

"Well, when is that?"

"Soon," Persephone chided. "You were just saying that you're overwhelmed with everything that's happened. You really want to go to work right now?"

Makaria scoffed angrily, even though her words had no heat. "Well...no." She pouted a little at her own tone, even though what Persephone said had struck a chord in her. When she spoke again, her voice was quiet. "I don't even know where to begin." She swallowed more wine and avoided making eye contact with the other two goddesses, feeling like she was going to cry again. Persephone reached across the table and grabbed her hand.

"Listen here." She was firm. "Don't think for a second that

you're doing this alone, okay? I know there is a *lot* of information coming at you, but we'll help you figure it out piece by piece." Makaria smiled at that, wiping a tear from her cheek. Hecate continued.

"When you do meet with Thanatos, just remember, he's probably just as nervous as you are."

Makaria rolled her eyes. "Is this like when you're afraid of spiders and your parents say, 'They're more afraid of you, than you are of them?'"

"Oh no," Hecate said calmly. "Everyone should be more afraid of Thanatos."

Makaria's eyes widened, and she sputtered for something to say, trying to keep up with the goddess's change in tone.

"Or," Persephone's face lit up with a devilish expression, "you can spend a year ruining his life—"

"Not helping, Seph," Hecate chided with a groan, running her hand through her hair. "Don't listen to her. She's been stringing Hades along ever since she ran away from her mother and escaped down here."

"I am *not* stringing him along." Persephone turned up her nose playfully. "I am simply making sure that Hades realizes how mad he is for me before I acquiesce."

"Oh, he's mad *at* you all right," Hecate scoffed, but Persephone was unbothered.

"Listen to me, Makaria," Persephone popped another pomegranate seed into her mouth. "The secret to the men of the Underworld is this…" She paused, commanding the kitchen table like it was a stage. "Shades of mortals and immortals alike find their final haven here. It's the ultimate repose for every soul. Hades, Erebus, Charon… They're all looking for their own safe place, too." Silence settled over the kitchen.

Makaria didn't know what to think. She couldn't imagine someone who sounded as commanding and terrifying as Thanatos looking for a refuge.

"Even Thanatos?" she asked quietly, sounding timid. Persephone nodded slowly.

"*Especially* Thanatos. Now what do you say we head up topside? It's almost the Feast of Dionysus after all, and it sounds like you could use a good party."

5

The God of death didn't take breaks. Occasionally, there were moments when Thanatos would slow time and send fractals of his own shade out into the world to do his job. It kept the cycle of life and death in its perpetual motion but granted him pockets of serenity. It was in one of these brief reprieves, after he departed Delphi, that he appeared in his own hall.

Thanatos was hardly ever home. When he was there, he always took up residence on one of two great thrones. They had been a gift from his brother, Hypnos, and were made of bone, which didn't make them any less comfortable. The second throne had always been empty. Thanatos assumed that it had been a cruel, mocking trick of his brother to give him a consort's throne, which was rather unlike Hypnos.

He had said nothing about it, had accepted the gifts, and placed them in the receiving space. In some ages past, before men even had fire, Thanatos would occasionally hold council in his own halls. There were some souls and shades that, if they hadn't made it to Charon, would plead their case that their death had been in error. Thanatos had been a young god and mortality had been even messier than it was now; there had been some accidents and deaths that had seemed a little *too* premature. Thanatos was not too egoistical, like many of the other gods in the pantheon, to admit that he had made a mistake. If it hadn't been for the early judgements of Thanatos, mankind likely wouldn't have survived.

After the gods began interfering with men like playthings, and mankind evolved, Thanatos stopped holding council. He knew which deaths were just, and the immortals of the Underworld had fallen into an impervious routine millennia ago. There was no need now to listen to the complaints of the dying and the dead. Thanatos was always as gentle as need be, but there was never a need for a redux. Besides, if he ever did that these days, he would be questioning the Fates themselves, and that was an argument he was too smart to get into.

Thanatos bristled and let out a shaky breath as he slipped down into his body like a pillar of smoke. He was trying to eradicate all thoughts from his head as he stepped into the receiving hall. The great room was empty as always, and he could almost see the dust covering the tapestries that hung from the ceiling. The alcoves for altars and offerings were despondent and half-used while burnt incense sticks were littered in one corner.

Nyx had tried for a few centuries to encourage Thanatos to make the place more welcoming; she thought it would ease some of the wildness she saw in his eyes. Nothing had worked. Like any mother, she had spent the next hundred years wondering how she could make Thanatos happy—until she realized that *happy* was too trivial. It was fleeting. She wanted Thanatos to feel secure, to feel loved. There was a darkness in his gaze that was all too different from the blackness that overtook him when he became sickle and scythe.

Thanatos brushed off the memories of those conversations like cobwebs as he stepped up the dais, slipping into his chair with a deep sigh of contentment. His eyes had only been closed for a few seconds when the room was filled with the scent of poppies, and petals started raining down from the rafters.

"Oh, for *fuck's* sake, Hypnos!" Thanatos groused, rubbing his hand over his eyes as he sat up. The hall was already covered in a thin layer of poppy petals as they continued to fall down around him, getting stuck in Thanatos's hair and cuirass. He heard Hypnos's laughter before he saw him. He emerged from a particularly tall pile of flowers in the corner.

Thanatos and Hypnos were twins, yet there could not have been two individuals more different. Thanatos had dark hair and blue eyes that looked like ice; Hypnos had hair so blonde it was almost white, and his eyes appeared like warm embers. It was fitting—Thanatos was the God of death, and Hypnos was the God of sleep. Hypnos was also, if you asked his twin brother, infinitely more annoying. Sleep did have a tendency to be elusive when you needed it and showed up in spades when it was inappropriate. Death, Thanatos always argued, was always on time.

"You cannot tell me that you're missing this party," Hypnos said by way of greeting. Thanatos nearly growled. The week before the Feast of Dionysus, Dionysus himself took full control of Mt. Olympus. There was nothing but feasting and drinking for days, and when the gods got to drinking, Thanatos worked overtime. Tonight was going to be one of those nights.

"You know why I'm not going. A feast of the gods means that I'll be needed in the mortal realm, and why would I go spend time with those pompous fools? They don't want me there." Thanatos didn't even bother to look at his brother. He knew that he was standing in front of the dais with a permanent, soft smile on his face and angelic charm.

"That's exactly why you should go!" A second voice chimed in, and Thanatos turned his head, grinding his teeth when he saw Hesperus.

Hesperus was the God of the Evening Star, but more

importantly, he had been Hypnos's consort for the past two-thousand years. He was taller than Hypnos, with dark auburn hair that permanently looked wind-swept. In Thanatos's social circles, Hypnos and Hesperus were more synonymous with one another than Castor and Pollux, even more so than Thanatos and Hypnos, his *literal* twin.

Nyx couldn't have been more excited that her son had chosen a god of the night sky as his lover. It was another reason that Thanatos thought his mother was so hellbent on matchmaking; she had seen those two together and thought that it was what Thanatos was missing.

It's not, he hissed to himself.

It is, a different part of his brain hissed back.

Thanatos had seen the look on his brother's face whenever Hesperus was around, and how his expression relaxed every time he fell asleep on Hesperus's shoulder—which was often.

"Oh, good, there's two of you here," Thanatos deadpanned. "In my house, where I did not invite you, to bug me about going to a party on Olympus. Of all places."

"You know you'd get a kick out of seeing the look on their faces!" Hesperus shouted with glee, rubbing his hands together with so much mischief in his eye, he looked like he was channeling Hermes.

"I've seen enough shocked and appalled expressions to last an immortal lifetime," Thanatos countered although he saw the disappointment on Hypnos's face and felt his resolve crumbling. He always caved to his younger brother. It was why he had kept the two thrones in the great hall, after all these years. Hypnos shrugged.

"Well…" he yawned, "the rumor is that Apollo is telling people *he's* the reason you won't go." Thanatos nearly jumped out of his chair, some of his weariness evaporating when he thought of that childish god and his incessant lyre.

"Apollo is doing *what?*" Thanatos's voice nearly shook the rafters.

Hypnos's eyes got wide, and a devilish smirk appeared on Hesperus's face.

"Told you that would get a response," he whispered under his breath to Hypnos, who waved him off and focused back on his brother.

"Apparently, Apollo has been telling people that he's gotten the best of you. He's the god of the sun—"

"That's Helios," Thanatos snapped, but Hypnos shrugged.

"Zeus says that the job belongs to Apollo. Anyway, Apollo has been telling people that his bright light has frightened you off Olympus, casting you at the bottom of the mountain only to deal with mortals."

The idea made Thanatos's blood run cold and he felt his hands shifting into their dark claws.

"What the fuck did Hades say about that?" Thanatos stormed off the dais.

"Do you think Hades gives a fuck what anyone on Olympus says?" Hesperus laughed with a scoff. "Plus, he's been wrapped around Persephone's finger since she showed up down here."

Thanatos twitched again. He certainly didn't want anything to do with Apollo, but he'd be damned if he let Apollo get away with directly insulting him.

It's not like it will do anything to change your reputation, that mocking voice in the back of his head chimed in. Thanatos pulled at his hair in frustration, pacing while his brother and Hesperus watched in anticipation.

"Fine!" Thanatos finally shouted, dropping his hands to his sides. "We'll fucking go."

Hypnos and Hesperus both cheered in their enthusiasm, Hesperus leaning over and kissing Hypnos's cheek in victory.

"Do you want to come with us or escort yourself?" Hypnos asked kindly. Thanatos nodded.

"I'll go with you." He stormed past the pair and out the door, unleashing bits of his power around him. If he was going to show up on Mt. Olympus, then he was going to make sure that he did it right.

▸▸▸

MAKARIA WAS a bundle of nerves as she followed Persephone inside. This was her first trip to Mt. Olympus. Now at the steps to the great acropolis, she was worried that a drunken party wasn't the best time to make a first impression.

As Persephone whisked them up through the Underworld and to the front steps of Zeus's heavenly temple—Hecate had laughed raucously and declined the invitation, disappearing with her consort before Persephone and Makaria could leave—she had insisted there was no better time to meet the rest of the immortals.

The temple was lined with shining columns, with nearly a dozen steps up to the great doors. Each step was mosaicked with brilliant tile that shone with gemstones. Makaria knew they cost more than a year of a mortal man's wage. There were great basins of fire that stood taller than her, and the air already smelled of smoke, ambrosia, and wine.

"Now," Persephone squeezed Makaria's hand as they materialized together in front of the doors. "Remember, it's not a successful party unless someone wants to fuck you and someone else wants to fight you."

Makaria's eyes got wide.

"Do you like spending time with these people?" She couldn't help but wonder why Persephone cared at all. She seemed to fit in so well with the Underworld. Makaria was shocked that the goddess had suggested they go to Olympus.

"Oh, absolutely not. They're horrid, each and every one of them." Persephone shook her head and made a retching noise.

"I've learned it's best to play the part of bubbly, kind-hearted goddess of spring." Persephone winked. "They never suspect *her* of anything." She threw the doors open, and Makaria was immediately overwhelmed by the sights and sounds of a raucous party.

Every god that she knew by name and image seemed to be packed inside, as well as several immortals that she couldn't identify. Dionysus was seated on Zeus's throne, holding an amphora nearly as big as he was in his lap. Everyone was holding a cup or a chalice, and there was a fountain in the very center of the room that was flowing with wine.

The festivities of Dionysus were one of the few times that his more *wild* group of acolytes were allowed on Olympus, further packing the hall with a myriad of wood nymphs, satyrs, and forest sprites.

Makaria followed Persephone inside, nearly awestruck with the ebb and flow of power in the room. As soon as they crossed the threshold, drinks appeared in their hands. Makaria turned to look at Persephone, but she was already gone. It only took Makaria a second to find her shining blonde hair, and she was hidden in the corner, discussing something animatedly with a god Makaria didn't recognize.

In an opposite corner, there was a mortal man playing the lyre and singing. He had the most beautiful voice that Makaria had ever heard, and she found herself slipping through the crowds to get closer. She leaned up against a pillar and took a long sip of wine, hiding out of sight from the rest of the gods and listening to the musician.

"He's one of mine, you know." A deep, melodic voice cut through the party's din behind her. Makaria startled, turning around and blushing a harsh shade of red. Apollo was standing in front of her, looking like an overgrown cherub, with a smile like sunlight, hair that curled at his temples, and eyes that were not to be trusted.

"I'm s-sorry?" Makaria forced the words out, taking a step backwards.

"The singer." Apollo pointed in the man's direction and stumbled, and Makaria realized how drunk he was. "Orpheus. He's one of mine."

"Oh," Makaria nodded, her lips pulling into a thin line. "How nice for you." She picked up the folds of her skirt and turned to leave when Apollo caught her arm and pulled her closer to him.

"You're *new*," he grinned lecherously, looming over her, "and you're immortal. Tough news about that one-year trial period, hm?" His voice darkened, and he pulled Makaria even closer so her body brushed up against his. "You know, you could be one of mine too. I could make sure that you prove your worthiness."

There was an unmistakable look in his expression that let Makaria know he was not interested in her choral abilities. She shook her head, pulling her arm from his grip.

"No, thank you—"

"No?" Apollo's entire face darkened as he yelled in response, the noise of the party drowning him out. "What do you mean, no? I'm one of the twelve! You're hardly a demi-god. You can't refuse me."

"I think I just did," Makaria spat, taking another step backward. "Now, if you don't—"

"Don't what?" Apollo glared at her, making up the ground between them.

Makaria hadn't realized that he had been slowly backing her up against the wall. Orpheus was only a stone's throw away, but he played on blindly, clearly charmed by Apollo to forget his surroundings in order to perform on Olympus.

"Just let me go." Makaria squirmed, praying with everything in her that she could find some way to channel her power. Any power, so long as it tossed Apollo on his ass.

"I don't think I will." Apollo put his hands up on the wall above Makaria, boxing her in.

▶▶▶

FROM ACROSS THE PARTY, Thanatos had finally set his sights on Apollo. The glowing, incandescent light that always seemed to surround the childish immortal betrayed his location. Thanatos got closer, and he felt his hands clench into fists as he realized that Apollo had cornered a woman. Thanatos wanted to be angry—he wanted to look at Apollo and immediately feel nothing but rage—but every wicked thing that he thought couldn't find purchase as he took in the mystery woman and studied her.

He was enamored with everything from her long, shining white hair to her bright, gray eyes—eyes that were currently filled with fear, which made Thanatos growl under his breath as a shockwave of power released from every pore of his being.

There was something in Thanatos that latched onto her and wouldn't let go; it tightened around his chest until he thought he couldn't breathe. His power called out to her like a song, which rocked him to his core. His power didn't react to *anyone*, not even Nyx or Hades, with whom he shared the most kinship. It twisted his heart as he realized there was a part of him, however small, that felt like it was a fit with her. He felt the blood rushing in his veins as his head nearly went empty at the sight of her. As much as he could sense her power, he knew that it was new. It still stirred in her veins like water cooling off from its boiling point.

They didn't mention a new goddess that was so...beautiful. Thanatos shook his head, almost violently bringing himself back to the present. He cursed himself viciously. *How dare you! There's a job to do, and you're busy staring at the new goddess like that damn Cupid has been fucking about.* Thanatos hissed and picked up his pace as he crossed the party, knocking over goblets and immortals alike.

❦❦❦

MEANWHILE, Makaria screwed her eyes shut and waited for an opportunity to kick Apollo between the legs when there was a deep shout and a gust of wind. Makaria sensed a shadow come over the party, and when she blinked her eyes open, she realized that there was just a shadow over *her*. A large, looming shadow. Someone was now standing between her and Apollo.

"Who are you?" Makaria breathed, feeling her entire body relax in relief.

There was something dangerous about the stranger, but somehow, she knew that he wouldn't hurt her. His body was blocking hers more effectively than any barrier. She couldn't see his face, but she could tell that he was furious.

He was wearing his full hoplite armor, but there were no weapons at his side, his fingers extending into claws. Clouds of dark blue and black power emanated off him, and the air around him was cold. She watched with glee from behind his massive torso as Apollo, the alleged Sun God, shivered.

"Apollo." The stranger's voice was full of barely contained rage. He looked ready to rip the god's shade from his body where he stood. "I know you weren't imposing yourself on the goddess."

Makaria couldn't help but shiver when she heard the other god use such a commanding tone. Apollo blanched, all the anger and bravado stripped from his face.

"I d-didn't know you were coming tonight." His words

were clipped. The god nodded once. "Of course. I meant no harm —"

"You absolutely fucking did," Thanatos lip curled up into a sneer as he bent down so he was eye-to-eye with Apollo. "If I were you, I'd leave this hall right now before I decide, for the first time in my immortal life, to fuck the Fates and take your shade to oblivion right now."

Makaria felt even her blood run a little cooler at that threat, although parts of her flashed hot.

Apollo nodded rapidly and turned on his heel, even running away a few paces before he vanished into thin air, taking Orpheus with him. Makaria felt the last of the tension leave her body as the god turned to face her—and she got her first look at him.

Her new magic had flared to life at the sight of him, and its strength had shocked her. There was a pulsing in her veins that called out to him. It had *recognized* him, and it warmed her from the inside out. A crushing feeling of relief and repose had blanketed her, her newfound powers confusing her and addling her brain, but one thing was certain—the magic rolling around in her body was made for this god. Yet, she didn't even know his name, and something on his face was unreadable. That palpable disdain pivoted the feeling on its head, and she felt like her heart had been cleaved in two.

"Oh, thank the gods," Makaria let out a soft sigh, looking up at the god in front of her in a slight state of shock. "Well, you, thank *you*, You're a god. Not the other gods, they—" She started rambling almost incoherently, and the stranger cut her off with a gentle smile.

"The other gods, in my experience, aren't good for much more than what you see before you now. Are you...new here? I'm presuming."

He gave a little nod towards the rest of the party. Makaria looked past him and saw that they had descended even further into madness. Everyone was holding at least two cups, most of the immortals were in various stages of undress, and there was wine flowing from some of the cracks in the walls.

"Oh." Makaria gasped quietly, her mouth popping open at the sight of the debauchery. "I suppose it's a bit obvious that I'm the newest one of the lot, isn't it?" The god offered her another smile that almost acted like a balm to her nerves.

"Trust me, standing out from this crowd is a good thing. Do you..." The god's voice was almost hesitant. "Do you want to go somewhere quieter?" He seemed nervous, and even though Makaria didn't know him in the slightest, she got the feeling that it was out of character for him.

"Yes." Makaria nearly felt her neck snap at how quickly she nodded in her agreement. The god held out an arm and ushered her away from the dimly lit corner, his body making way for her as they shoved their way through the party. As soon as a door was in sight, he stopped. Makaria let out a small squeak as she barreled into his back.

"I'm so sorry!"

He turned around and shook his head once. "No need, but..." His head turned, and he looked off to a table on their left, where Makaria noticed a very sleepy blonde god was leaning on a very drunken satyr. She heard him warbling through, what sounded like, very intoxicated yawns. It was a sound that Makaria wasn't sure she had ever heard before. "I think I need to go help him." The massive immortal ran a hand through his hair, looking down at her with a slight grimace on his face.

"Y-you're not Hesperus-s..." The sleepy god hiccupped, and Makaria's eyes widened.

"That might be for the best."

The god nodded. "Will you...just step outside? Down the stairs and to the left, there's a garden that wraps around the building. I can meet you there in a few minutes?"

Makaria blushed, warmth building in her stomach again. "Yes! Yes, that sounds perfect."

"It's a date," the god smiled and veered off to his left, easily hoisting the sleeping immortal onto his shoulder. He gave her a wink before vanishing off into the crowd, presumedly to take the drunken man home.

Makaria didn't take more than a step outside before she felt a warm hand on her shoulder, tugging her back. She turned around, jerking her arm away, immediately filled with fear that Apollo had followed her outside. Relief flooded her when she realized it was only Persephone, who was now staring at her with a curious look.

"Are you okay, Makaria?"

"Yes," Makaria answered, probably a little too quickly. "I'm all right. Are you enjoying yourself?"

"It's great…" Persephone answered slowly. Her brow furrowed as she took in Makaria's stilted tone of voice and ruffled appearance. "We need to go, though. Ares just pulled out his weapons, which means this is going to turn into a drunken brawl faster than you can say *Aphrodite*."

"Aphrodite? What does she have to do with that—" Makaria was cut off with the sound of a massive crash and a flash of lightning, followed by a chorus of angry shouting.

"That's our signal to leave," Persephone said firmly, grabbing hold of Makaria's hand to pull them back to the Underworld. Makaria opened her mouth to protest but already felt herself disappearing on the air, being yanked back to the safety of Hecate's home.

I didn't even get his name.

•

6

After they abandoned the party, the rest of Makaria's evening was spent in Hecate's kitchen. Nyx had joined them, leaving Erebus on duty in the night sky, and they all kept the nectar and wine flowing. Makaria was soundly nestled between Hecate and Persephone as they continued to welcome her to immortality. Every time they congratulated her or made reference to her newly minted status, Makaria felt a small stone of dread sink deeper into her stomach. She tried to understand their explanation for why she couldn't have learned all of the conditions of immortality before accepting, but it made her anxious. It didn't help that her thoughts were now preoccupied by the god who had saved her from Apollo on Mt. Olympus.

How do you even prove that you're worthy of being immortal? And…who was that other god? He didn't have an energy like any god I've ever seen, not even the other immortals of the Underworld.

"I can see your thoughts from here," Hecate chided her gently, filling up her cup. "Don't think about it for one night, okay? You're worried about your immortality. Celebrate! Everyone is going to help you."

'Don't think about it for one night' means I will only *think about it for the rest of the night.*

Hecate looked at her with a raised eye, and Makaria wondered if she really was reading her thoughts. She smiled softly, toasting her wine in Hecate's direction before swallowing half of it down and chasing it with more sweets. She had never been one for wine and bakeries while she was alive; now she was wondering why she had spent so long denying herself little joys. What had been the purpose of her commitment to stoicism? How could she have been so uptight in the land of the living when baked honey and bread existed?

Nyx pushed the plate closer to Makaria with a smile. "There's nothing better for a shock than bread. Eat up, child."

She finally started to feel the tension in her shoulders ebb and relaxed more as the evening went on. The goddesses regaled her with stories of their own immortal infancies, which mainly consisted of accidents that they had caused. Persephone did a dramatic reenactment of the first time she met Hades, followed by the lie she told Demeter about the pomegranate seeds.

"Could you imagine if that were true? If eating food in Hades's house kept you here forever?" Persephone broke off into giggles. "Poseidon would be the God of Styx instead of the God of the sea! I'd be in more trouble if my mother *knew* as much about the Underworld as much as she *hates* it."

By the time the women were generously full of wine—which required a lot of wine for immortals—the stories got more and more outrageous until Makaria was nearly falling off her seat, her face pink with laughter.

Every so often, Thanatos would make an appearance in one of the goddesses' stories. Makaria would feel her attention pick up, as if the mention of his name was calling to her beyond her awareness that he was the other god of death.

Hecate recalled when she was learning necromancy, one time she accidentally summoned Thanatos directly. Thinking she had died, he was shockingly kind—until he learned of her error. Nyx rolled her eyes, refilling cups and making note of the time she had been so close to finally finishing off Zeus that Thanatos had appeared in the corner. When he had to leave without Zeus's shade, he sulked for a year.

"A year?!" Makaria startled, wondering what kind of person would keep a bad temper for so long. Nyx patted her arm gently with a glint in her eye.

"He felt that it was an injustice that Zeus be allowed to live," Nyx explained, "because of all the atrocities he's committed over the eons. Especially against women."

Oh. Makaria said nothing and found herself taking yet another long sip. As the sun was beginning to rise, Nyx finally stood and said her farewells, suddenly looking remarkably sober. Makaria stood on shaky legs, the goddesses laughing as Hecate wrapped an arm around her waist.

"It's the nectar, darling." Hecate grinned. "You'll get used to it…" The women were cut off by a sudden off-key chorus of male voices hollering from the courtyard.

"Oh, that I would be a cup of wine—"

"That your lips would land on *miiiiine!*"

The drinking song rang out through the columns, interjected with rather intoxicated laughter. Hecate, Persephone, and Nyx seemed to identify the voices immediately, everyone rolling their eyes and looking at each other with a deadpan expression.

"You did tell him to go visit his parents," Nyx shrugged, adjusting her peplos as dark tendrils of her power started to gather around her. Hecate groaned.

"I didn't think that meant drinking with Hermes."

"Is everybody drunk?" Makaria hiccupped, standing a little straighter and removing herself from Hecate's supportive grip.

"It's not an…uncommon pastime." Nyx smirked as if there was history there that she didn't have time to divulge. "The closer we get to the Festival of Dionysus, the stronger everyone's going to feel his influence. You'll start to pick up on the other god's influences and powers before long."

Without saying another word, Nyx smiled at Makaria and dissipated, dark shadows disappearing out through the cracks in the stone walls. Makaria gasped at her sudden departure, and Hecate squeezed her hand warmly.

"You'll get used to that too. There's so much coming and going, it would take us forever to get anywhere if we always had such formal goodbyes." Makaria nodded, feeling overwhelmed again now that the wine had stopped flowing and was settling in her stomach. There was an acidic taste in her mouth as her buzz turned into a sour, intoxicated feeling. Hecate nodded in the direction of the doorway. "Let's get you upstairs. You're staying here for the night and tomorrow, it's your first day on the job."

Before Makaria could even react, two large male bodies burst into the kitchen. They both tried to go through the door at the same time, causing them to get stuck and struggle against one another before collapsing to the floor. Apparently, this was the funniest thing that had ever happened, and they broke out into a fresh bought of laughter. Makaria recognized Aeëtes from earlier, the one who was intimate with Hecate. The second man—no, he was definitely a god—was a shining, golden tangle of curls and limbs. It only took her a moment to see the winged sandals kicking about in the air, and she knew —Hermes.

"Gentlemen, please," Hecate muttered. "If I can even call you gentlemen at present. Did you have a lovely visit with your mother, dear?" Hecate put the emphasis on 'mother,' indicating that she was very aware that Aeëtes had not gone. Yet, there was a bit of a softness in her eyes that let Makaria know she wasn't upset. She noted the relationship between them seemed playful, and Hecate's stern attitude had virtually no effect on her lover.

Aeëtes detangled himself from Hermes and jumped to his

feet with surprising athleticism for someone so intoxicated. Hermes whined on the floor, spreading himself out like a starfish.

"No fair," he pouted. "Now I've no one to cuddle with." Hermes's gazed landed on Persephone, and his expression flipped. "Oh, sweet Goddess of spring, come down here and let me show you what it's like to have a lover who's not bound by darkness." He wiggled his eyebrows in what was most likely an attempt at looking salacious, but only looked utterly deranged.

"I very much happen to like being *bound by darkness*, as you so aptly put it." Persephone winked, finishing off her cup. Hermes sat up with a faux, shocked gasp, looking scandalized.

"How adventurous of you!" He clapped his hands together. "Here I was, thinking that the sweet Persephone, who the flowers hold dear, wouldn't be…"

"A little wicked?" Persephone winked at Hermes, and Makaria thought he might fall over again in his adoration of her. "There are poisonous flowers, too, you know?"

"That's it!" Hermes clapped his hands together and jumped to his feet, all traces of his drunkenness gone. "Hecate, my maiden of manslaughter, I regret to inform you that the prestigious title of 'Hermes's Underworld Mistress' is no longer yours."

"Oh gods," Hecate playfully kicked her foot in Hermes's direction, "how ever will I go on?" Aeëtes crossed the short distance to Hecate and wrapped his arms around her waist, pulling her in for a kiss. Makaria felt a pang of longing as Hecate smiled into the embrace, and she turned her face to give them the semblance of privacy. Hermes was dusting off his short chiton as he looked at Makaria with a wild grin, his attention already off Persephone.

"Hello, hello, hello," he clapped his hands and stepped towards her. "Aren't you a fetching young thing."

Makaria's eyes got wide as she took a step back, somewhat confused by his forwardness. "Excuse you! I'm practically an old woman…" she stopped herself. Makaria still wasn't used to her new appearance, to the youthfulness that had been returned to her when immortality flooded her bones. She realized she had entered a world that had made her mortal age utterly pointless. Her face now defied time.

Besides, Hermes is a god. Everyone is young to him. Makaria floundered for a second, still unsure how to approach each Olympian. She had always known Nyx and Hecate welcomed her with open arms, but this was the infamous trickster himself. He seemed to sense her deliberation and waggled his eyebrows at her.

"Oh! You're a very young thing, indeed. Welcome to immortality." He gave her a short bow. "Whatever you need to know, ask me. I'm the only god who will give you a straight answer." He stepped towards Makaria and looped his arm through hers. "I'm Hermes, in case you didn't know."

"She knows. You just like the sound of your own name." Hecate pulled away from Aeëtes. "Get your flirty hands off her, Hermes. I thought you were in love with Persephone now? This is Makaria, and she's under Nyx's protection." Hermes blanched slightly at that and then blushed, dropping Makaria's arm as he took a few steps back.

"Well," he recovered almost instantly, "I'm still the only god who will give you a straight answer." Makaria blushed at his accompanying smirk.

"That's a lie," Aeëtes interjected, clapping Hermes on the back. "He's the trickster, Makaria, and the only thing you need to know about Hermes is that nickname is *very* well-deserved." Hermes slung his arm over his friend's shoulders and sighed dramatically.

"Do you see how they continue to assassinate my character?"

She laughed in response, the anxiety ebbing out of her once more in the presence of the mismatched group.

"You two are worse than gossiping nymphs." Hecate made

a shooing motion with her hands towards the door. "Makaria has been immortal for less than two days, and you're already in her face."

Aeëtes's face twisted in an expression of mock horror. "I didn't do anything!"

Hecate sighed, staring at her consort with an unamused expression. "You brought him here." She looked at Hermes pointedly, and Aeëtes had the good sense to look chastised.

Makaria was drinking up every interaction, trying to keep up with the relationships and the way they spoke to one another. It was, yet again, another sense of warm familiarity that she had never been a part of.

"What's the new job, sweetness?" Hermes hiccupped and looked at Makaria, who couldn't help but smile.

"Drop the nicknames." Persephone raised an eyebrow in warning at Hermes, who bowed his head to her, causing his curls to fall into his eyes. He didn't make any effort to move them as he looked towards the young goddess again.

"I stand corrected. What is the new job?" He held a dramatic pause, as if to emphasize the lack of a pet name, and looked at Persephone expectantly.

"Very good," she deadpanned.

Aeëtes sauntered away from Hermes and pulled Hecate closer to him, beginning to whisper things in her ear that made her blush. Makaria turned from them and focused on answering Hermes's question.

"The Goddess of blessed death." Her voice was hesitant when she spoke, and that ball of anxiety returned in her stomach. Hermes looked genuinely shocked when he heard her, furrowing his brow slightly.

"A death goddess?" He took a step towards her, cocking his head to the side.

"Well," Makaria wrung her hands together, "the goddess of blessed death. *B-blessed.*"

There was a severity in Hermes's tone that made her think

there was something else that the others weren't telling her. Hermes spoke slowly as though he wanted to be very explicit in what Makaria was saying. "But…a death goddess? You've become a death goddess?"

"Y-yes," Makaria squeaked. Hermes's face had twisted into something else, an expression that made Makaria understand he was also the god of dark mischief and thievery. The gaiety in his eyes had bled away, and he was deadly serious when he stared at her.

"How are you going to prove your worthiness?" Hermes pushed again, his voice sharp.

"I-I don't know," Makaria stumbled as the anxiety in her stomach spread to her chest. The tight feeling threatened to take her over, making her breathing escalate. "I think Thanatos is supposed to teach me."

Hermes cursed, nearly spitting the words as he leaned back from Makaria. Her eyes went wide in shock, and she blushed, staring at the angry god. He shook his head as he looked at her, deadly serious.

"Thanatos is not to be messed with," he spoke low to keep the other immortals from overhearing him. "If I were you, I would find another way to learn the ropes."

"I d-don't think there is anyone else!" Makaria squeaked as the weight of everything that had happened that day started to crumble around her. Her mouth went dry as she forced the words out. "He's the only god of death…"

"I know how the gods work," Hermes snapped. "You don't need to lecture me on the pantheon." His eyes turned dark as he pointed a finger at her. "I'm looking out for you here. If you want to prove your worthiness as a death god, *find another way*. Thanatos feels possessive about his job, and he will not help you."

Makaria startled. Hermes's warning seemed off. She trusted Nyx and Hecate. They had said that he would teach her. She had spent all day listening to stories that Thanatos had been interwoven in while this was the god of tricksters, after all. She stomped her foot beneath her hem to steady herself, straightening up and summoning whatever bravery she had.

"Stop it," Makaria hissed back at Hermes, and her tone surprised him. "You say not to lecture you on the pantheon, but you aren't a god of the Underworld. I am." She paused, but she had said it so finitely, Hermes found himself impressed with the young goddess. Makaria took a deep breath and started again. "I am a goddess of the Underworld now, which means, affairs between the immortals of hell are *my* business, not *yours*." She poked Hermes in the chest, feeling herself getting swept up in her anger. Makaria had been on the outskirts her whole life, and she wouldn't stand for anyone spewing judgements from the outside looking in—no matter where they were or who they were.

"I won't hear anything rotten about Thanatos," Makaria said simply as if she was making a passing statement about the weather. "Not from you, not from anybody. The mortal world is full of enough awful rumors. I won't listen to any from the immortal world." Makaria finished with a sharp nod, and her confidence suddenly left her in a flash as she waited for Hermes's response. There was a beat of silence between them before Hermes broke out into raucous laughter.

"Oh! You're a delight." He clapped his hands together. "You are simply a delight. By all means… I can't wait for you to meet him." There was a spark in Hermes's eye and mischief in his tone that made Makaria uneasy, but she ignored it.

Hermes's laughter had broken Hecate and Aeëtes out of their trance, and Hecate stepped towards Makaria. She glared at the trickster.

"Stop scaring her." Hecate's eyes glowed white for a brief moment. "No one needs whatever nonsense you've been filling her head with, Hermes."

"All right, all right," Hermes waved his hands in mock surrender as he took a few steps backwards toward the door.

"I'll get going. Makaria, it's been lovely. Hecate, you remain a delicious night terror. Persephone, I await the day you realize that *Big H* is *my* nickname, not Hades's." He bowed low and then snapped to attention, as if he had forgotten something. "Aeëtes, my friend, remember if you two are ever looking for a third…"

"Out, Hermes!" Aeëtes waved his hand in the air once with an exasperated shake of the head, and the god vanished.

Makaria jumped at the sight of Hermes disappearing in front of her, and Hecate rubbed her arm gently. "Like I said, we really do come and go in a flash. He didn't say anything egregious, did he?" Hecate looked at her with a protective and gentle gaze.

Makaria shrugged. "I'm not sure what the bar is for *egregious* when it comes to Hermes."

The rest of the room laughed, but Hecate seemed to sense Makaria's anxiety. She wrapped her up in a tight hug, squeezing her close. Makaria let out a long sigh, feeling some of the uneasiness in her chest unraveling.

"Come on, sweet goddess," Hecate smiled, grabbing her hand, "it's already morning. I think it's time we all retired."

7

The next morning, Makaria was pleasantly surprised to find that she wasn't hungover. *If that's a side effect of immortality, then consider me doubly intrigued to make this work.* She sighed, rolling over in the warm bed and burying her face further into the pillow. Hecate's guest room was as well-furnished and welcoming as the rest of her home. Whether it was the wine or the magic, she had passed out as soon as her head touched the pillow.

It took her a second to get her bearings when she had woken up. For a few seconds, she thought she was back at the temple. Everything had come rushing back to her at once—her new immortality, drinking the evening away with Nyx, Persephone, and Hecate, Hermes's strange warning to stay away from Thanatos, and her mystery savior at the party. She felt herself flush with secondhand embarrassment when she recalled how she had snapped at the messenger god. That was yesterday; this was today.

It was her *first* day.

Now, she was absolutely terrified. *How do you even prepare for your first day as a god?* Her anxiety had an iron grip on her spine.

Makaria thought it was entirely unfair that gods didn't get hangovers, but they still had anxiety.

"That makes you one of the good ones." Hecate's voice surprised Makaria, who turned around to see her standing in the doorway.

"Oh!" She stood up quickly and smiled sheepishly at the goddess. "I guess I said that last part out loud."

Hecate nodded. "You did. However, I meant what I said. If you're nervous or anxious about this…" Hecate waved a hand in the air. "It means you're one of the good ones. Do you think Zeus has ever been anxious a day in his life?"

Makaria grimaced. "No. That would imply that he cared about anything."

"Exactly," Hecate encouraged. "I don't want you to let it run your life, Makaria, but remember this—your anxiety doesn't make you any less capable. If anything, it means you care about this. If you care, that's half the battle of being deemed worthy."

Makaria looked down at her feet, fiddling with her fingers again. "What's the other half of the battle?" When she picked up her head, there were tears in her eyes. Hecate crossed the room towards her and gently grabbed her face.

"Even I don't know. Only you can know this, and it will become apparent once you've achieved it." She let go of Makaria's face and grabbed her hand, leading her out of the bedroom. "Nyx is engaged elsewhere today, so let's get some breakfast in you. You don't necessarily need it, but I've found that it's helpful for young immortals to keep up with their old habits. Then it'll be time for you to get to work."

"How will I know where to go?" Makaria chewed on her lip as she followed Hecate into the kitchen. The goddess shrugged, grabbing some small branches off her mantle and tossing them into the lit hearth.

"You'll know."

▶▶▶

THE FEAST of Dionysus hadn't even started yet, and people were already acting foolishly. Thanatos had taken far too many souls to the Underworld today already. From his perspective, they were gone before their time due to reckless behavior.

If the Fates are cutting their strings, I guess that means it is *their time.* Thanatos mused, trying to console himself over what seemed to be so many avoidable deaths. *Maybe they would've gone on to do something that harmed others in the future. Still.* He shook his head as he swept over the city's rooftops on his way to where the latest casualty lay dying.

His heart broke on these occasions, and he treated them carefully. It was a rude awakening to go from celebrating one moment and learning you were dead the next. He had a late start to the morning—something he despised—and found his thoughts drifting to the new immortal he had met the night before.

Correction: the new immortal who had stood him up. He didn't even get a chance to learn her name since she never appeared in the garden after he took Hypnos home. Thanatos waited there until he dared not wait any longer, watching the sun rise as something akin to hope dried up in his chest. New immortals weren't exactly uncommon, but they were rare enough that he should be able to quickly ascertain who she was. It was his own insecurities that kept him from doing so, worried that he had been rejected before he'd introduced himself.

Still, that power within her. There's no way that she's a creature of Zeus or Aphrodite or even Artemis… But anyone in the Underworld would've spread the word about a new goddess in Hades's realm.

Thanatos solidified into his mortal form and dropped to his feet, taking special care to always make sure that it was the first thing that the mortal soul laid eyes on. He was preparing himself for the worst as he turned a corner, stepping into the alley where the young man was…and he felt his world drop out from underneath him.

There was the body of Alexandros Athanidis, who had drunkenly grabbed a glass of wine that wasn't intended for him and started a fight with the man who had bought it. It had been a brawl that resulted in Alexandros lying face down in an alley, an argument that likely would have never escalated this far had it not been for the excessive influence of Dionysus permeating the air.

That didn't shock Thanatos.

It was the woman next to Alexandros who was having an animated conversation with the man's shade that stunned him. She, on the other hand, was very much alive, and she was immortal. He felt his heart began to race as he stared at her, his jaw nearly dropping to his feet.

It's the goddess from last night.

Thanatos's entire field of vision condensed to a single point as he stared at her. A million different conflicting emotions arose in him, ranging from fury and frustration to attraction.

What in the name of the gods is she doing here? She can't think that this is her job! Thanatos felt his anger wavering as he took in her gentle aura and that kind face, those gray eyes that had been full of fear when he first saw them.

No, no, no! He snapped at himself, fighting the urge to knock himself upside the head to get himself back on track. *Whoever she is, there has been a mistake. There is no other immortal who deals with death, and she's flagrant enough to step all over where she doesn't belong!*

Thanatos watched as Alexandros's hands flailed dramatically, pulling him back to the heart of the matter—the shade he had come to collect. The shade that this new goddess was trying to collect for him. Thanatos took a few seconds to gather himself, for Alexandros's sake not the goddess's, and listened.

"Now, hear me out," Alexandros started, his voice pleading. "You've got it all wrong! It's easy, you can definitely just drop me back into my body…"

"I don't think that's how it goes." The new goddess's voice was wavering, her nerves manifesting physically as she wrung her hands together and cracked her knuckles.

"It is! I know it is. Come on, goddess, you must believe me. This was an accident!"

"Well, okay…"

Absolutely not! Thanatos growled as he snapped his fingers, freezing time but leaving the goddess out of it. She startled and looked around, noticing that the shade in front of her had stopped moving. She looked around nervously and realized *nothing* was moving.

For a second, Thanatos almost felt sorry for her, but hearing her bargain with the dead had infuriated him to no end. It would only mess up the mortal's life irrevocably in the long run. Allowing them to beg and barter was similar to a cat playing with its food. The realization that she was arguing with a shade poured over him like a bucket of cold water. When he spoke, Thanatos's words were sharp as iron.

"You're doing that wrong."

The goddess's attention snapped to the edge of the alley where a tall, dark-haired god emerged from the shadows. He watched as her expression shifted from confusion to recognition…then something he didn't recognize. Was it relief?

She can't possibly be relieved to see me. It was one of the few times he had ever seen someone look at him that way, and he reeled with it.

"It's you!" She clapped her hands together and smiled.

Thanatos felt his stomach twist at her expression, but he buried it, steeling his face and keeping his features stoic. She stood up and adjusted the hem of her skirt, taking another step towards him. She felt her power, as foreign as it still was to her, jump to the surface of her skin. Her mortal form was covered in gooseflesh as she tried to keep her shiver from being too apparent. Between the warm feeling that she got when she looked at the god and the way that her power reacted, Makaria felt like she was drunk all over again.

If this is Thanatos, then surely, that's going to be the answer to all of my problems! What luck. Her thoughts were optimistic as she thought back to their encounter the night before and her need of his help. She was practically beaming when she spoke again, not noticing Thanatos's icy expression. "Oh, thank the gods. I'm assuming you're Thanatos? I was so hoping that you'd—"

"That I'd what?" Thanatos growled as he got closer, taking long strides and stepping in front of Makaria. "Do my fucking job?"

Her eyes got wide, and she shook her head rapidly. She spun at the intensity of his tone.

"Oh, well, no." She was visibly flustered as she pointed to the shade. "I was just discussing with this man—"

"He has a name. Use it. The dead aren't nameless. They aren't forgotten." Thanatos crossed his arms over his broad chest, staring down at Makaria with fury in his cold, blue eyes.

"I-I was just speaking with Alexandros—"

"You were *bargaining* with Alexandros," Thanatos cut her off again, his face contorting into something akin to barely contained rage. "You should never, ever bargain with the dead."

"I thought—"

"You thought wrong. You shouldn't be here."

The goddess's eyes widened with shock as she leaned back as if she wanted to put more space between herself and the God of death. She had been relieved as soon as Thanatos had arrived and was awestruck at his handsome appearance again in the broad light of day. That sour feeling returned to the pit of her stomach.

That morning, Hecate had helped Makaria slip into a meditation, where she could access her power for the first time. All she had to do, Hecate had claimed, was focus on it, and it would take her exactly where she needed to go. Makaria had assumed that meant it would immediately take her to Thanatos. Instead, it had taken her to the newly dead Alexandros, whom she had no idea what to do with.

"I didn't know," she offered up meekly. Thanatos grimaced.

"Of course you didn't. You don't know a thing about collecting the shades of the dead, but you thought you'd give it a try?" His voice was sharp and cold, and Makaria felt it like knives. She so desperately was trying to hold onto this new place in the world after a mortal lifetime of being the outcast. She was embarrassed by her initial attraction to Thanatos, and now he was making her feel unworthy.

It was almost the same feeling that Thanatos struggled with at the sight of a new death god, the idea that his place in the world was now replaceable. There was betrayal stewing in the back of his mind. Briefly, he had argued with Hypnos about being assigned a partner, but he thought he'd put an end to it. No one had discussed her arrival to immortality with him, and now he had been blindsided. Thanatos and Makaria's insecurities were now front and center, dictating their emotions.

"I did what I was told!" Makaria hissed, jumping up to her feet and taking a step closer to Thanatos. She buried her anxiety and the decrepit feelings of being unwanted that lurked in the back of her mind, letting anger take over to fight her battles.

"Maybe if *you* got here sooner," she accused Thanatos, "then I would've had a second to talk to you!"

"Are you accusing me of something?" Thanatos's voice dropped even lower as he closed the gap between them. The tension between them intensified, and Makaria swallowed thickly.

"I'm only accusing you of being an asshole."

Thanatos scoffed in response, giving her a once-over. He shook his head as if he didn't like what he was seeing. "I'll forgive you because you're new, but you're going to have to get used to that."

"What? That you're an asshole? Trust me, I'm pretty certain that it's your most prevailing quality."

Thanatos felt his heart twist at the barb, but he buried it quickly.

It doesn't matter if one more person thinks you're the villain. It doesn't matter if you thought, even for a few moments…

He tried to rationalize with himself, but he knew that it was inevitable. In trying to make sure that a mortal shade had the most painless transition to the afterlife possible, he had gone and made yet another enemy. *Even if she's a very beautiful enemy —fuck, stop it.*

"My most prevailing quality is being the God of death," Thanatos snarled, "something that you would do well to remember. One question that I'd love answered, however, is who the fuck are you?" He punctuated each word like it was an arrow.

The goddess furrowed her eyes at him, her hands going to her hips. She opened and closed her mouth a few times, as if she couldn't decide on what to say. Finally, she dropped her arms and looked up at Thanatos.

"My name is Makaria. I was a priestess of Nyx's. I died two days ago, and now I'm supposed to be the Goddess of blessed death. I don't know what else to tell you. I have a year to make…this," she waved her hands around, "work." She gritted her teeth together and swallowed what remained of her pride. "I need your help to make that happen."

A goddess of blessed death?! Thanatos's ability to keep his face impassive as he got the news from Makaria was impressive. He kept his features as still as stone although his eyes gave him away—they glowed their bright, shining blue, and Makaria shrank back a little at the sight. There was something greater than fury in those eyes, something even stronger than rage.

Makaria felt herself blanch further and was also met with a strange sense of betrayal.

Did no one bother to tell Thanatos? Oh gods, and I was going to leave with him last night...

"Why would I want to help you?" Thanatos raised an eyebrow at her, scoffing slightly. "You seem to think that you can just show up and do it yourself. I don't know who told you that I was looking for help, but they were wrong."

Thanatos officially knew he was being an asshole and didn't care. Makaria had shown up and tried to do his job without waiting or asking for any help at all, which to him, meant that she hadn't cared if she messed it up. The rush of attraction he felt as soon as he had seen her made it worse.

In reality, Makaria had been concerned that Alexandros's shade would get confused if a death god didn't show up. She had indeed been trying to help. Now, she was too insecure and felt too threatened by Thanatos to explain herself.

"That would be your mother," Makaria snapped at him, and Thanatos's expression broke as his lip curled. "Are you going to help me or not?"

"No." Thanatos's answer was so quick, Makaria couldn't keep some of the shock off her face. Thanatos didn't react in the slightest. "Keep away from the shades, *blessed* or not. Which, for the record, a man who dies at the Feast of Dionysus in a fight over a glass of wine? That's hardly a blessed death."

He emphasized *blessed* in such a way to leave no doubt that he was mocking her. She felt a cold rush of fear threaten to take her under, coming up to meet her where she stood in an onslaught of panic.

If he's not going to help me, there's no way that I can make this work.

"You really aren't going to help me." Makaria shook her head. It wasn't a question. She looked around, forcing herself to take slow, even breaths.

Did I really say that I wasn't going to help? Thanatos nearly groaned aloud, his thoughts were ricocheting all over the place as he argued with himself. *No, I'm doing my job. I can't get distracted because she's a pretty face. No one warned me about this, so it's hardly my responsibility.*

"Here's some advice." Thanatos's voice was softer when he spoke. "Don't ever bargain with the dead. We don't cut the strings; the Fates do. If it's time for someone to go, it's time. If you bargain with the dead, it only prolongs their suffering."

"We?" Makaria's face was so full of hope, Thanatos almost caved.

"Slip of the tongue," Thanatos grunted, both of them ignoring the innuendo. "Look," he ran his hand through his hair, "you seem like a nice person. I'm not sure how you got mixed up in this, or what my mother offered you, but trust me. This isn't the job for you."

Makaria shook her head. "I don't…I don't have a choice."

"There's always a choice."

"You want me to decide to *die?*" Makaria's eyes got wide as they filled with horror as she looked at him, and Thanatos suddenly felt tired.

There's the look that they all eventually give you.

"No, although I can say I'm partial to the subject." He shrugged. "There's always a gray area when it comes to immortality. Goddess of blessed death can mean…something else. I don't know. Figure it out." Makaria's face brightened a little as she chewed on a fingernail, sorting through everything that Thanatos was saying.

"Well, do you think—"

"No," he cut her off with a shake of the head. "I'm not going to run through this with you. Just…figure it out and stay away from the dead. This is my only warning."

Makaria opened her mouth to respond, but Thanatos snapped his fingers. There was a bright flash of light, and then both Thanatos and Alexandros were gone.

8

Makaria watched the empty space where Thanatos had just been with blinking eyes. She tried to wrap her mind around her first interaction with the God of death, and a mix of shame and anger ran through her newly ichor-filled veins. It was no secret that she was struggling to keep up with the rapid changes that occurred in her life, and this was even worse. Thanatos was supposed to be the only god who could *help* her, but he only suggested that she try and find a *different job*.

She had been lonely in life, and for a few short hours yesterday, she thought she'd found a family in death. It was sudden, but she was now filled with a longing to prove herself worthy of her immortal companions. The thought of letting down Nyx, even Hecate and Persephone, made her spirit wilt. Makaria took a deep breath and stood up, dusting the edge of her chiton, and swore under her breath.

No one is going to take this opportunity from me. She stopped herself before she made a vow in Nyx's name. It was a habit left over from her mortality that she rightfully assumed would be misplaced now. *Not even some ridiculous, avenging death god.* There was a twinge of something unfamiliar in her stomach, a sense of building heat that she experienced when she had locked eyes with Thanatos. Whatever it was, she cast it aside, determined to prove her place in the Underworld—with or without Thanatos's help.

Besides, there's nothing blessed *about that man anyway,* Makaria sneered, turning her nose up at her own thoughts. *How could I possibly need his help? They swear he cares* so *much for the mortal realm, but I don't see it.* As soon as she said it to herself, it felt wrong. She had seen Thanatos's anger when she didn't refer to the dead shade by name. He had been furious with her that she almost—accidentally—prolonged the man's suffering.

Still. Makaria began walking towards the edge of the alley, merging in with the crowds as they mingled before the Feast of Dionysus. She had spent most of her mortal life knowing her place in the world and confining herself to it. Now that she had the world in the palm of her hand, she found herself almost wishing for her small, isolated corner of existence. Yet, the loneliness and fear of a life un-lived warred with her insecurities about where she fit in this new universe. Makaria responded by shaking her head once, standing up taller, and deciding to get lost in the crowd.

I guess there's nowhere I need to be at present… The gods mingle in the mortal realm all the time.

Hecate had given her a quick rundown of interacting with living mortals—not the dead ones, unfortunately, which was supposed to be Thanatos's job—and what to do. Makaria had dressed in a gray chiton with a black himation wrapped over it, and she wore golden sandals that complimented the thin, gold band that circled her forehead.

It took a second of concentration, but Makaria was able to wield her power and make her most immortal features slip away. The circlet disappeared from her brow and her sandals turned to leather. Her waist-length white hair took on a more natural blonde color, and some of the luster left her gray eyes.

Makaria fidgeted for a second, realizing that it felt odd

being in a mortal form. It felt like wearing clothing that was almost too small, but not quite. She sighed, once again feeling overwhelmed with the seemingly never-ending list of immortal intricacies.

That's enough. You're practically young again, and it's the Feast of Dionysus. What's stopping you? Makaria took a deep breath and pushed herself out into the crowd. It should be a very normal experience, mingling with others and enjoying a street festival, but for someone who had never done it, she felt like a teenager trapped in a deity's body, learning social graces that most mortals had adopted by the time they were fourteen. She pushed through the barrier of shame that her own inexperience provided her and approached a merchant for a cup of wine.

And a second cup of wine.

And a third.

By the time she was—how many?—four pours in, Makaria was wondering why no one had ever told her before how *fun* it was to meet people. She flirted her way through the crowds, accepting drinks, doling them out to others, even conjuring a coin or two to give to performing singers and poets. At present, she was leaning heavily on a soldier—at least, she thought he was a soldier—and helping herself to a plate of cheese.

Now, I'm starting to see what this immortality thing is all about, she chuckled pleasantly to herself and grabbed a bite of food. Makaria paused with the snack halfway to her lips, catching the eye of a small child who was standing a stone's throw away from the table. Anyone could tell that they were starving, their clothes dirty and torn, and they stared at the piece of bread in Makaria's hand like it was a banquet.

The sight pulled Makaria from her stupor. She stood up and pushed off the soldier. She grabbed a second piece of bread, as well as some cheese and dates, and went over to the small child. Makaria bent down to their eye level and smiled, extending a hand full of food towards them. They eyed Makaria with a sense of mistrust initially, but when she made no move to ridicule or taunt them, they grabbed the food in both hands and ran away. Makaria stood with a sigh, her heart clenching as she watched them disappear. She condemned herself.

What sort of a blessed goddess gets drunk on a feast day? I'm acting like a priest. I could be helping the living, even if Thanatos won't let me help the dead.

Makaria stood up and promptly headed off for the nearest alley, disappearing amongst a stack of barrels and abandoned, empty amphoras. She closed her eyes and focused, letting herself slip into a meditative state to access her power. Hecate had assured her that meditating wouldn't be necessary once she got a hold of her abilities, but in the beginning, it helped to give into her powers.

"*Magic is almost sentient,*" Hecate had warned her, "*It's fine to let it hold the reigns in the beginning, but you should learn quick.*"

Here we go, Makaria muttered silently to her powers. *I want to help the hungry, the thirsty. We're so close to the Feast of Dionysus and bodies starve. Take me where I'm needed.*

She wasn't sure if praying to her powers worked the same way that she had once prayed to the gods, but it was worth trying. It must have worked because merely a few seconds later, she felt her body beginning to dissipate. Her immortal features came back, flickering onto her face. She was effervescent as she drifted away on the wind, not knowing if she was succumbing to her powers or the wine.

❦❦❦

When Makaria felt her feet forming on solid ground, she blinked her eyes open to see where her magic had taken her. It was dusk, and the sky was mottled with colors of orange and pink. Makaria couldn't tell if she was in the mortal realm or the Underworld. There was a soft sound of running water, and she turned, realizing that she was on a lakeshore. Tall, delicious smelling fruit trees covered the bank. The trees grew so close to one another that Makaria could hardly see through them, and she caught glimpses of the water through their branches.

The air was perfumed with jasmine and lily, and Makaria wondered if she had stumbled into the land of Pan and his nymphs. She made her way down to the lake, feeling the soft, sandy soil beneath her sandals. The sensation was so delicious, she leaned down and untied her sandals, kicking them off and walking barefoot. Fruit blossoms drifted down to the earth below all around her. Makaria could've sworn that she could even hear the faintest sounds of a lyre on the wind. It might have been the remaining effects of alcohol in her veins, but Makaria decided that this would be an all-too-pleasant place to stay awhile.

Makaria ducked under a low-hanging branch and emerged at the water's edge. She picked her head up, and she was so horrified by what lay in front of her, she screamed.

This wasn't a paradise—it was a prison.

In front of her, a dying man was chained to the trunk of the largest pear tree. He was emaciated; his eyes were nothing more than dull holes in his head. His body was twisted, each joint swollen, while his skin was drawn tight over his bones. Makaria realized in pure horror that she could count every one of them. The prisoner's hair, or what little of it remained, was hanging in limp, wispy strands. Even the chain that bound him by the ankle seemed impossibly small in order to hold onto his frail ankle.

The man still possessed his shade—Makaria could tell that much—but he hadn't moved since she stumbled onto the sand. Not even when she screamed. He seemed permanently outstretched, reaching towards something, until Makaria realized he was reaching for the *water*. Undoubtedly dying of thirst, the man's extended fingers came within a hair's breadth of the water's edge. A large, ripe pear hung low from the closest branch, right out of his grasp.

Makaria felt another shudder of horror run through her as she bent down near his face.

"Hello?" she said softly. "Can you—" Makaria was cut off with an awful scream as the living corpse jerked to life. He swung his arm out towards her and caught the end of her skirts, tugging her to him with a dogged strength she didn't expect he could possess.

"Water!" he bellowed at her, his voice sounding clear and commanding. It was not at all the sound that she expected to come out of a dry, cracked throat. *What sort of damnation is this? Let someone die if they must, but eternal, living torment?* Makaria was appalled.

"Y-yes, yes, of course!"

At her agreement, the prisoner released her, and she stumbled towards the lake's edge. She scooped up as much water as she could in her cupped hands, bent down towards the prisoner, and as she was about to pour it into his waiting mouth when—

"Makaria! Don't!"

Makaria let out a sharp cry as strong hands grabbed her around the waist, pulling her down onto the sand. She landed with a heavy thud on top of a muscled chest, sending her pitiful offering of water into her disruptor's face. The prisoner behind them started to wail like he was being branded with hot pokers. She blinked her eyes rapidly and let out a sharp gasp, realizing that she was lying on top of Thanatos.

He wiped the water off his face and glared at her, those blue eyes freezing her to the spot. Makaria's entire body was tense as she couldn't help but notice the warm, hard contours of Thanatos beneath her. He felt as good as she had imagined he would, and she was embarrassed that her thoughts went there—however briefly. For whatever reason, he had ripped her away from giving the ever-dying man water at the last minute.

The dying man! Her thoughts were pulled from the feel of the god underneath her and refocused on the stranger who Thanatos had insisted go thirsty. Makaria sat up with a scoff, crossing her arms over her chest as she straddled Thanatos's waist.

"What in the Hades was that for?" she snapped angrily at him, pointing towards the prisoner. "That man is—"

Thanatos shook his head, his face morphing into something furious as his hands flexed at his sides and turned into claws. He propped himself up on his elbows so they were face-to-face, and Makaria felt her measly attempt at showing bravado slip away under his penetrating stare. It was like the first night that she had met the God of death, and she found herself completely under his spell. The hard lines of his face and the fury in his eyes did nothing to distract from his attractiveness. If anything, they added to it, and there was an angry glint in his expression that made her sweat.

"Makaria," Thanatos spoke slowly as if he was barely containing himself, "do you know who that is?"

Makaria blushed and shook her head once. "No."

"Do you know where *you* are?"

"No." Makaria hung her head.

"Do you know who put him there?" Thanatos's voice was barely audible, dropping into a low growl that made Makaria shiver. She shook her head. "Answer me. Out loud. Do you know who put him there?"

"No," Makaria whimpered.

Thanatos wrapped his hands around her waist and pulled her off him, depositing her on the shore so he sat between Makaria and the prisoner. He let out a long breath, shaking his head almost in utter disbelief as he stood. Thanatos looked back at the prisoner, who was still bellowing like a cow.

"Be quiet," he commanded, and the man obeyed without hesitation.

Makaria looked up at Thanatos, and she saw glimpses of the reaper for the first time. There was something holy in his anger, a quality to his rage that was built on a foundation of vengeance. He turned to look at her, and she shivered.

"This is Tantalus," Thanatos snarled.

Makaria felt her previous embarrassment increase tenfold, mixing with fear and threatening to consume her. Makaria buried her face in her hands. She didn't know how she could be so foolish. She had heard of Tantalus, who had fed his own son to Zeus in an attempt to punish the gods. Zeus had cursed the wicked king to forever go thirsty and hungry, next to a pool of water and surrounded by fruit trees. As Makaria confronted her shame, her feelings of inadequacy made her want to dive underwater and not emerge until Thanatos was gone.

"Do you know," Thanatos continued, "that if anyone feeds Tantalus, not only will his curse end, but they will be forced to take his place?"

Makaria nodded her head slowly like a repentant child. She dared not meet Thanatos's gaze. Another few minutes of silence stretched on as Makaria fought back tears. Finally, after what felt like an eternity—even though she hadn't come close to experiencing that yet—Thanatos let out something between a grunt and a sigh. She heard his big body moving towards her, almost silent on the sand.

Makaria picked her head up in surprise when he extended a hand out to her. She sheepishly accepted it, sliding her hand into his as he helped her to her feet. Her fingers were entirely encased in his palm, and she felt his power coalescing with hers. It was a sensation that was so cold, it almost burned hot, but it somehow relaxed her. That warm, churning feeling returned to the pit of her stomach as he held onto her hand for a moment too long. Their powers sparked in their hands, wisps of smoke and sparks dancing between their fingertips.

Thanatos coughed at the same time that Makaria gasped, and they both let go. There were another few dreadful moments of silence before the God of death cleared his throat.

"Go back to Hecate's, Makaria." He used the same commanding tone on her that he had on Tantalus, but somehow, it didn't have the same sting. "If you had been pulled into Tantalus's curse…not even I could have saved you."

Makaria nodded, picking up her hem and walking towards the grove of trees. She would find a secluded place to attempt to whisk herself off to the Goddess of witchcraft.

Her mind reeled. Had that been *concern* in Thanatos's voice? Surely not. She only made it a few paces before Thanatos called out after her.

"You don't know the way, do you?" He groaned, any trace of warmth now evaporating from his voice. Makaria let her head fall back as she sighed, wondering when she would be able to stop making herself look a fool in front of him.

"No," she uttered that damn word again, *no*.

Thanatos was at her side, his hand on her shoulder as he directed her between the fruit trees. She tried not to pay any attention to how the smallest touch from him anchored her.

"I'll escort you," he murmured gruffly. "Gods forbid, you find where we hid Ixion."

Makaria looked up at Thanatos's face in shock and thought that she could see the slightest hint of a smile on his face.

9

After sending Makaria on her way to Hecate's, Thanatos vanished back home. He manifested into his chair of bone and took one… two… three deep breaths. They did nothing to keep the rage at bay. It was boiling in his veins. The arrival of a partner meant that everything he knew in the world was changing, and the God of death wasn't particularly good at change. Death was a constant; it was something that had been untransformed since the dawn of time, and bringing another god into the mix was enough to make Thanatos threaten to cleave the Underworld in two.

Thanatos slammed his fist down on the heavy armrest and bellowed, his voice shaking the walls. "Erebus!"

He knew that wherever his father was, he would hear him. It only took a few moments before Thanatos could detect Erebus as he slid through the walls and poured down from the rafters in columns of smoke and night. Erebus slowly materialized in front of the dais. Thanatos picked his head up and sat straighter, adjusting himself so he wasn't hanging off the armrest.

After a few thousand years, their father and son relationship had evolved into one of contemporaries—a common occurrence amongst immortals. Still, he always had a healthy level of respect for Erebus as both the God of darkness and his father, but now, he was one furious god facing off with another.

"Thanatos," Erebus smiled warmly, "what marks the occasion?"

Erebus's attempts at nonchalance were abysmal. Thanatos's responding growl was a loud sound that seemed to echo off the walls and emphasize how empty his home was. Erebus was wearing his typical black chiton while his dark bands of shadows curled around his arms. His power reacted accordingly and flared up at the threatening noise.

"You know exactly why you're here."

"A father can't visit his son without pretense?" Erebus's expression bordered on playful.

"I called you here." Thanatos shrugged as he stood, stepping down off the dais and stalking towards his father. Thanatos's tone was now lighter, always preferring the route of coercion to violence, even though most people wouldn't expect that from him. Erebus let out a long sigh and shook his head slowly, tilting his face as he looked at his son.

"I'm assuming that this is about Makaria then?" Thanatos stiffened at the name, which Erebus wisely took note of. "I promise, it was not my idea. I have no agenda."

Thanatos let out a bark of laughter. "You always have an agenda. You just like to deny it. I feel like we've just gone through this with you and Nyx, and the whole…" he waved his hand around, "you know, uprising against Kronos that almost brought about the end of the world."

Erebus looked sheepish. "Fair enough, but that was enough politicking for me for a lifetime."

"For an immortal's lifetime or a mortal's?" Thanatos hissed. "I have extensive knowledge of both."

"Ah," Erebus clapped his hands together. "Well, that

remains to be seen." Thanatos groaned, sounding like a petulant teenager, which was both amusing and out of character. There were some paternal dynamics that persisted regardless of immortality, and vague answers was one of them.

"Let's get this over with then." Thanatos looked towards the ceiling. "I've got to get back to the mortal realm." He plastered his face with a saccharine smile, his teeth sharpening ever so slightly. "Do you want to tell me who the fuck Makaria is? Or better yet, what was Mother thinking?"

It was Erebus's turn to look petulant, but he shook his head, unfazed. "You can stop time if you need to, son. This is important. Your mother sent me."

"I called you here!"

Erebus raised a brow. "I was on my way."

That got Thanatos's attention. He had love for his father and often worked quite well with Erebus under his cover of darkness, but he had a special bond with Nyx.

She was one of the few other creatures of the Underworld who had suffered her reputation being maligned. Hades, Hecate, even his brothers, Charon and Hypnos, all had fearsome reputations, but they were respected, and their own lore was rooted mainly in fact.

Nyx and Thanatos had suffered in a way that was almost entirely unique to them, in that they had been constructed in the minds of mortals and immortals alike as beings of great evil. Ironically, it was the opposite. Nyx and Thanatos, who cared the most for the mortal world, Thanatos even more than his mother. It was a pressure and a pain that Thanatos bore and only Nyx had ever come closest to understanding. If Erebus was coming with a message from Nyx, then Thanatos was paying attention.

He flicked his fingers aimlessly in the air, effectively bringing time to a stop. Erebus nodded once in recognition and began again.

"Your mother is worried about you. I am, too, for what it's worth. You know that..."

"Hypnos already told me this," Thanatos growled as his temper rose. His eyes flashed with bright, blue light. "Mother agreed to back off after I told her that I refused to work with someone. A *partner*," he spat the word out like it was poisonous.

Erebus sighed, running a hand over his face as he shook his head.

"We're serious, Thanatos. This could be good for you. You have to nearly stop time to take a reprieve or split your own soul in pieces to rest."

"And?" Thanatos snapped. "This is my job. I was made for it. I don't need to split the responsibilities with some minor deity because mother wishes I was around more. Did no one think to tell me?"

Thanatos felt the little bit of kindred that he had with his family beginning to slip away from him like sand in an hourglass. When Hypnos had first come to tell him that he was getting a partner, Thanatos had nearly brought down the Underworld. It had taken a long conversation with Nyx to bring him back from the ledge, in which she promised to drop the subject. Thanatos had been infuriated with the entire notion, so he bid Nyx to promise on the waters of Styx that she wouldn't bring it up again.

Which explains why she sent Erebus to discuss this now. Thanatos fought the impulse to throw one of the thrones across the hall.

"It was discussed..."

"Oh, it was discussed. Please, let me know what you decided regarding *my job.*" Thanatos took another step forward, hardly a foot away from his father.

"We knew that you'd react like this." Erebus was calm. "We thought you'd have a little bit more decorum if you learned about it from Makaria herself. If the whispers on the wind are to be believed, that's not what happened."

Thanatos was barely keeping a lid on his power, his fingers

rapidly turning into claws and back again, flickering between the two forms like a flame. He also now felt thoroughly chastised, but his thoughts turned violent.

No one can do this job! Especially *another god. They will never have the gifts required to do it.*

Thanatos had poured all of his affection into his job; for eons, there had been nowhere else for it to go. He had put every last piece of his soul into his work, treating each passage and every soul like a part of himself, a family member, or even a loved one.

There was no one who waited for him on the consort's throne in the empty stone hall. That lost love bubbled over into every mortal that Thanatos transitioned over to the Underworld, and he kept that standard up throughout the centuries. Now, facing the idea of a partner once more, his blood boiled. Every part of him wanted to lash out at his parents. If he had poured everything he had into being the God of death and they thought he needed a partner to get the job done, what did that say about Thanatos? What did that say about the love he had to offer?

"This isn't a critique." Erebus could read the emotions on his son's face. He initially told Nyx that he wouldn't approach Thanatos with the idea of a partner again—that was until Nyx had laid out her entire plan in front of him. It was a little underhanded, a bit sneaky, and a smidge too similar to some of the schemes that their contemporaries enacted in Olympus. Nyx was convincing, however, and Erebus had agreed to it.

"What else could it be?" Thanatos growled, his hands now permanently shifted into claws, blue flames dancing between their sharped points. Erebus took a deep breath. The last thing that he wanted to do was get in a brawl.

"We're doing this because we love you." Erebus pleaded with him, but Thanatos nearly split his face in two with the severity of his snarl.

"Do you know how many times I've heard mortal parents

say that?" he hissed the words, and the temperature in the room dropped. "And do you know how many times I've had to collect their children shortly after?"

Erebus gawked. "You can't honestly be comparing the worst of the mortal men's sins to this! Infanticide! Really, Thanatos? You're normally cooler headed."

"I'm normally left to my own devices! It seems to me that I'm one of the few gods around who has a job that the world depends on them doing."

Erebus raised an eyebrow as his mortal form grew a few feet taller, his feet disappearing into clouds of black smoke. The light in the room briefly went out, and Thanatos knew that he had overstepped.

"Do not forget your mother's and my place," Erebus spoke with a deadly, commanding tone that shook the room.

Thanatos took a deep breath and nodded, his claws disappearing, and the flames going out. He ran a hand through his dark hair and sighed.

"I don't like it." He sounded more like a child than a god.

Erebus shrank back down and embraced Thanatos again, pulling him in tighter. "I know, but can you trust us? Can you give it a try?"

Thanatos fidgeted before disentangling himself from his father's grip. He took a few steps away and began to pace, chewing on his bottom lip. Erebus could practically see Thanatos's mind racing. When he turned to look back at his father, his eyes were haunted.

"Do you think she will care for the mortals as I do?"

Erebus waited for a moment, weighing different answers in his mind. "I think that anyone who sees you do your job will be touched. They will be changed in ways that they were perhaps unprepared for, but they will be honored to work alongside you."

Thanatos grimaced slightly. "That wasn't a yes."

"I can hardly speak for others, Thanatos. I trust Nyx, though, and I know that you do, too."

"That is a low blow."

Erebus merely shrugged, finally taking a few steps over towards Thanatos. "Listen to me." He placed his hands on his son's shoulders. "If you're worried they'll be frightened of your reputation…"

"I worry about the mortal shades who are frightened when they die," Thanatos cut his father off. "I don't give a damn what the latest immortal thinks of me."

Erebus simply nodded in acquiescence although the emotion in Thanatos's voice betrayed him.

"Understood. However, isn't that why you'd rather have a partner?" Thanatos's brow furrowed in confusion as he looked at Erebus.

"What do you mean?"

Erebus gave a slight grin. "If you're worried about the shades and souls of mortals, you should want to have a partner. There's a new god with death responsibilities, whether you want to work with them or not. It seems to me that if you were worried about them doing a good job, you'd want to keep an eye on them, no?"

Thanatos's expression contorted to one of confusion, to shock, to a new level of rage. He huffed out an angry puff of air, his fingers elongating to claws again while his eyes flashed with their deadly blue power. He knew that he had been caught, trapped by his own logic, but he forged ahead anyway. He wouldn't be manipulated by his family or a young, new immortal.

"No," Thanatos hissed the word under his breath. His whole body was bristling as he recoiled from Erebus's embrace like he had been struck by lightning. "I won't work with this *partner*," he spit the word. "Makaria already tried to help herself."

"You know the rules," Erebus warned him. "Any new

immortal has one year to prove their worthiness. If they do, then they're good at their job. If not, then you get your precious solitude back when you're the one who must end her shade."

I never said it was precious, Thanatos argued in his head but knew better than to make that declaration out loud. He nodded, taking the steps back up the dais and settling himself on his throne. "I said no."

Erebus sighed, his body slowly beginning to dissipate as he began to depart. His voice became a lasting echo around the great hall. "She's going to be around for a year, at the very least, Thanatos. Whether you like it or not. It's up to you what you do with that time."

Thanatos conjured up a hundred thoughts of things that he would *like* to do to Makaria, none of them involving work, before he let out a low curse. He pulled time to a slow, inching pace around him, settling back in his chair for what he figured was a well-deserved nap.

If his dreams were haunted with images of gray-eyed goddesses and their white hair, he wouldn't tell a single shade.

10

It had been a few days since the disastrous party on Mt. Olympus and a horrendous first meeting with Thanatos. After Thanatos had returned Makaria to Hecate's home, both Persephone and Hecate had been waiting for her. Makaria, who found that her tears had dried and given way to anger, recounted everything.

They had been mortified to learn what had happened between Makaria and Thanatos, including the events that transpired at the Olympian's party. Persephone apologized profusely for leaving Makaria alone, having assumed that no one would have been *that* brazen while there were other Underworld gods in the room.

"Then you don't know Apollo," Hecate had scoffed in response, muttering something about how Helios was just as terrible. "Sun gods. They think the world revolves around them."

Makaria didn't go out the next day, or the day after, and spent most of her time assisting Hecate. By the third day, she was starting to feel utterly useless, and panic began to blur her thoughts when she reminded herself of her temporary immortal status. Hecate had said nothing, giving her gentle encouragements that her time would come.

My time is very limited, unlike the rest of you. Makaria had wanted to snap back. *If someone would just tell me what to do, I could do it!* She had slipped out to the courtyard that morning, craving a little bit of space as she watched the dawn. It was different in the Underworld, the red and orange tones of the sunrise seemed more muted but nonetheless beautiful.

It was there that Nyx found her, holding onto a cup with a heavy shawl wrapped around her shoulders. Makaria felt Nyx before she saw her, her dark, stardust-filled power making itself known as she stepped out of a black pillar of clouds. Nyx always looked like she didn't have a hair out of place, even though she was coming back from her night's work.

"Makaria." Nyx smiled warmly and crossed the courtyard to greet the young goddess. Pieces of nightfall were still trailing behind her hem, and Makaria watched in awe as stars and constellations disappeared into the skirt of her peplos. She returned the embrace and sighed, feeling comforted by the primordial's presence. "What troubles you?" Nyx asked before she had even pulled away. Makaria couldn't help but pull a slightly confused face.

"Besides the fact that I'm supposed to be proving my mortality and Thanatos has refused to help me?"

Nyx raised an eyebrow, not in frustration but rather contemplation, and nodded her head gently. "Do you want this job?" Nyx inquired, studying Makaria with an analyzing expression. Makaria startled slightly, taking a few steps backward.

"Of course I do! I… I didn't always have a place on earth. I did in your service but not anywhere else. It feels like…" she sighed deeply, almost afraid to say the words out loud. "It feels like this is what I have been waiting for. *This* is what I've been waiting to live for."

Nyx smiled. "Then do it, child."

"How can you keep saying that?" Makaria huffed, her voice growing more frantic. "You and Hecate! I need to simply go out there and be this goddess? Thanatos was supposed to help me, and he won't. Now I'm supposed to do it? I don't even have control of my own power! I don't know what you want from me." Her voice trailed off into a whimper. Nyx's eyes were full of sympathy.

"I am regretful that Thanatos is taking a little bit longer to come around. I know this is a lot to comprehend in a very short period of time. Answer me this, how many times have you tried?"

Makaria's face contorted in confusion, and she shrugged. "I tried once with a shade, but the incident with Tantalus didn't make me feel any better, either."

"It sounds like you might have to try again." Nyx sounded every bit the stern mother when she said it, and Makaria was only a little embarrassed. "In the end, nothing happened with Tantalus. No one in the Underworld would let anything like that occur. We all keep eyes on these things, not just Thanatos."

Makaria nodded in response but said nothing, her eyes dropping down to her feet. The thought of disappointing Nyx outweighed the confusing things she felt over running into Thanatos again.

Nyx turned to go inside in order to give Makaria some space. As she passed, she leaned down and whispered, "You know, sometimes it's easier to ask forgiveness than permission. You don't need to be perfect at something right away."

Nyx was inside before Makaria could even react. She had always been afraid of being unwanted and strived to live in a perfect box for acceptance. The gentle push from Nyx was freeing. Makaria dropped the shawl, placed the cup on the ground, and walked right out of the courtyard. She closed her eyes, took a deep breath as the last of the night's darkness left the sky, and willed her power to take her. This time, she was more specific.

Take me to those in need of the face of blessed death.

▸▸▸

MAKARIA FELT a little dizzy when she opened her eyes, still adjusting to the feeling of re-forming in a corporeal body. It felt like she was sand, poured into a vessel. It wasn't an uncomfortable feeling, but it certainly was strange. She had a fresh determination about her as she looked at her surroundings, her face twisting in confusion. It was a graveyard.

It feels like this is a bit late... Makaria looked around and stepped out from between some mulberry trees, taking in the small clearing. Her face softened, and her heart went out to the couple that lay immobile on the ground. She realized that at a glance, their story appeared before her eyelids, up until the moment that the Fates had cut their strings. The man had gone first, believing that she was dead. She followed him promptly upon the gruesome discovery.

Oh, lovers!

Makaria almost wept at the sight of them, but as she got closer, some of her pain abated. She could see their shades, so tangled together in a mess of limbs that she almost couldn't tell them apart. They were weeping, but it was a joyful sound, and they each wiped tears off the other's cheek. These were two lovers who had rather die than live without the other, who had chosen the swift release of death than spend another existence tethered to a realm alone. She had seen in their story that there was no place for them together in the mortal world, but they were bound to be carried to Charon as one.

Charon! Her stomach lurched. The lovers, Pyramus and

Thisbe—she reminded herself of Thanatos's demand to always use the dead's names—had died apart from their families, and the circumstances might not be regarded kindly.

What if their families don't find them? Or don't bury them with a coin? Makaria was dread to take the lovers to the banks of Styx, only to have them wait there for all eternity. *Let them haunt the wretched souls who kept love apart in this world then,* her thoughts hissed, *if they can't be buried properly.*

Then another small piece of Makaria's job clicked into place. Her will manipulated her power to her accord, almost without her realizing it, and a heavy satchel appeared, tied around her waist. It was simple, but finely made, with gold thread that dangerously resembled the thread of the Fates. Inside was a seemingly never-ending supply of coins. Makaria's eyes got wide, and she grinned. *For the blessed! If I'm to be this goddess, then I say who deserves an assist when the wicked don't honor the bodies of the fortunate.*

The declaration snapped into place, and Makaria wobbled as a wave of magic washed over her and she managed to halt time. She had made part of the job her own, had found a way to honor the blessed dead, and a little more control over her powers was unlocked to her. She could feel it like fresh sunlight in her ichor, coursing through her body as it responded to her. *Oh, the gods. Is this what it's going to feel like as I prove myself worthy?*

She was pulled from her thoughts as an angry growl broke the clearing's sacred silence. Makaria, her eyes and hair glowing with a light like diamonds, spun on her heel. A sickle appeared in her hand, gleaming predatorily in the moonlight. The voice cut through the air like an additional blade.

"That's mine."

Makaria's face furrowed as she glared at Thanatos. He stepped into the clearing, the mulberry trees forcing him to duck under them. Makaria had to quell the warmth that reappeared in her stomach when he stepped into the full light of the moon, his eyes shining blue and his hands gripping a scythe. Makaria had to fight to keep the surprise off her face as she realized she wasn't holding a random sickle; it was the twin to the scythe that he was holding. Thanatos always appeared with the infamous blades, and now she had called one to her.

"Well," she stood her ground, "it looks like you're going to have to share."

Thanatos almost growled again. She could see him grinding his teeth and watched the muscles in his arm flex. He was keeping his eyes off her and fixed on the sickle, not out of distaste like she assumed, but because he wasn't prepared to find her there—glowing with her power, *owning* it for the first time. Even if it was just a fraction of what she contained.

When he had appeared next to the bodies of Pyramis and Thisbe, the last thing he had expected was to see her standing there, looking more angelic than even any creature of heaven dared.

"I don't share." His response was biting. "Now, if you'll excuse me, I have a job to do." He put the emphasis on job, and Makaria felt her power flare up territorially.

"They're blessed," she stepped in front of him and blocked him from the lovers' bodies. "I've said so. That means they're my responsibility."

Thanatos paused and looked at her in shock, wondering where this sudden onslaught of confidence had come from.

Damn, if it doesn't look good on her though... No! He almost had to physically shake himself to stay focused. She was still a new goddess and had no idea how to safely pull a shade from its body. *You could fucking teach her.* That annoying voice in the back of his head reappeared, and Thanatos shoved it away. *There might be a more fun way to go about it, though.*

Makaria eyed him warily as a smirk grew on Thanatos's face. He shrugged, his face turning into the picture of nonchalance, and stepped aside.

"All right. You have my sickle. It seems you've conjured

payment for Charon," he held his hands up, "which is a nice touch. I'm not above admitting that. So," he gave a little bow, and Makaria felt him restore time, "go ahead."

Makaria stood taller and walked past him. As soon as her back was to Thanatos, she grimaced. She didn't have any idea how this part worked, and now he was watching her—and she was desperate not to have a repeat of last time.

She assumed that the sickle had something to do with it and approached the shades with reverence as she palmed it.

"Pyramus, Thisbe," she called out their names, her voice morphing into something coaxing and melodic.

Thanatos was also glad that she couldn't see his face, as he nearly stumbled at the new sound of it. *No. She's a pointless, new immortal, who is going to be more trouble for the dead, and for you, than it's worth.*

The shades turned to face Makaria, and their eyes filled with joy at their reunion. Pyramus protectively slid in front of Thisbe.

"You are not Thanatos." His voice was cautious, and Makaria felt some of the wind fall out of her sails. She heard Thanatos snickering behind her. Pyramus couldn't see the God of death and kept speaking. "You carry the sickle when he is known for the scythe."

Makaria nearly rolled her eyes at the observation. *Men and their swords, for crying out loud.* Pyramus continued on in a voice that could only belong to a man inflated by love. "Do you mean us harm?"

"I would protect you from those who would raise a hand against you, in this realm or the next." Makaria didn't know where the words were coming from, but when she looked at the lovers, she was almost overcome with emotion. "Your dedication to one another has been recognized by the gods, and I come to you a servant, the Goddess of blessed death."

Pyramus and Thisbe's faces were stunned, Thisbe letting out a shocked gasp that sounded almost like laughter.

"We haven't been buried." Thisbe bit her lip. "I don't think our families—"

Makaria held up a hand and stopped her. "It would be my honor."

The couple nearly burst into fresh tears.

Thanatos watched from a short distance, stewing in his own insecurities as he begrudgingly admitted to himself that Makaria did care. He watched the shades until he felt time pause again, and he pivoted his gaze to Makaria.

She looked frustrated, holding the sickle awkwardly in one hand. He crossed his arms over his chest and waited. After a few, agonizing minutes, Makaria was silently begging her powers for all their worth to show her what to do. Parts of this job were coming easily to her, but this, not so much. She closed her eyes and pictured the shades being set free from their bodies, drifting away, the sound of a sickle as it tethered their tie to this realm—

"Don't go!" Thanatos's voice carried an emotion she had never heard from him before, and it shook her from her reverie. Makaria realized with a soft thud that her feet touched the ground. She had been floating.

"What?" she snapped, turning around to look at him with an expression of ire. "I was getting somewhere —"

Thanatos was standing right next to her and had his hands on his temples, looking exasperated. "You were about to send *your* shade to Charon, Makaria!" He held his hands out and nearly shook them in frustration. "Forget having a year to prove your worthiness. You nearly ended it yourself!"

Makaria was fed up with being embarrassed, and only felt herself coil tighter with anger. "Whose fault is that?" She dropped the sickle and put her hands on her hips. "Huh?"

Thanatos only stared at her without speaking. "Exactly. I'm *trying*, and if you aren't going to help me, you don't get to be mad when I mess up."

Thanatos remained silent, his lips pulling into a tight, thin line as he stomped past her. He pulled his scythe out from thin air, and with one, clean movement, sliced the shades from their bodies. He turned around and held out his hand to her. "Give me the coins."

"No." Makaria didn't care if she sounded petulant. "I'll do it."

She stalked past him, softening her expression as she reached into the bag and procured the tokens for Pyramus and Thisbe. Thanatos snapped his fingers and time resumed. With a subtle wave of his hand, a current of his power whisked the souls away to the Underworld. The god and the goddess were silent, neither of them looking at one another. It was finally Thanatos who broke the silence.

"I can't have you accidentally sending yourself to Charon or running around and potentially harming shades."

"I would *never* harm a shade!" Makaria spun to face him. Thanatos let out an exasperated groan.

"I can't have you going around accidentally harming shades. Better?" He raised an eyebrow at her, and she nodded for him to continue. He nearly screamed in annoyance before he let his head drop back, and he sighed.

"I will help you."

Makaria's face lit up so brightly, it matched her glowing hair, and her eyes filled with hope. Thanatos felt something in his chest twist. He couldn't afford any familiarity with her, and he steeled his expression.

"Let me rephrase. I will make sure you do not egregiously harm yourself, or *accidentally*," he said the word slowly, "harm a shade. We are not partners. I am not happy about this, and I have no chariot in this race or wager on the outcome of your immortality."

Makaria glared at him. "The stories have truly left your generosity out of their descriptions."

"You will only be a bigger thorn in my side if I have to keep coming to rescue you. You wanted me to help you? You got your wish. From now on, if you're dealing with the dead—blessed, cursed, immortal, anything involving the dead—and you won't breathe without me next to you. Got it?"

"I understand," Makaria muttered, suddenly feeling like she had signed up for something much bigger than she had intended. Thanatos shook his head.

"I don't think you do understand. I don't care if it is the first boy you kissed. You do not handle any shade without me."

"Philon died years ago." Makaria brushed him off, and Thanatos growled.

"I don't like you." His voice was cold. It was childish, and he knew it, but he couldn't help himself as he battled the different emotions she wrenched to the surface in him. Makaria scowled right back, wearing a look that Thanatos thought could freeze fire.

"I don't like you either. I don't like this whole arrangement."

"Then it looks like we agree on one thing, *goddess*."

Makaria reached down and picked up the sickle, toying with it in her hand to taunt him that the object had seemingly chosen a new owner.

"Great. I hate you, you hate me, and we'll spend the next year attached to one another." Her voice was rich with sarcasm. "How could this go wrong?"

Thanatos shook his head, watching as the goddess was coming alive in front of him. She had been eager to please and anxious when they first met, but what a difference a few days and some immortal powers could make.

"This time, you can get yourself home from here, I imagine."

"Now, you said—" Makaria interrupted him, but he was gone.

II

11

When Makaria agreed to Thanatos's tutelage, she never expected that it would involve such early mornings. If she had, she would've never agreed to it in the first place. Thanatos had started showing up at Hecate's house to collect Makaria before dawn every day for the past week, and Makaria was beginning to think of alternate options to her path to worthiness.

That particular morning, she had rolled out of bed and marched straight past Thanatos in the courtyard, not stopping for pleasantries. Immortals didn't *need* to sleep, but it was taking Makaria's newly ageless body a little bit of time to catch up to the idea. Besides, that didn't mean that Makaria didn't *want* to sleep. Sleeping was good. Great, even. If she could slide a nap in…

"Makaria!" Thanatos's barking voice cut through her tired mind, making her stand up straighter. They were on the outskirts of a village, standing somewhere in a pasture. Makaria didn't care for the specifics. It wasn't like she was even going to be allowed to *do* anything. She had watched Thanatos send souls to the Underworld nearly thousands of times by now—"*Curse his ability to stop time and this damn omnipresence!*" she had complained—and still wasn't allowed to help. Which brought them to this morning, one in which Makaria was particularly cranky and Thanatos was...himself.

"I'm paying attention!" she snapped back, flipping the sickle idly in her hand. The sight of it in her hands seemed to irk Thanatos, so she always carried it around.

"What did I just say?" He cocked an eyebrow as he gave her a once-over, making Makaria shiver.

"I'm going to wager that it was something about death." Makaria flashed him a winning smile, but Thanatos's stone-faced expression didn't budge. She had come into this partnership wanting to learn and desperate to prove her worthiness, but his reluctance to let her assist had grated on her nerves.

If he doesn't want to play nice, we won't play nice. She had resigned herself to that commitment, determined to match Thanatos's steely demeanor shot for shot.

"You need to follow me," he growled.

Makaria could almost see the power in his voice, watching it move over the grass on its way to her. She shivered slightly and nodded, dropping her eyes to her feet as she trailed after him.

"We're going to the village." He kept his eyes forward as they began to walk through the pastures. "Glamour yourself."

Makaria couldn't help but watch Thanatos as he shifted. Whatever magic he possessed called out to her—death magic always recognized its own—but as for Thanatos himself, not so much. Thanatos's claws disappeared, and his hair muted itself, going from its inky blue to a much more mortal black. His face softened ever so slightly, and Makaria found herself staring at the planes of his cheekbones.

Stop it. This is the last place you need to worry about having a crush. She rolled her shoulders and let her immortal features recede, her features dulling as they solidified into something entirely human. Well, almost human. They were both still shockingly beautiful humans, even if they did look like humans now.

As Thanatos and Makaria approached the small village, Thanatos let his power envelope both of them until they were obscured from mortal view entirely. Makaria always thought it was overkill, both dampening their features *and* obscuring themselves from view, but Thanatos thought differently.

"All it takes is one person who's a little more spiritually adept than the rest and..." His warning sounded like something that had come from experience and he had learned the hard way, but Makaria didn't press further.

If they could be seen, both mortal and immortal alike would comment on the strikingness of the pair. Makaria, with her gray peplos and winding chiton, her waist-length white hair and gold circlet. Her features were as pale as an angelic corpse, but her gray eyes glittered in the light.

Thanatos stood beside her. Where she only came up to his shoulder, his frame was nearly double her size. He looked like a striking opposite—all sharp angles where she was soft, hair as dark as night, and every inch of his clothing was black. The only similar thing was their eyes—gray and blue respectively—that looked like two halves of a whole in the broad daylight. It was apparent from their faces that they wanted nothing to do with one another, but those eyes told a different story.

Once they crossed onto the village's main road, Hypnos was waiting for them. He tilted his head to the side and tried to suppress a smile when he saw them coming. Their duality catching his attention.

What a pair they'll make if they figure themselves out.

Makaria's coloring was similar to Hypnos's, crafted to complement Thanatos.

"Hypnos." Thanatos acknowledged him by way of greeting, his scythe appearing in his hand.

Makaria noticed that Thanatos's tone had changed, morphing from agitation to one of a gentle solemnness, which told her that he was about to go to work. That was one thing that they could both be counted on for—Makaria and Thanatos left their bickering aside when it was time for a shade to pass on. Thanatos had noticed that about her and was grateful but didn't comment on it. Makaria had been studying Thanatos from day one, trying to understand his mood shifts, but she still felt as clueless as she did on day one, no matter what Persephone and Hecate had told her.

"Makaria," Hypnos said in return, ignoring Thanatos and extending his arms out to the goddess.

She smiled and slid her hands into his, and he greeted her with a soft kiss on each cheek. If Hypnos felt his brother's power flare up at that, so be it. If Hypnos had greeted Makaria that way on purpose to gauge his brother's reaction, well... *Interesting.*

Hypnos was grinning wildly when he pulled back from Makaria. "It's a pleasure to meet you, Goddess of blessed death."

"So you've heard of me," she winked playfully, and Hypnos decided that he loved her.

"Oh, I love you." He clapped his hands in delight before cutting himself off with a yawn. "All right, no time like the present. Unless you're Thanatos of course," he waved a hand in his brother's direction, "Then time becomes irrelevant in all its forms."

"Let's get to work or I'll make *you* irrelevant," Thanatos grumbled. He knew that his brother was woefully in love with his consort, but he didn't like seeing anyone kiss Makaria. The fact that he didn't like seeing that also made him uncomfortable, and he didn't know which sensation was worse.

Hypnos rolled his eyes and turned away from them, beckoning them to follow with a wave of his hand. Makaria looked confused and leaned in closer to Thanatos as they trailed after his brother.

"What is Hypnos doing here?"

"Ah," Thanatos responded without looking down at her as they walked, "We're relieving Hypnos."

"Relieving? What do you mean… Oh." Makaria quickly put it together and kept walking, Thanatos's quietness extending to her. She was surprised when he spoke again, his voice even lower and filled with tenderness.

"These can be some of the gentlest or some of the roughest departures." Thanatos swallowed thickly. "If someone is asleep when they die, they can either be grateful for such a quick, blessed transition or…" he trailed off. When he didn't finish his sentence, Makaria couldn't help but inquire.

"Or what?"

Thanatos let out a long breath, and she could see his eyes twist in pain. "Or they think it's a nightmare."

Makaria's face twisted up in confusion.

"That's not so bad. A lot of shades try to barter with you or are confused…"

"No," Thanatos cut her off with a shake of his head. "They think *I'm* the stuff of nightmares."

Makaria was shocked into silence. She could barely manage a nod as they kept walking, both of their gazes going to Hypnos, still leading them through the village. Makaria had seen the crack in Thanatos's armor, and she knew it. He wasn't worried about the job being difficult in terms of its execution; it was difficult *on him*. It bothered him when people thought he was the very literal stuff of nightmares. It was so far from the gentle Thanatos that she had come to recognize. Of course, she had seen him in his full furious form when excising a murderer and a kidnapper a few days prior. That image would always stay with her. Now, she knew that wasn't who Thanatos *was*. She just didn't know how to tell him that. Or if it was even her place.

Finally, Hypnos stopped outside the low door to a small cottage. The walls were stuffed with mud and straw while the thatched ceiling looked ready to cave in. Hypnos turned to

Thanatos and Makaria and nodded, holding back some of the coarse wool that hung in lieu of a door.

"There's only one?" Thanatos looked at Hypnos, who nodded in assent. Thanatos stepped inside. Makaria stood in the doorway next to Hypnos, giving Thanatos space as she had learned to do. Suddenly, Thanatos looked behind him and silently beckoned her with a finger. Makaria felt her eyes widen in shock, but she walked in after him, a nervous wave crashing over her.

It took a second for her eyes to adjust to the low light. As soon as she did, she zeroed in on the shade almost immediately. It was an old woman, who was covered in wrinkles that told the story of a life well lived. She was made up of memories and smile lines, and Makaria felt her heart swell. This was a woman who had loved and been loved in return, and her departure to the Underworld would likely be met with cheers from those who went before her. Makaria watched in silence as Thanatos went down on one knee, placing his hand on the woman's shoulder. He shook her gently as if to wake her from sleep although Makaria knew it was an awakening of a different kind. A small wind picked up inside the space, and Makaria watched as Hypnos's influence was sucked out of the room.

The woman blinked her eyes open and sat up slowly, a small smile crossing her face as she took in Thanatos. Makaria felt herself release a sigh; she realized that she had been hoping that this wouldn't be a shade who mistook Thanatos for a nightmare.

"...are you ready?"

Makaria focused as she heard the last of Thanatos's conversation with the shade. She nodded, with tears in her eyes, and Makaria was flooded with anticipation. She knew that she was picking up on the shade's feelings, and that this was a blessed soul. It could have been one that was marked for Makaria, but she kept her mouth shut. There was a look in Thanatos's eye that told her this was more important than her right now, that there were days he needed this to counteract the days that weren't so pleasant.

There was a glint of light and a swift motion, and by the time Makaria looked up, the scythe was already disappearing from Thanatos's hand. The shade was gone, likely already halfway to Charon. Thanatos stood up and walked past Makaria without a word. She trailed after him, but he was already gone when she stepped outside. Hypnos was waiting for her.

Makaria scoffed in frustration. "I don't know what I'm supposed to learn by following him around like this."

Hypnos yawned and tilted his head to the side, chewing his lip as if he were weighing his options.

"You knew that this shade was marked blessed." Hypnos shrugged. "Why do you think that Thanatos took responsibility?"

"Because he always takes responsibility."

Hypnos made a *tsk* noise. "That's true. He told you why it's sometimes difficult when his job means relieving me?" Makaria nodded. "So think harder. If it wasn't a blessed death, that means it would've likely been someone who would've been terrified or angry to see Thanatos."

"I don't know what I'm supposed to do about that." Makaria felt herself getting defensive.

"You both need to find balance." Hypnos sounded like an aggravated parent. "If Thanatos thinks that you're going to be taking all the blessed deaths from him, he'd never have any peace again. He'd be forced to work the rest of his days as the *nightmare*."

"No!" Makaria shocked herself with the strength of her rebuttal. She blushed and tried to temper her tone. "I mean, that would be awful. I don't want that for him. Besides, not every good person who dies is blessed…"

Hypnos shrugged, his eyes drooping ever so slightly. "I

don't care for the semantics of this. I'll let you and my brother battle that out. A word of advice, though…" Makaria found herself leaning in. "*Blessed* doesn't always mean they were blessed with *goodness.*"

Before Makaria could ask Hypnos what that meant, he was gone.

12

Apollo was foul-tempered. This had nothing to do with his mood on any particular day. It was simply a character trait. It was now the day before the Feast of Dionysus, and he had been stewing since Thanatos had run him out of the party on Olympus. It was hardly the first time that any of the gods had quarreled, but Apollo always had a particular distaste when it came to Thanatos.

Apollo had picked up a mantle of superiority as he assumed all things relating to light, music, and the sun were the very opposite of death and destruction—the latter having nothing to do with Thanatos, but Apollo wouldn't hear of it. Apollo nursed his one-sided rivalry with great care, letting Orpheus trail him for days in the mortal realm and sing songs of Apollo's greatness.

Thanatos doesn't have a bard. I bet he wishes he did. I have songs that are sung about my excellence.

Thanatos would've been tempted to kill a bard if one followed him around while dictating his actions in song. Again, Apollo wouldn't hear of this and added his propagandist lyricist, in the form of Orpheus, to his long list of alleged superior traits.

Apollo was still licking his wounds in a small clearing outside of Athens when a group of satyrs came stumbling in through the tree line. Orpheus was sitting at Apollo's feet, humming away, as the god scoffed at the intrusion. He *hated* satyrs—Pan, the father of all satyrs, and even by extension, Hermes, Pan's own father. However, it would be a shorter list to focus on the few that Apollo didn't despise. Currently, the list read:

1. Orpheus
2. Artemis

The satyrs were drunk, although this was not unexpected, as almost every immortal and mortal soul was drunk the closer they crept to Dionysia. They stumbled over one another, their hooves getting tangled and their cheeks ruddy as their laughter filled the clearing. They got louder and louder as they got closer, moving towards the tree stump where Apollo was sitting, until they drowned out the sounds of Orpheus and his lyre.

"Will you knock that off?" Apollo snapped, getting the attention of the satyrs. There were four of them, three male and one female, all carrying cups of wine that were undoubtedly enchanted to never run dry. They looked at Apollo as if he had just declared the sun would rise at night. One of them, who looked to be the youngest, stepped forward. He carried himself like their leader, touching his hand to his breast as he spoke.

"Oh wise Apollo," the group behind him snickered, "in such a joyous time of feasting, surely you do not—"

"Stop speaking like that," Apollo hissed. He sat up straighter, kicking Orpheus in the back and not stopping for a second to see if he had harmed his devotee. "This isn't a formal gathering. You're drunk in the woods, and you're disturbing my peace. I can't even hear Orpheus playing my lyre."

The satyr looked at him for a moment, his head turning to one side. A devilish smirk crossed his face, and Apollo felt himself grow tense with anger. *How dare these half-immortals smirk in the face of a* god?

"My name is Marsyas." He gave a mocking bow. "I am bereft to hear that a god of music like yourself, Apollo, is so morose before the holiday."

Apollo growled. "You do not need to concern yourself with the likes of me and mine. If I want to hear my own blessed lyre and take a moment of peace, I will. Be gone with you."

For a second, it looked like Marsyas and the satyrs might listen to Apollo. He gave another short, little bow, and they began backing away slowly. Then Marsyas grinned wildly and snapped his fingers.

"I have an idea! A little…wager, perhaps. In honor of the holiday."

Apollo felt the last of his patience disappearing on the wind. Orpheus looked between Marsyas and Apollo with a look of shocked silence on his face. Apollo turned the idea over in his head. There was nothing that a god loved more than a wager, especially when they were betting against anyone but another god.

"Do go on." Apollo raised a brow.

"Well, I see that you fancy the lyre."

"Everyone knows this," Apollo growled. "What is your wager?" Marsyas chuckled as if he was entirely unbothered by Apollo's threats of violence.

"I'm rather proficient on the flute myself," Marsyas hiccupped, betraying his increasing level of intoxication. "I wager that I can play a prettier tune on the aulos than *you* can play on the lyre."

The other satyrs gasped behind him, and the rest of the clearing went deadly still. It was as if the trees, the grass, and the wind were afraid to move. It was a tale nearly as old as time itself—everyone knew that you did *not* challenge a god.

Marsyas knew it too, and were it not for his enchanted cup of wine, he would have never suggested it.

Apollo stood slowly, his face unreadable.

Foolish, foolish satyr. His thoughts were dark and violent, as another nearly fatal blow to his ego stood in front of him in the form of Marsyas. Apollo was out for blood.

"The terms?" Apollo asked gently.

Marsyas shrugged, clearly not having thought this far in advance.

"Um," he stuttered slowly, taking another long draught of his wine. "The terms, yes. The winner…can do whatever he wants to the loser!" Marsyas trailed off in laughter, sounding like a child who wanted to bother his older brother. Apollo grinned, his mind turning with all the possibilities. After challenging a god, the second dumbest thing that you could do was leave the terms open for interpretation.

"I accept." Apollo stuck his hand out, and Marsyas grabbed it, shaking it eagerly while Apollo eyed him with disdain.

Marsyas cheered as he released Apollo, the other satyrs shouting their exuberance alongside him. Only Orpheus had a look of horror etched into his face, knowing firsthand that Apollo's cruelty was deep under the surface. There was a wickedness behind that bright aura, the sun god whose soul was black as tar. Apollo turned around and looked at Orpheus, licking his teeth and scoffing in amusement.

"Hand me my lyre, Orpheus," he commanded.

Orpheus did so at once, standing up and passing him the instrument before he took a few steps back to the edge of the clearing.

"Who is to judge the contest then?"

Apollo rolled his shoulders like an athlete preparing for a race, strumming a few opening notes on the lyre. Marsyas had been whispering in a huddle with the satyrs. His speech was slurred, and his teeth were now stained red with wine when he spoke.

"W-we have t-two—two!—problems, your g-godliness." Apollo sneered but did not answer. Marsyas continued. "W-we cannot have O-Orpheus judge the contest, a-as he is predisposed to you. As the satyrs a-are to m-me. Also…" Marsyas patted his sides like he was searching for his pockets or a satchel, only to remember that he was a satyr. Satyrs didn't wear clothes. "I s-seem to be without my f-flute." He hiccupped so forcefully that he stumbled backwards and fell on the ground.

Apollo's face twisted up in a mockery of a smile. "Not a problem. Why don't we let the satyrs decide?"

Marsyas's eyes got wide, thinking that he would now undoubtedly win. "I-I am sure that they could be impartial," he giggled, quickly backtracking on his earlier statement. Apollo nodded, giving the satyr what looked to be a respectful nod.

"Excellent," he said to the other satyrs. "I'm sure you will be fair, judging between a god and your friend."

The satyrs cheered and called out their affirmations back to him, toasting one another and sipping wine, spilling it down their chests as they all answered, "Yes!"

Apollo smiled. "And, my dear opponent, surely you know the god of music always comes prepared. I would be happy to lend you my flute for the occasion." Apollo pulled a golden aulos out from the folds of his chiton.

Marsyas nearly drooled at the sight of it, grabbing it between stained fingers and practically leering at the solid gold instrument. Marsyas thrust his hand in the air like he had already won, the flute sparkling in the sunlight.

Orpheus felt dread, heavy like a rock, sink in his stomach. He knew that everything Apollo did was likely laced with trickery—and he was correct. Apollo happily handed over a cursed flute to Marsyas, knowing that no matter how aptly he played or how hard he blew on the pipes, no sound would come out. He was doomed before he even began. Orpheus was nearly sick as he watched the drunken, innocent satyr's dance of celebration before the contest had even begun.

Apollo clapped his hands twice, getting the satyrs' attention, and beckoned for Marsyas.

"I would be happy to begin if you please." Apollo's tone was saccharine, and it made the hair on the back of Orpheus's neck stand up. The satyrs all cheered again but immediately quieted down, piling on the tree stump where Apollo had been sitting. The god walked towards the center of the clearing, held up his lyre, and began to play.

There was no doubting that Apollo was wicked, but there was even less room to deny that he was the god of music. Every time he stroked the lyre's strings, ethereal notes rang out through the clearing. Apollo began to glow, his hair and fingertips radiating golden beams of light, the scent of oranges and smoke permeating the wind.

The music was almost visible in the air, translucent, shining notes sailing up to the heavens with every hum. The trees and the grass began to sway in time with the music. A few of the trees even shed their disguises, appearing as gorgeous dryads, practically melting as their petals fell right off them at the sound. Apollo was hardly even paying attention to the tune, wickedly studying the dryads and ignoring the shocked looks on the satyrs' faces.

There was no telling how long Apollo played. The crowd that had gathered in the clearing was entranced with the music. Orpheus, the only one who had some immunity to the tune, looked positively green as he stood away from the others. He knew what Apollo was doing as he coaxed more of the satyrs' brethren out of the woods, luring them in with the lyre. He wanted an audience.

When Apollo was finally finished, he brandished the lyre like a newborn babe and clutched it to his chest. The crowd that had gathered in the clearing all cheered as flower petals and fruit were tossed down at Apollo's feat.

The satyrs squirmed uncomfortably as they waited for the noise to die down before summoning their courage and pushing Marsyas forward. They whispered encouragements to him, promising Marsyas that they would always choose him over Apollo. The god said nothing as he passed Marsyas, who stepped in the center of the clearing, swallowing thickly as he eyed everyone who had gathered for the performance.

Marsyas took another long sip of wine—to which, the satyrs cheered—and dropped his cup on the ground. He smiled until his whole face lit up with it, grabbed the flute, slapped his leg once, brought it to his lips, and…

No sound came out. There was only a diseased, raspy breathing sound that emanated from the pipes. The entire crowd gasped, and Apollo laughed, watching as the color drained from Marsyas's face. He coughed a few times and stood up straighter, waving his hands with fake bravado to get the crowd to quiet down. They did and everyone leaned forward, waiting. Marsyas picked up the flute, brought it to his lips…and again, not a single sound came out. Everything lapsed into chaos.

The accusations of cheating were quick to fly, with satyrs and dryads and wind spirits demanding that Apollo answer for his trickery. Marsyas was filled with panic as he attempted to play the flute again, and again, and again…only to be met with the sounds of his own labored breathing. Apollo stood, his arms crossed over his chest, watching the sight unfold with glee.

"It's cursed!" a dryad yelled, pointing to the flute. Apollo stepped towards Marsyas and plucked the aulos from him. He looked right at the dryad and blew a perfect note on the instrument, causing another round of shocked gasps and shouts to come up from the crowd. Apollo shrugged as he turned and looked towards the group of satyrs.

"Well? Surely, you are prepared to judge this contest."

There was a sinking feeling in the atmosphere as everyone

knew of the trickery that had occurred. It must have been a cursed object, but of course, Apollo would be able to manipulate his own magic and play the instrument. The satyrs, acting as judges, would have no choice but to declare Apollo the winner, unless they wanted to face his wrath themselves. The entire clearing got quiet as the female satyr stood, her eyes full of tears and her voice quiet.

"We declare the winner to be...Apollo."

The din that arose from the crowd was a sad and melancholy cry as the observers gave half-hearted yells in support of Apollo. They were too afraid of the god to speak out now that a winner had been determined. It was a sham, but those were the shady rulings of making deals with gods. The other forest visitors quickly departed back to where they had come from, refusing to bear witness to what was to come.

Apollo turned towards Marsyas and clapped his hands. "Come here then, you wicked satyr, and let me decide what shall be done to you."

Marsyas, to his credit, raised his chin and stepped forward until he was toe to toe with Apollo. The god laughed, a cruel sound if there ever was one, and he tossed the flute into the air. When he caught it, it had transformed, and now Apollo held a hunting knife made of solid gold. The punishment of Marsyas happened quickly, but also devastatingly slowly, while the satyrs shrieked in fear, and Marsyas cried out in utter torment until his screams shook the trees.

Apollo pinned the satyr to the nearest tree that he knew to be a dryad and chose specifically in his wickedness, and sang a jaunty tune of young love as he flayed the satyr alive. When the wicked deed was finally done, Apollo stepped back, his face flecked with blood and his smile manic. He waved his hand and transformed the skin of the satyr into a wine flask. Without a moment's hesitation—and still whistling—Apollo picked it up and threw it at the other satyrs' feet. They screamed and ran from it, evacuating the clearing until it was only Orpheus and Apollo left.

Orpheus shook his head, his complexion pale. "I renounce you," he said simply, but with conviction, and fled off into the forest.

Apollo raised an eyebrow in surprise, not entirely bothered by the thought of losing just another human acolyte, and shrugged. He took a sip from the cursed flask and sang another damned tune.

"Then I curse you, Orpheus."

13

Apollo was still sitting on the tree stump when Thanatos and Makaria arrived. He paused, the damned flask halfway to his mouth and another wicked grin spreading across his face.

The gods of death were pulled to the sight at the clearing. In life, Marsyas had been a drunk and a gambler, but his death was so afoul with trickery that it had redeemed him in the eyes of the Fates. There were many deaths during the Feasts of Dionysus that proved questionable, and the Fates tended to be as magnanimous as they allowed themselves when all the world was tipsy.

Thanatos appeared in the clearing first, the grass around his feet turning to frost when he landed. He sensed Apollo's sickly power in the air as soon as he landed, causing his armor to manifest over his chest and his eyes to flash black as the whites of his eyes were swallowed up by his power. Thanatos's presence caused the forest to still, not in fear like it had when Apollo had shocked them, but in gentle repose. The great equalizer had arrived.

Thanatos looked around the clearing and took in the sight before him, shaking his head in ire at Apollo.

"You're a wretched god," Thanatos spat. Apollo merely shrugged, leaning back on his elbows.

"What do I care of your opinion, Thanatos?" Apollo taunted him. "No one wants to be on Death's *good side*," he jeered. "Then you'd be hanging out with me all the time."

"I assure you that wouldn't be the case," Thanatos hissed.

He felt his temper stewing inside of him as he sensed the disrespect that had occurred to Marsyas in his final moments. Thanatos tightened his grip on his scythe, prepared to beg the Fates to cut Apollo's string for this, when there was another soft breeze in the clearing. Thanatos's eyes got wide as he spun around, watching as Makaria materialized a few paces away from him. Her satchel of coins was tied around her waist and her sickle—*his* sickle—was in her hand. Thanatos had hoped that she wouldn't have been beckoned for this, that the sheer violence of the death firmly put it in his territory. He spun around and dropped his scythe, stepping in front of Makaria as she dropped into her body and blocking her view of the clearing.

"Makaria, go home." His voice was taught.

Makaria rolled her eyes, assuming over the past few days that they had at least moved past this argument. "Thanatos, I thought we were over this…"

"Go home," Thanatos commanded her, and Makaria ignored what that voice did to her insides. "You don't need to see this."

There was some wickedness in the world, in these games of life and death, that Thanatos found himself suddenly desperate to shield her from. Makaria couldn't push past Thanatos, but swiftly ducked under his elbow to get around him.

"I'm a goddess of death. I can handle a little—*oh my gods!*" Makaria shrieked when she laid eyes on the sight of Marsyas's disfigured body, his shade clinging onto it.

His shade was only apparent to Thanatos and Makaria, and Marsyas wept, traumatized by his violent final moments.

Makaria felt her hands beginning to shake as she couldn't stop staring, couldn't rip her eyes away from the bloodied tree in front of her. The sound of her fear made Thanatos's blood run cold, and he almost cracked the wooden handle of his scythe with the strength of his grip.

Fates… he prayed. *Grant me this.*

The sing-song voices of the Fates rose up to greet him almost instantly. Thanatos was the only god that they would always answer. He carried more of their favor than even Nyx. They did not answer to him, but so crucial was his work to them that they would at least always answer him.

You may frighten him. You may frighten him. You may frighten him. The Fates' response carried its signature triple-echo. Thanatos felt some of his frustration unwind in his chest at the permission.

He may taste death. He may taste death. He may taste death.

He must not swallow it. He must not swallow it. He must not swallow it.

Thanatos grumbled only slightly at that, but he knew they were indulging him. He wasn't allowed to take Apollo's life, but he was allowed some recourse. Thanatos didn't stop to reflect on the fact that he wanted vengeance against Apollo more for Makaria's sake than Marsyas's. Thanatos pulled himself back to the present moment, coming up behind Makaria. He placed his hands on her shoulders, and she sank under the weight of them, leaning back towards him as she searched for support.

"Who would do such a thing?"

Apollo's cold, nefarious laughter echoed throughout the clearing. Thanatos felt Makaria's entire body go tense. She turned her head slowly, and when her eyes landed on Apollo, Thanatos watched proudly as her grip on the sickle tightened.

"I should have known something this debased could only come from something you touched."

Makaria's words were laced with power, and Thanatos

could see it dancing on the wind as she spoke, a ripple of icy blue magic disappearing over the grass. He kept his face stoic as he leveled his gaze at Apollo but felt something warm spread in his chest—something akin to pride—as Makaria stepped towards the god, now unfazed.

Apollo feigned sadness and clutched at his chest. "You wound me, young goddess!" His face contorted into a displeased sneer. "Do your job and away with you to the Underworld. There's nothing for you here."

"Unless I decide to take you with me," Makaria quipped, crossing the space between them until she was halfway in between Thanatos and Apollo. Apollo's brow furrowed in confusion, but Thanatos caught the slightest blip of fear in his eyes.

That's a girl. Thanatos grinned from behind her, rolling his head to the side as he let himself expand. His fingers morphed into claws, his teeth elongating into fine-tipped points. The wildness in his eyes was back again, and a soft aura of dark, deep blue power cascaded around him. The frost at his feet melted as the grass died, the blight slowly spreading out from Thanatos like slow-moving water, killing all the greenery it touched.

"You can't do that," Apollo's voice was filled with false bravado. "Only the Fates decide."

"Do they?" Makaria took one more step closer, and Thanatos swore he saw Apollo flinch. "Maybe I've forgotten that little fact. I am such a *young goddess*, after all. I'm sure they would find it in their hearts to forgive me while I adjust to the learning curve." As she said the words 'learning curve,' she ran her thumb across the curved blade of the sickle, a thin bead of golden ichor appearing on her finger. Makaria promptly licked it off, eyeing Apollo with a dead stare. Thanatos was not unaffected by the sight. Apollo seemed frozen, but then he shook himself free of his stupor and stood. He pointed a finger at Makaria.

"Listen here, I don't take kindly to threats from—"

Thanatos's transformation into his most powerful form was almost complete, and he walked forward and took his place behind Makaria again. At the sight of the God of death, his teeth gleaming in the sunlight and power dripping off of his armor like tar, Apollo paled.

Makaria, without looking at Thanatos, assumed the reaction was aimed at her. She grinned with pride. "Threats from who? Did you forget that I was a goddess of *death?*" She twirled the sickle. Thanatos mimed *yes* to Apollo from behind Makaria.

"Y-yes," Apollo nodded without moving another inch, his eyes firmly fixed on Thanatos.

"You'd do well to not forget it again," Makaria hissed. She turned around, and in an instant, Thanatos was back in a mortal form. Makaria looked at him, in the body that she was used to, and sighed. Her features contorted back to sadness once she took her eyes off Apollo, and she walked towards Thanatos, keeping her tears at bay.

"What do I do?" she asked gently, and Thanatos nodded in the direction of Marsyas.

"Go. If anyone has earned a blessed death, it is him. Go and —do not move, Apollo!" Thanatos cut himself off and shouted over Makaria's shoulder at Apollo, who had begun to try and sneak away. Apollo stopped moving and sat back down on the tree stump with a *hmph* that sounded like a child. Thanatos turned his attention back to Makaria. "Go and see to Marsyas. See past his body and tend to his shade. He could use your kindness." Thanatos encouraged her, and Makaria nodded rapidly, steeling herself to the grisly sight beyond them.

"What… Will someone bury him?" she whispered. Thanatos sighed, his gaze moving from the mutilated Marsyas to the sulking Apollo.

"Yes, I imagine that Pan and the satyrs will."

"Then…why do I…why do I need to give him a coin?"

Makaria looked up at him in confusion, the intricacies of the job still weighing her down.

"Look at Marsyas," Thanatos encouraged with a nod in the satyr's direction, and Makaria knew that he meant for her to look at Marsyas's shade. He was still crying, his face contorted in a grimace of fear and pain. Thanatos's voice was as soft as she had ever heard it when he spoke again. "Do you think he should wait a few days for Pan and his family to assemble the funerary rites?"

Makaria balked at the thought. The idea of leaving Marsyas's shade attached to his body for any longer than necessary made her queasy. "No, no, of course not." She shook her head and walked away from Thanatos, who kept an eye on her as she proceeded with her work.

Makaria was gentle and quick with Marsyas, explaining to him what had happened and where he was bound for next. While she was busy, Thanatos turned back towards Apollo, unleashing his immortal form again in a blink and putting up a wave of power in between him and Makaria. He felt a flicker of shame as he did it, as he sought to hide himself from her, but something in him cringed at the idea of her seeing him in his most brutal of apparitions.

"Apollo," Thanatos bellowed, his claws making a sickening clacking sound as they tapped against the scythe's handle. "You will answer for this." Thanatos vanished and reappeared directly in front of the other god, who shrieked and fell backward.

"I-I did what was within my rights!" Apollo screamed back, not in anger, but in fear. "It was a wager and I won!"

Thanatos shook his head slowly, pulling the scythe back above his shoulder. A nasty grin spread across his face and revealed his wicked teeth. There was a fresh wave of power that undulated off him, flattening Apollo to the ground and making him cower. There was such a finality in everything that Thanatos said and did, it struck to your very bones and held you there. Fear gripped

Apollo's heart like he had never known, and he whimpered on the ground. His own power tried to answer Thanatos's display of strength, but the meager rays of light were devoured by shadow.

"You know as well as I," Thanatos's voice dropped even lower, shaking the trees around them, "that you took advantage of a drunken satyr, who came at you in jest, and gave him a cursed instrument."

The events of the wager had played out before Thanatos's eyes before he had even arrived as the events of all deaths did. Apollo shrieked at his own deception.

"T-that doesn't mean you can kill me!"

Thanatos bent down, and with his free hand, he dragged a solitary claw up Apollo's chiton, ripping it in a clean line.

"I think… I can do whatever I want."

Suddenly, without any of the tact or grace that he showed others, Thanatos swung the scythe down and violently cleaved the shade from Apollo's body. Apollo let out a cry of pain as his power exploded around them, but it dissipated on the wind as it was quickly outmatched by Thanatos's magic. Thanatos held the shade of Apollo in his hand, leaning his head down over Apollo and opening his mouth wide, as if he was ready to devour it. Apollo wept, squirming in Thanatos's sharp grip, every inch of him feeling like it had been ripped apart.

When Apollo finally screwed his eyes shut and consigned himself to the end, he felt a massive impact that nearly broke every bone in his body. Thanatos slammed Apollo's shade back into his mortal form, leaving him a panting, shuddering mess on the ground. The gods healed quickly, even though they still felt pain, and Apollo cursed Thanatos and all he was worth as he crawled away. Thanatos watched in sick satisfaction as Apollo's joints hung in wrong directions and his body tripped over itself trying to repair the damage.

It was a violent thing to have your shade pulled from your body, especially if the Fates had not cut your string, only to be slammed back into it. It was the most pain that any immortal or mortal could likely feel, being pulled in between the land of the living and the dead. God or not, it would take Apollo days to feel fully himself again.

Thanatos watched with a satisfied smirk, slowly decompressing back into his mortal form, as Apollo finally garnered enough of his own power to vanish. He heard Apollo's curses on the wind but only smiled, waving his hand and removing the barrier between himself and Makaria. She was waiting for him, her hands on her hips.

"What was that about?" Her brow was furrowed. "Where's Apollo?"

Thanatos waved a hand in the air. "Don't worry about it. Did you tend to Marsyas?"

Makaria nodded but looked rather sheepish. "Yes, but there's something you should—"

"Thanatos!" A deep, rich voice rang out through the clearing, and Thanatos rolled his eyes.

"Oh, not today," Thanatos sighed heavily, and Makaria grimaced.

Pan stumbled in from the tree line, and Thanatos could see his disciples quickly attending to the body of Marsyas behind them.

"What is the meaning of this?" Pan bellowed, going right up to Thanatos and sticking his finger in his chest. "How dare you allow…"

"You know that I don't have any power over how someone dies or even when," Thanatos growled, but it was without threat, and Makaria got the impression that this was a conversation he had had many times prior.

"Well," Pan stuttered, "who did this?" Thanatos stepped towards Makaria, putting his hand on her shoulder and beginning to pull them back to the Underworld. "Don't you go without answering me!" Pan's threat echoed on the winds around them, and before Makaria could blink, they were standing back in the fields of Asphodel.

"Why didn't you answer him?" Makaria spun around and demanded answers of Thanatos. "He cared for Marsyas. That wasn't very fair…"

"I'm always fair," Thanatos cut her off as his eyes glowed blue. Makaria took a small step back, knowing she had touched a nerve.

"Still," she muttered, looking down at her feet and kicking at the ground there. Thanatos rolled his eyes and let out a disgruntled sigh.

"Pan will figure out who did this soon enough. That doesn't matter to us." Thanatos pointed his scythe at her, as if to drive home his point. "The less that you can involve yourself in the drama of the living, the better."

Thanatos turned on his heel and began walking off, muttering under his breath.

Makaria couldn't help but notice that he had said *us*.

14

Makaria was still thinking of the way Thanatos had referred to them as a team—*Well, he used* 'us', she bargained with herself—a week later. The early wake-up calls were bothering her less and less. She didn't know if she was simply getting used to existing beyond a circadian rhythm or if she was looking forward to seeing Thanatos. She felt *something* whenever she looked at him, and it was harder than ever to tell herself if it was disgust or frustration.

The past few weeks had been grueling, and she didn't do nearly as much as she wanted to, but she couldn't deny that Thanatos was a thorough teacher. His patience had gotten better over time too, something that made Makaria's anxiety ease ever so slightly.

She slipped out of Hecate's house without a word, waiting for Thanatos in the courtyard. It had become a steady routine. Except this morning, she was holding two portions of bread in her hands, which was making her exceptionally nervous for such a small gesture. There had been fleeting moments of tension between them, and Thanatos had shown her kindness in their tougher moments on the job, but it was a wall that Makaria was determined to break through. There was something holding Thanatos back, keeping him from relaxing around her. Makaria wasn't even concerned if he fully opened up to her, but she knew that he still acted particularly reserved when he was around her. It was a small token, and she hoped it would act as a semi-literal olive branch.

"Good morning," Thanatos's low voice got Makaria's attention, and her eyes snapped up to meet his.

"Morning!" She smiled, immediately thrusting the small bundle out towards him. "I brought you breakfast. Well, a snack, I guess." Makaria paused and forced her smile a little bit bigger, suddenly feeling like this might have been a mistake. Thanatos said nothing, and she started talking to fill the silence. "You really should try it. Aeëtes makes the most divine bread. Who would've thought? I certainly wouldn't have—"

"Thank you," Thanatos cut her off and accepted it from her outstretched hand. He still wasn't smiling, but there was a softness in his eyes that Makaria was only used to seeing when he looked at mortals. "I don't think anyone has ever…brought me breakfast before." He said the words slowly as if they were in a foreign tongue. Makaria tilted her head a little, choosing her sentiments carefully.

"There are a lot of reasons that working with me might not be so bad."

Thanatos looked remorseful as he turned away from her, walking out of the courtyard and beckoning her to follow him. They went a few paces in silence, Makaria's nerves getting worse by the minute, worried that she had overstepped a boundary. She didn't want to carve out her place in this world by pushing Thanatos out of his. When Thanatos finally spoke, his voice was low, as if he was sharing secrets.

"It's not…personal."

Makaria raised a brow. "Well…to be honest, I didn't think that it was. You have to admit that you weren't exactly forthcoming when we met."

"I wasn't." Thanatos shrugged but offered no further explanation. They were walking along the shores of the river now, quietly pulling off pieces of bread. Makaria decided that there was little to lose.

"Why do you hate the idea of working with a partner so much?" Thanatos stopped short, releasing a long breath before he turned to look at her.

"I've been teaching you, haven't I? Do you feel like I have been keeping secrets from you or denying you critical pieces of information?" he spoke quickly and analytically, and Makaria could almost see his walls going up.

Their relationship had been full of nothing but stops and starts, filled with moments of fleeting familiarity and then pivoting back to near contempt.

I've had enough of this, and it stops today. I'm tired of not knowing where I stand with him.

"No," Makaria sighed exasperatedly. "That's not what I mean. Although, beyond delivering coins to the blessed, you really haven't let me do much."

Thanatos stiffened. "You can file a complaint with my mother if you'd like." Makaria wanted to shake him, and she fought the impulse to stomp her foot.

"You're insufferable," she groaned, and Thanatos looked away from her. Makaria cursed herself, realizing that she was still going about this the wrong way. *What is it that Persephone said about the men of the Underworld?*

"Look," Makaria sighed slowly, looking up at Thanatos, "I don't want to take your place. I know that this is difficult, but I think we can figure it out…together."

"Together?" Thanatos snapped his head back towards Makaria, fixing his eyes on her.

The air seemed to get thicker around them, and a lump formed in Makaria's throat. There were very few times when Thanatos would look her dead in the eye, and every time he did, it caused chills to run down her entire body. His breathing picked up as if he was similarly affected, and both of their powers began manifesting between their fingertips.

Something shifted in her soul as Thanatos bored his gaze into her, and Makaria found herself wanting to throw herself into his arms. There was an emptiness in his eyes, and she was overcome with the desire to fill it. Thanatos studied her and was overcome with a vision of her in his home. No, not just in his home—on the other throne. The consort's throne. He was so terrified by the sudden revelation of how well she might fit there that he refused to move a single inch, refused to breathe.

As the black and blue tendrils of smoke curled around their wrists and reached for one another, the pair gasped, both of them taking a few steps backward as if they could yank their magic away.

"As friends!" Makaria squawked the word out, sounding as though she was breaking the surface of water and coming up for air. The power dissipated around them, and Thanatos looked around as if he was trying to determine where it went. There were a few more moments of terse silence as neither of them dared speak or even look at each other.

"Friends," Thanatos repeated.

"Friends." Makaria nodded, thrusting her hand out towards him awkwardly, as if to shake.

Thanatos looked down at her extended hand and let out a low chuckle, the tension seemingly broken between them. He reached out and accepted the gesture, encompassing her entire palm in his. If they both held on for a minute longer than was socially acceptable, neither of them commented.

"Well," Makaria looked up at him, "where are we off to today?"

Thanatos flicked his fingers in the air and Makaria felt the familiar pulling sensation that let her know they were headed to the mortal realm.

"This one is going to be interesting." Thanatos turned to

look at her and winked, his expression fading on the wind as they drifted off to the land of the living.

▶▶▶

WHEN MAKARIA FELT her feet touch the ground and blinked her eyes open, she almost fell backwards. They were standing in a clearing that looked remarkably like the one that held Tantalus. Thanatos turned to her and smiled, chuckling softly. He must've known that she recognized the small pool and its grove of fruit trees, and he shook his head.

"Fear not, this isn't where Tantalus is kept."

Thanatos led the way through the branches, holding them back for Makaria as she walked behind him. She tried not to read too much into the gesture.

You're friends now. He's just being friendly.

Thanatos, on the other hand, had felt like a lit flame ever since he'd met Makaria. There were so many things about their relationship that needed to be handled with caution — she was a new immortal who knew nothing about this world; she might take over his job or leave him the worst parts of it, and if she didn't prove herself worthy, he'd be the one to take her shade. At least, those were the things he told himself. He disregarded that most of that could be avoided if he got over himself and worked with her, *really* worked with her. The real problem was admitting to himself that he could see himself *working* with her for a very long time. In a lot of ways. A lot of different —

Stop it.

Thanatos corrected his thoughts as he held another branch away from Makaria's face. He was still ridden with the fear that he'd let someone down, let her down, in the matters of life and death. That was something he'd never come back from, but if she wanted to be *friends*, then friends it was. He had almost scoffed in her face when she mentioned it, but telling her that he was torn between a shockingly intense desire for her and the fact that he might have to be the one to kill her was out of the question. In the end, all of his teaching wouldn't matter. She was the only person who could prove herself worthy.

When they finally stepped out to the water's edge, Makaria zeroed in on the shade who awaited them.

"Narcissus," Thanatos murmured, looking down at his arm and reading the name off it.

The man was kneeling over the water's edge, about to fall in. He was the most stunning man that Makaria had ever seen, at least by mortal standards. He had a frame built like an athlete, full of poise and grace, which she could determine even by how he held his body above the water. His hair was a deep brown, shining with golden highlights, as if the gods couldn't decide what color it should be. Makaria couldn't see his face, but she got the feeling that it also looked like it was crafted by Aphrodite herself.

Neither Makaria nor Thanatos moved as the man fell into the water, and after a few, quick moments, drowned. Makaria always felt her stomach turn when the last moments of someone's life were violent, but she knew that there was nothing they could do to intervene. Narcissus's shade pulled itself from the watery depths, collapsing on the shore and breathing heavily as though it was still in a mortal body.

"Did he just..." Makaria trailed off as the events of Narcissus's life flashed before her eyes. Thanatos laughed quietly, his shoulders shaking, as he started walking towards the shade.

"Drown because he was staring at his own reflection? Yes."

Makaria felt her mood sour as she scowled at the shade, the depressing story of Echo playing out in her mind. They both approached the shade, scythe and sickle appearing in their hands respectively, and Thanatos looked at Makaria.

"Well? I think this one is yours." He had a playful grin on his face.

"What?" Makaria crossed her arms over her chest, careful to not poke herself with the sickle. "I think not! He's just drowned himself because of his own vanity. You can't be serious."

"He was *blessed* with other-worldly beauty, Makaria." Thanatos's tone was playful, and it made Makaria flush. He had taunted her with the idea of *blessed* death before, but never like this. Not as if they were...equals. Friends. A lazy smile crossed her face, and she scoffed.

"He was *blessed*," she gave a poor impersonation of Thanatos's low voice, which caused him to laugh, "in life with those good looks. There's nothing here about his death that's blessed." The mood between them had shifted to something that was undoubtedly playful, almost flirty.

Friends, friends, we're friends. Makaria repeated the phrase in her head.

We're being friendly. So friendly. Thanatos nearly beat the phrase into his consciousness. Their attraction was so strong, albeit confusing and sudden, that it was hard for either of them to find the *friendly* line.

"You're getting hung up on technicalities," Thanatos chided, tapping his temple. It made Makaria think back to when Nyx had accused her of the same thing, and Hypnos's advice that *blessed* could have different meanings. There was an ember of something in her mind that clicked into place, but Makaria was distracted by a wailing sound at their feet.

Narcissus's shade was openly sobbing now, his face contorted into an expression of disdain.

"N-not to make this about *me*," he sniffled harshly, "but I'm the one who's died here!"

Thanatos rolled his eyes. His empathy ran out when it came to the vain and entitled.

"Are you sure this one is mine?" Thanatos looked down at

Makaria again, both of them trying to contain their laughter. "He certainly thinks that's blessed."

"I am cursed!" Narcissus cried out in response, causing both of the gods of death to frown at him in distaste. He continued on, remarkably unbothered. "Cursed! What else makes sense? I had everything—everything—and now I'm *dead.*"

"Okay," Thanatos let out a low whistle, "I'm done here. Point made, Makaria."

Before she could even respond, Thanatos flicked his scythe through the air and sent Narcissus's shade to the banks of Styx. They both burst into laughter again as Narcissus's wailing complaints were carried off on the wind. When they finally stopped, Makaria looked up at Thanatos with a studious expression.

"What?" Thanatos looked around as if there was something he wasn't seeing, confused by Makaria's shift in attitude. She only smiled, slipping the sickle into the sash around her waist and beginning to walk back towards the fruit trees.

"Oh, nothing," she called out over her shoulder. "However, I do think this is the first time I've ever seen you smile so much."

Thanatos begrudgingly felt his heart leap at that, and he jogged to catch up with her.

"Well, if that's the case," his tone was rife with mock seriousness, "we'd better not tell Narcissus. He'll think it's because of him."

Makaria was still laughing as they were pulled off to their next death.

15

In the following two weeks, Thanatos had slowly—very, very slowly—started to let Makaria step in more as she shadowed him. There was hardly a moment where she wasn't near him, standing next to him or sitting beside a shade they were assisting. They had meant it when they agreed to work together as friends, but both of them struggled with replaying the memory of the first night that they met.

If only I had let my brother sort out his own drunken escapades. Thanatos wasn't full of many regrets, but he found himself singularly focused on this one. Makaria wasn't much better off, wondering if the party had only been a day later, would she have had a little more confidence in the world of the immortals to stay at Olympus without Persephone?

Probably not, but curse Ares and his horrible timing.

Each shade that called out to the realm of the dead were met with the presence of Thanatos and Makaria, their arrival starting to blur together. It helped that their physical forms were so complementary to one another, and it wasn't long until their auras were practically emanating the same energy. That very morning, when Thanatos showed up at Hecate's front step to meet Makaria, it had only taken one quick glance from

Nyx before she raised her brow in a pleased, suspicious way. She gave her son a once-over and then promptly did so to Makaria, who apparently had gotten over her disillusionment with early mornings—judging by the way she practically floated down the steps.

Hecate and Nyx watched the pair leave. Hecate laughed to herself before tossing a handful of ash in her hearth's open flame.

"I don't always approve of your scheming…"

"Yes, you do," Nyx interrupted her with a scoff, crossing her legs at the kitchen table and picking at a loaf of olive bread. "In fact, if we look at it historically, you've got a longer track record of *schemes*."

"It's not scheming when it's your job," Hecate said primly, straightening up. "Like I was saying, I don't always approve of your scheming, but those two? Smart."

"We'll see," Nyx murmured to herself, watching Thanatos and Makaria through the small window. They walked so closely next to one another that a strong gust of wind would make them touch. Their hands swayed as they walked, their fingers coming desperately close until one of them inevitably pulled away at the last minute. Nyx shook her head in disbelief as Thanatos summoned his power, and the pair disappeared on the wind. "It's not enough that we see it. They'll have to see it for themselves."

Makaria was getting more accustomed to traveling as a god, which was drastically different from getting from point A to point B as a human, and hardly noticed it when she was swept off the ground. The one thing that she could not ever get used to was the feel of Thanatos's power when he ushered them from place to place. It licked up her ankles as she dissipated, encompassing her whole body before she very literally sank into it and disappeared. She had seen it happened with enough of the other immortals that she knew no one else felt like a touch of another god's power might incinerate them.

It wouldn't be a bad way to go.

Although, there were probably some awkward technicalities around her death if it was caused by Thanatos. Their *friendship* was driving them both insane, now that they had gotten over the initial territorial disputes of their second meeting. Thanatos wasn't doing any better, feeling his demeanor soften and part of his heart melt a little bit more every time he brought Makaria closer to him. She was still getting used to her power, she had been a goddess for barely over a month, so she still required a lot of assistance. It nearly drove him mad, how much *touching* it required.

Their fears and insecurities had caused whiplash, but they were both happy to just spend the past few weeks working together without an ever-present argument.

Makaria looked up and was surprised to find that they were standing in a receiving hall. She knew they were still in the Underworld and took a quick glance around the space. It was made of black stone and was covered with inlaid jewels; tapestries the colors of gemstones hung from the rafters.

It would've been fit for Midas himself—Makaria and Thanatos had dealt with that rather unpleasant lesson a week ago—if it wasn't so clearly built for a god. There were tall basins full of oil and lit with fire, covering the entire room not in firelight, but with the soft glow of all the riches that seemed to be pouring out of the walls themselves. The room was full of people, all of them gods, and Makaria could identify a few of them at first glance.

At the head of the room was a small dais, only a few steps up, where two massive obsidian thrones were carved out of the ground itself.

In one of them, unmistakably, was Hades.

Makaria hadn't met Hades yet, but his presence spoke for itself. His ankle-length black chiton and black leather sandals were synonymous with the God of the Underworld, but it was the brooch at his shoulder that gave him away. It was nearly the size of a child's fist, made of pure silver and embellished with a garnet.

The stone's red color was so dark, it was almost black. The rest of Hades's look hadn't changed in millennia either—a short, trimmed beard, and waves of dark, curly hair. He was distracted, his bident laying lazily across his lap. It was a wicked weapon, and Makaria knew that no matter how relaxed he looked, Hades could wield it with dreadful accuracy.

"If you stare at him any longer, I might get jealous." Thanatos's voice was playful and quiet as he leaned down and whispered in Makaria's ear. She scoffed playfully and rolled her eyes at him, cocking an eyebrow in disbelief.

"Jealous of what, pray tell?" Makaria teased. *Tell me. Tell me directly you're jealous, so I'll know for sure this isn't a game.*

Thanatos smirked in return but said nothing, straightening up and nodding towards the dais as if to scold Makaria and urge her to pay attention. She flicked her hand dismissively in his direction, but the gesture had no intent behind it. This was what their *friendship* had become, dropping hints and flirtatious comments that went right up to the line. As soon as one of them would ask point blank to try and force some sort of solid response, the other would pull back. Makaria had tried it, knowing that Thanatos wouldn't admit that he might be jealous of how she looked at Hades in approval.

"What are we doing—"

Makaria realized she had no idea why they would be in Hades's receiving hall, but she was cut off when there was a loud knock at the doors. Thanatos's hand slid to her back, the light, warm touch sending a shiver down Makaria's spine, but he pointed in the direction of the doors. They swung open, and Makaria was shocked to see Persephone walk in, her gait light and her expression untroubled, as if she didn't have a care in the world while the heavy doors slammed shut behind her.

Makaria knew that look was part of Persephone's arsenal.

She kept up the charade of a unmotivated, ditzy goddess of flowers and spring, but she was devastatingly powerful. Especially now that her bargain with Demeter had been struck and her relationship with Hades, and position in the Underworld, had been secured.

Persephone's peplos flowed on the ground a few feet behind her, black petals appearing on the floor where it dragged. It was fitting for her dueling titles—Goddess of Spring and Queen of the Underworld. She seemed unfazed as she slid up the dais, all of her movements graceful like the breeze.

Persephone kissed Hades's cheek sweetly, causing his face to soften considerably, before she sat down on the throne next to him.

"By the gods," Thanatos laughed so only Makaria could hear him, "look how soft he is for her."

Makaria bent her neck to look up at Thanatos, her expression challenging and teasing as she hid her mouth behind her hand, whispering.

"Do you really think that Persephone makes Hades *soft*?"

As soon as she said it, Makaria blushed furiously and then looked away, her eyes downcast as if she was immediately embarrassed by the taunt. Thanatos's mouth dropped open in a wide smile that was equally amused and shocked. He bent down again to offer a retort when Hades clapped his hands once and got the room's attention.

"Bring them in!" When Hades opened his mouth to speak, he didn't talk, he commanded.

Makaria felt a shiver as the god's power swung the doors wide open for the second time. There was a wave of murmurs and whispers that spread over the crowd as footsteps entered the hall, but Makaria couldn't see over the heads of the gods in front of her. She went up on her tiptoes to get a closer look, and barely managed to hold back a squeak as Thanatos wrapped his arm around her waist. He hoisted her a few inches up until they were waist to waist, her body flush with his. Makaria felt her insides turn to fire as she tried not to think about how he was holding her up with only one hand.

"A shade has entered Hades's realm willingly to claim a shade we've taken," Thanatos whispered in Makaria's ear, and her eyes went wide in shock. Thanatos's power handled most of the mortal shades although she incarnated directly with him at every death that they could.

From the sound of it, they hadn't been present at this passing. Now that the shade had made it to the Underworld and past Charon, they were solely under Hades's jurisdiction. The footsteps got closer until they crossed in front of Makaria and Thanatos, kneeling down at the dais.

"It's Orpheus!" Makaria hissed, squirming in Thanatos's grip until he placed her back on the ground. He whisper-yelled at Makaria as she began pushing through some of the other immortals in attendance to get to the front of the crowd.

"Wait—" Thanatos called after her, not focusing on whatever it was that Hades was saying as he followed Makaria through the masses. She stopped short of breaking free from the crowd, and Thanatos came up to stand behind her.

Orpheus was kneeling in front of the thrones, his arm wrapped over the shoulders of a woman by his side. She was also nearly prostrate in front of Hades and Persephone, and it was apparent from her slightly muted coloring that she was the one who had died. Orpheus still held on to some of the color of the living, blood still pulsed underneath his skin. He was pleading with Hades, a lyre hanging off the crook of his arm.

Where the hell is Apollo? Makaria felt herself grow tense when she realized he might be in the room. Thanatos moved closer to her again, his hand gently resting on her back, as if he realized the same thing. She relaxed immediately under his touch, and they focused on what the gods were saying.

"She wasn't supposed to die," Orpheus was pleading. "You

have to believe me. Apollo cursed me. He bargained with the Fates, so her string was cut…"

"Careful," Hades silenced Orpheus, his tone was sharp as granite. "Every string is cut at the time it was always going to be cut."

All the gods knew that on occasion, there was bargaining with the Fates. It was very seldom done successfully—Nyx was one of the few goddesses who managed to pull it off more than once. It was rare to get the Fates' attention, so if it happened, it was decreed that said bargain was likely always part of a mortal's fate. Thus creating a gray area, where Hades emphasized that *'Every string is cut at the time it was always going to be cut'*, which was true but did not discount the god's influence. It was simply too foolish to debate the Fates, and Hades didn't tolerate disrespect towards them in the Underworld.

"Hades." Persephone's voice was a soft contrast to her husband's, but it carried no less power as she leaned over the armrest to get his attention. He raised a brow in her direction, and Persephone looked at the lovers. "Let him plead his case." She didn't command that he release the shades, just listen. Hades looked at the bent figures of the mortals in front of him and nodded once.

Orpheus and Eurydice took turns and proceeded to tell the story of their love to the crowd of immortals. Persephone's face contorted as she listened with rapt attention while Hades remained stoic. Makaria felt herself gasp when she heard about the snake that bit Eurydice on her wedding day, and by the time Orpheus recounted his journey to the Underworld, she was unable to stop her tears from falling on her cheeks.

Thanatos looked down when he felt Makaria's shoulders shake, his hand going from her back to wrap around her waist as he realized she was crying. It was truly an awful story—anything involving young love always was—but Thanatos had lived too long and seen too many deaths and rebirths to be particularly moved. It was painful, but either Orpheus would move on or he wouldn't. Eventually, he'd be reunited with Eurydice in the Underworld, one way or another. He could tell from Makaria's body language that she didn't feel the same way.

"…and now, I humbly ask you to release us both." Orpheus finished his story and bowed his head once more.

Hades looked around the room, and Thanatos recognized the god's expression. Hades was a strategist, through and through, and that was the face of a man who was judging the expressions of the other immortals in the room. He was gauging how effective Orpheus had been in pleading his case.

Hades doesn't make deals. Thanatos's thoughts were melancholic but resigned. *Poor Orpheus, you've come to barter with the one god made of stone. Any other god of the twelve would've indulged in human games.*

It was Persephone's expression that Thanatos overlooked. Her eyes were wide with compassion. It hadn't been easy getting to the point where she was able to sit next to Hades on that dais, and those memories were too fresh for her to ignore them.

It did catch Thanatos's attention when Persephone scanned the room, her gaze landing on Makaria. The goddesses greeted one another with the subtlest of nods. Thanatos knew that they were friends; he had heard how it was Persephone who pulled Makaria away from Olympus that first night, which was something he had to actively remind himself he couldn't be mad at her for.

Persephone raised an eyebrow and ever-so-slightly, tilted her head towards Eurydice. Thanatos felt his body tense as he waited for Makaria's answer. A few, paralyzing seconds later, he watched as another tear fell down Makaria's face, and she nodded. It was a fleeting interaction, quick enough that no one caught it other than Thanatos, but it made his blood run cold, and he felt some of his power pull back from where it was intermingled with Makaria's.

She was asked to choose between life and death...and she chose to cheat death. Thanatos didn't move a muscle, but he felt himself almost physically recoiling, his mind running away with the idea. *She would never choose you. No one ever has, not like that. You're friends, and that's all it will ever be.*

Hades's voice rose above the all-consuming nature of Thanatos's own insecurities, pulling him back to the present moment. Hades was openly arguing with Persephone, and although their voices were muted enough that no one heard specifics, the fight was apparent. Thanatos felt a wave of power ripple across his skin as Orpheus and Eurydice's names were repeatedly written and erased down his arms. As Hades and Persephone argued about the fate of the mortals, their threads shifted. Thanatos couldn't keep up from one moment to the next with the outcome.

He gritted his teeth and let it happen, even though it caused him great physical pain to stand so close to the mortals while their destiny was in flux. Allegedly. This was one of those gray areas that became practically undefinable, nearly impossible to answer the question about what determined whether an outcome was predestined.

Makaria sensed the shift in Thanatos's energy and turned to look up at him, her expression full of concern. Thanatos shook his head and directed her back to Orpheus and Eurydice, unable to look her in the eyes. He was equally as upset that she had encouraged Persephone to argue for this, for Orpheus and Eurydice's release.

For choosing life.

Hades finally stood, holding out his hands for quiet while he gripped the bident. His face was resigned, and behind him, Persephone seemed accepting, but not pleased. The energy around Thanatos cooled off as he felt the lovers' fate settling.

Interesting. Thanatos pursued the different options in front of them, which they were currently unaware of. *Very interesting. It's rather crafty of Hades.* Thanatos's mood lightened considerably although he had slightly built up the wall in between him and Makaria again.

"Orpheus." Hades's voice was like oil, and his wide frame nearly blocked the sight of Persephone behind him. "You have made it to the Underworld without the messages of Thanatos or the blessings of Charon. You've willingly entered my domain, choosing of your own free will to place yourself in my dominion for judgement."

Thanatos always got a little enjoyment out of watching the other gods, especially the seldom few he considered friends, using their *god voice*. He leaned down and elbowed Makaria softly in the side.

"He is really laying it on thick, no?"

Makaria turned to him, giving him a small smile before steeling her expression. *Stop acting like you're flirting with a local boy during temple services.* The voice in her head sounded suspiciously like her mother's. She did the right thing and promptly ignored it.

"Are you still acting jealous?"

"He's basically evangelizing!"

"You cannot possibly be fussing about another god of the Underworld taking his job too seriously, Thanatos!" Makaria could hardly keep her voice down.

They both stopped as they heard Hades clear his throat, snapping their attention back to the proceedings. The god was staring at him, a slightly stunned expression on his face when he realized that it was Thanatos, of all people. Makaria flushed so thoroughly that she nearly glowed with ichor, and Thanatos had the good judgement to look sheepish. Hades continued speaking, but Thanatos knew that he would be having a conversation with the god later.

"...so you may go. Remember, Orpheus, Eurydice may follow you. She cannot walk beside you or in front of you, and you will go through the darkness. You will be escorted by

Erebus himself, so in the dark you will remain. If you manage to trust Eurydice..."

Thanatos didn't hear any more, as the same cold, sweeping realization from a few minutes prior flooded him. He couldn't ignore it. Makaria, even in the most subtle of ways, had encouraged Persephone to bargain for this.

She had argued for *life*.

Thanatos didn't wait to listen to the rest of the conversation. He knew that he would be needed, personally, to wait for the outcome of Orpheus's trial. There was a chance that Eurydice would be designated for Makaria, but if that was the case, it was time for Makaria to determine that for herself.

Thanatos turned slightly, ready to depart, trying to rationalize the shockingly strong feelings of betrayal that he felt running through him at Makaria's simple, quiet advocacy to Persephone. It shouldn't have mattered. It was one time. In the beginning, there were plenty of times that Thanatos listened to the bargains of souls before the Underworld established a rhythm...but he wasn't thinking rationally.

He didn't know what was more upsetting—the fact that he was irrational or because he was starting to come to terms with *why* it was Makaria that made him act that way.

16

Thanatos left Hades's throne room without waiting for Makaria. He sat silently on the banks of Styx, hiding himself away from the arriving shades and Charon, his own brother. There had been a large entourage that escorted Orpheus and Eurydice to the cave at Taenarum, where the lovers would make their fated ascent. It didn't matter to Thanatos. If he was needed to bring Eurydice back to the Underworld, he'd be called there. Over the years, Thanatos had built up a resistance to the rejections of man and immortals alike. In his heart of hearts, he couldn't say that it didn't matter to him, but he had eons of practice ignoring it.

When he saw Makaria advocate for life, that illusion shattered. Thanatos still didn't put any weight in the opinions of the Olympians, but he had realized in that moment how much he truly cared about what Makaria thought of him. That realization had nearly gutted him where he stood, and it took all of his strength to calmly exit the crowd.

Makaria knows the Underworld well enough by now. If not, Persephone was there. He felt guilty at leaving her behind and tried to assuage the dreadful feeling without much avail. He was thoroughly burrowed in his own thoughts—his brothers would accurately say that he was sulking—when a solitary name appeared written on his arm.

Eurydice.

Orpheus hadn't managed the climb. Thanatos was needed to go and collect Eurydice and bring her back to Hades. A sick sense of satisfaction rolled through Thanatos, and he felt himself cringe slightly at his own self-righteousness.

Somewhere, deeper in his heart, he was more upset that Makaria would likely be heartbroken. He steeled his expression as he drifted up on the winds towards the cave entrance, knowing that Makaria would meet him there. Until she had proven herself as an immortal, the dead called out to them equally. It put the pressure on Makaria, and also somewhat on Thanatos, to carve out a position in her new world and prove her worthiness. There wasn't a doubt in his mind that she would seek to reintroduce Eurydice to the Underworld. He couldn't say that he blamed her.

When Thanatos arrived at Taenarum, he began the ascent up the rocky, subterranean tunnel that would eventually deposit him in the mortal world. The more he climbed, his heart sank, realizing how close Orpheus had gotten. Thanatos rounded the last corner and sighed, feeling a deep, unpleasant churning in his gut appear at the sight in front of him. Makaria was already there, her white hair nearly translucent from the rays of the sun behind her. The lovers had been *that* close. Orpheus was in shambles, his body thrown on the ground and half-lying on top of Eurydice. Her shade stood a few meters away, conversing quietly with Makaria.

The look on Eurydice's face was almost calm, disappointed but not surprised. She seemed to have resigned herself to this outcome before the wager was made, almost as if she didn't trust that Orpheus would ever be able to accomplish the task.

Thanatos didn't approach as he saw Makaria pulling a gold coin from her pouch, handing it over to Eurydice. The shade smiled at her with tears in her eyes, before turning and starting to walk away. Makaria went after her, and Thanatos stepped forward, revealing himself from the shadows, both of them concerned as Eurydice seemed content to walk herself back down to the Underworld.

"Please." Eurydice held up a hand. All of her movements were choppy. Thanatos could see it now; there *was* great sadness in her eyes. "I am the one soul that already knows the way to hell."

Makaria and Thanatos were both stunned by her admission, and Eurydice gave them a small bow and turned around. She disappeared into the darkness before either of them could protest. Makaria spun on her heel, her eyes full of confusion as she took in Thanatos.

"Did you have somewhere else that you needed to be?" she demanded, scowling at him. "You certainly left Hades's in a hurry."

Thanatos grunted. "I don't answer to you." He crossed his arms over his chest, fighting the temptation to kick at the rocks beneath his feet like a child. Makaria let out a bark of laughter.

"Are we back to this then?" She motioned between the two of them. "I can't seem to keep up, so if you'd be so generous as to let me know where I stand with you, I'd appreciate it."

Thanatos wouldn't meet her gaze, but a flicker of dark blue magic danced over his skin. Makaria couldn't tell if he was angry or upset, although, she reckoned it was probably both.

"What we are has always remained the same, Makaria. You are here to take over part of my job, one I have held for millennia, and—"

"Nope," Makaria cut him off, her voice as sharp as the sickle she now carried. "Thanatos, I need you to think very fucking seriously about the next words out of your mouth because I have had it."

Thanatos nearly fell over with the strength he used to bring his head up, staring directly at Makaria. He had never heard her speak in such a way before, and especially not to him. She had slowly come more into her own over the past few weeks, but this was something entirely different.

He looked her over and tried to put a finger on what looked different, until he realized—it was more of her power. It was slotting into place, pieces of it wrapping itself around Makaria like jewelry. Every god's power looked slightly different when it manifested, and Makaria's magic…

It made Thanatos's heart stop. It cascaded from her, white and golden rays, hanging off her like earrings and curling around her wrists like bracelets. It slowly solidified until it took the shape of coins, coins of passage, representing the blessing of her gift—the gift of tokens to give to Charon for those who were deemed worthy. Makaria didn't seem to realize it was happening, only that she felt a rush of confidence that she hadn't felt even a few minutes before. Her willingness to know when it was the time for death and when it was the time for life, her council to Persephone, and her attendance to Eurydice must have gotten her closer still to proving her worthiness.

At that exact moment, however, Makaria wasn't interested in that. She was more fascinated by the hot and cold attitude of the god of death in front of her, who was now—she would agree with Thanatos's brothers—absolutely sulking.

"Did Eurydice take your tongue back to hell?" she snapped at Thanatos, and there was a flicker of death's power in her voice that Thanatos recognized. His brow furrowed as he shoved his feelings of awe and affection down deeper, shaking his head as he responded.

"You chose life, Makaria." Thanatos's voice sounded miserable, and he hated it. Her fury remained as she waited for him to continue. When he didn't, she took another step towards him, her eyes glowing brightly in her newly acquired well of power.

"Excuse me? What part of sending Eurydice back to Charon looked like choosing life to you?"

Thanatos thoroughly felt like he was being chastised, and

rightfully so, as he fought the urge to curl in on himself. Crippling waves of rejection were running down his spine, and it took all of his strength to keep his expression as impassive as ever. Makaria didn't buy it.

"Don't you go all 'brooding death god' on me. I've seen it already, and I can do it, too. Use your words, Thanatos." Makaria was practically growling at him. Thanatos straightened up to his full height, refusing to say a word as he crossed his arms over his chest and tried to look as imposing as possible.

Makaria let out a deep sigh and dropped her hands from her waist, realizing that a different tactic was required to get through to him. She closed the distance between them, gently wrapping her hand around his wrist. Thanatos's eyes went wide in surprise, but he made no move to stop her. Makaria played with his fingers for a moment before wrapping up his hand in hers, looking up at him with a tender expression.

"What do you mean by that? Tell me. You have to tell me so I can understand you, Thanatos."

There was something in her plea that sent a wide crack through his defenses. He didn't know the last time someone had tried to understand him. Even his parents, although he loved them, made their own assumptions about his wants and needs. Thanatos's stoicism faltered. For a brief second, Makaria saw the amount of pain that he was holding behind those blue eyes, and she almost wept.

"Tell me," she encouraged again, rubbing her thumb over his palm. "Don't lock me out. Not again. We were doing pretty well, you and I."

Her voice lifted at the end in a slightly playful and suggestive tone, making the smallest of smiles appear briefly on Thanatos's face. He let out a long breath and nodded. He was quiet and rough as sand when he finally started speaking.

"In Hades's hall, I saw you encourage Persephone to bargain for Eurydice and Orpheus's life. You... You chose life." He didn't say any more than that, and he didn't need to. Makaria could see the rejection written all over his face.

"Thanatos," she pleaded, "I wasn't choosing life over death. I wasn't..." she took a deep breath, "I wasn't rejecting *you.*"

His gaze snapped to hers, and he held his breath. Makaria tugged them down to the ground, forcing Thanatos to sit. After only a moment's hesitation, she decided to ride out whatever fresh way of confidence she was experiencing, and she settled herself in his lap. Thanatos's entire body froze at the contact. He didn't move a single muscle until Makaria put a hand on his chest.

"Is this okay?" Thanatos didn't respond for a few seconds, his entire mind going blank. In her brief time in the Underworld so far, Makaria had seen how the other gods—even the ones that cared for him—treated him. It always felt like there was a boundary around Thanatos that no one would cross.

That must be terribly lonely. Her heart ached at the knowledge, so she waited patiently for him to adjust to the contact. Eventually, he nodded, and Makaria continued speaking, keeping her voice low like she was talking to a wounded animal.

"My grandmother was a priestess at one of Nyx's temples. She was there when Hera committed her slaughter. My mother lived there too, but she was only a child and hadn't yet devoted her life to Nyx's service. When the looters and pillagers arrived, my mother watched from her hiding place as the priestesses all dropped dead where they stood."

Thanatos cringed and opened his mouth to offer his condolences, but Makaria shook her head.

"Let me finish. Nyx knew that those women were going to die. She had a chance to bring them gently down to the Underworld, or they would be assaulted first. Their last memories of their mortal lives would've been...unbearable. My mother escaped, and eventually, Nyx saved her too when she was pregnant with me. That's how we made it to her last temple."

"Sometimes I wish that Hera was still alive, if only to take her soul again." Thanatos growled, the sound echoing in his chest. Makaria shrugged, looking up at him again.

"Listen to me," she pleaded with him. "Death doesn't frighten me. I know that it is not a terrible thing. That day, what Nyx did... It saved them. It saved my grandmother from an awful fate. You have to believe me when I tell you that I do not wish to cheat death—cheat you—of its duty. I know when the time comes, it is almost always for the best."

"And when it isn't?" Thanatos looked at her, pleading. "You saw Marsyas. There are times it is not a quiet, holy process."

"No, not always, but it is not inherently evil. In those times when the Fates make decisions that are greater than even you or me, that's when we're there to make it easier. I know this. You know this. I just don't think...." Makaria sighed. "I don't think you trust me."

Makaria stopped but was met with only silence. Thanatos couldn't look her in the eye as she sighed and started again.

"The only reason that I petitioned for Orpheus and Eurydice's life is because I have a feeling that Apollo was involved. Orpheus was one of his chosen. Maybe he still is. I'm not sure. They deserved another chance, and if the Fates decided it wasn't to be, which they did, we show up to do our job." Makaria's voice had slowly gotten louder.

"I don't know how this is going to work." Thanatos's confession was heavy, and he swallowed thickly as he turned to look at Makaria. "I don't know how to share these responsibilities. I've never had to. It's all I have. Then I think about the other immortals and their disdain, what it would look like if they turned their ire towards you..." Thanatos trailed off, biting his tongue as he got too close to admitting something he wasn't ready to say to himself, let alone out loud. Regardless, Makaria sensed it, and her heart jumped up into her throat. He was looking away from her again, and she gently pulled his gaze back to hers, her fingers lingering on his cheek.

"I don't care what the other gods think of me, either, Thanatos. When it comes to this job, I only care what *you* think of me."

For a moment, neither of them spoke. The tension between them stole their breath away as their powers began reaching for one another again. Thanatos searched Makaria's eyes and found only truth—a clear, burning desire to be by his side.

But as what? He found himself tripping over prayers to Aphrodite that Makaria might want to stand next to him as… something more.

Makaria thought that she was going to burn right out of her skin. Her power reached out to Thanatos and mixed with his, smoke and sparks coming together in a dark cloud of white, gold, black, and blue all around them. Time itself seemed to stop and Thanatos couldn't be sure if that was, indeed, his own power that was responsible for how long the moment seemed to go on.

In this reprieve, there wasn't a force in existence strong enough to tear him away from Makaria's face. Her hands moved of their own volition, curling around his neck as she sat up straighter in his lap. Makaria leaned ever-so-subtly forward, until there was no mistaking her intention. Thanatos thought that he was truly captured in between life and death, that this was a dreaded purgatory or extended wait that every soul dreaded before judgement.

"No more games, Thanatos," she whispered against his lips.

The words sent chills down the god's spine until Makaria pressed her body against his and kissed him. Thanatos froze for a second before his whole body turned to heat, his arms wrapping around her waist. He cupped a hand around the back of Makaria's head and leaned into the embrace, kissing her back with every bit of him that he could summon forth. Her lips slid over his until they were locked in a soft embrace, surprisingly tender compared to the outpouring of emotion they were both sifting through.

Makaria pulled back slightly, and Thanatos let out a breathy whine of protest, so she leaned in and bit at his lip. She smiled at the sound, taking great pleasure in how it was so different than the Thanatos she was used to. He let out a low groan as he opened his mouth to her, her tongue teasing his. Thanatos tightened his touch on Makaria until he thought it might almost be painful, and he quickly loosened his grip. It was her turn to whine as she encouraged him, and Thanatos quickly understood and held on tighter.

Makaria relished in the security of it. Her place in this new world was still undecided, but there was nothing partial about the way that he held onto her. Power flowed out of the both of them in waves, and Thanatos breathed her air into his lungs like it was his last. It was the kind of kiss that was simultaneously desperate and timid, rife with contradiction as they embraced each other in a way they could never put into words.

When Makaria finally pulled back, her fingers went to her lips, tracing the outline of them as if she couldn't believe that had happened. Thanatos was practically panting, desperately hoping that she wouldn't comment on his arousal as she shifted in his lap. They stayed like that for a few moments, both of them breathing hard, almost silently waiting to see if the other would call foul.

Neither of them dared.

"Well," Makaria said softly, pushing some of Thanatos's hair off his forehead. "Truce?"

Thanatos looked at her for another long second, her hair mussed in every direction, before his face nearly cracked with the width of his smile.

"Truce."

17

Makaria had hoped that after the *friendship* line had been thoroughly crossed in the cave, Thanatos would lighten up around her. She wasn't looking for them to have an entire conversation about what they were doing, beyond what she should be doing as a new goddess, but she did have an expectation that his mood would shift, and their flirtation could escalate. She felt like she should have been more embarrassed or nervous. After all, this had the potential to complicate her entire situation as a new goddess. Somehow, the new pieces of her power that settled into her body must have pushed her doubt out of the way. For once, Makaria felt...positive. Hopeful. She couldn't even bring herself to chastise the infatuated way she thought about Thanatos—thoughts that she had previously spent most of her time trying to temper.

Makaria pieced through her thoughts as she waited for him the next morning, as always, at the entrance to Hecate's courtyard.

You made out with Thanatos. *Of all the gods to kiss. It might be an utter disaster moving forward, but I can't say I wish it never happened.*

She felt Thanatos's power before she saw him, her eyes searching for his presence on the horizon. Dark, blue clouds appeared in front of her, and although she had seen it hundreds of times, she felt her stomach flip when Thanatos materialized out of the smoke. She looked up at him with a wide smile, her smile still giddy…but stopped short when she saw the typical, stoic expression etched on Thanatos's face. He stood there for a moment, waiting for her to join him so he could whisk them off, but Makaria didn't move. She felt her stomach sink a little farther, but this time it was out of dread.

"Are you coming?" Thanatos sounded impassive and bored.

Makaria felt her face flush with embarrassment. *Is he rejecting me?* She felt a sharp sting of fear, but it was quickly replaced with confusion. *If he was so worried about rejection yesterday, he better not be trying to back away from this now.* As Makaria walked forward and joined Thanatos, she said nothing, waiting to see what he would do. He grabbed her hand, and she felt them beginning to drift up on the wind, on the way to their next, most pressing assignment. Thanatos said nothing else.

Makaria fought the urge to openly reprimand him as they traveled. She knew him well enough by now to know that his moods were hardly ever as savage as they appeared. If he was hiding from her after their kiss the day before, it was because he was afraid, and Makaria was already willing to fight for her position as a goddess. She'd fight for Thanatos, too.

If you think you can hide from me behind your claws and your blank expression, you're wrong. You aren't ready for someone who knows you, to go toe-to-toe with you.

It didn't take the gods of death long to arrive in the mortal realm. As soon as the clouds faded away and Makaria stepped into her corporeal form, she took in the sight in front of her. One of the things that Thanatos had taught her was how to take in a scene quickly and efficiently. She scanned over the forest clearing that they had stumbled into and immediately began categorizing everyone she saw, as well as the shade in question.

Thanatos and Makaria had arrived to a boar hunt. Hunters were scattered along the tree line, some of them leaning on their spears while others held onto the hound's leashes. All of them looked anxious. Makaria realized that the men were a mixture of both mortal and immortal. The loud, broken sound of a woman weeping caught her attention, and she turned towards the edge of the hunting party. She felt her face contort into a grimace before she could stop it.

Aphrodite was lying across a large boulder, the dead body of a beautiful man strewn across her lap. She was begging and praying to the gods, calling each of them into question, as her hands ran over the youth's face repeatedly. It didn't take much for Makaria to realize that he had been gored, presumedly by the very boar that he had tried to kill. From the looks of it, the offending creature had gotten away too.

"Oh, for the love of the Fates," Thanatos hissed under his breath, rubbing a hand over his brow before he turned to look at Makaria.

"You don't want to handle this one, trust me. There's nothing blessed about this process."

His tone was clipped and professional, and it made Makaria want to scream. She bid her time, however, and simply nodded, holding out a hand for Thanatos to commandeer the situation. He let out another dissatisfied sound and stepped forward, the glamor disappearing from his and Makaria's appearances. As soon as their power was palpable, Aphrodite's attention snapped toward the God of death. Her face contorted from sorrow to rage, pointing her finger accusingly at Thanatos.

"Don't you *dare!*" she shrieked, her aura lighting up with a display of her power, shockingly pink and scented of roses. "Thanatos, you wretched creature of the Underworld—"

He held up his hands in surrender as he stepped forward. "Aphrodite, listen to me. You know that I don't choose."

Aphrodite clutched the man's body tighter to her chest, screaming through her tears. Makaria's heart would have gone out to her if she was not so thoroughly hellbent on blaming Thanatos. There was true ire in Aphrodite's words, and it didn't sit well with her. She was still cussing and ranting at Thanatos as he stepped towards her, her face going red with fury.

"My Adonis," Aphrodite sobbed, burying her head in his neck. "My Adonis!" She turned her eyes back to Thanatos. "If you take him, it will be war upon you! I shall use everything at my disposal to make your life…"

"What?" Thanatos cut her off, his gentle demeanor beginning to chip away after Aphrodite yelled insult after insult at him. "You'll make my life a living hell?" He raised a brow at Aphrodite, pulling the scythe from his waist.

"No!" she shrieked again, holding on tight to Adonis's body. His shade already floated above it, however, and all it took was a flick of Thanatos's wrist to fully separate it. Adonis's shade disappeared almost instantaneously, flying away on the wind towards Charon. Aphrodite seemed to sense the moment it happened, dropping the body and charging towards Thanatos.

She pulled a slim dagger from the folds of her chiton, a wicked, sharp thing, and threw her arm at him. Thanatos caught Aphrodite's wrists easily, holding them firmly as she writhed in his grip. He looked like a patient man trying to get control of a drunkard. Aphrodite was no match for his strength and quickly wore herself out, sliding down to the ground and dropping the blade. As soon as it hit the soil, Thanatos released her, and she fell over and sobbed in her hands.

"For what it's worth," Thanatos said gently, "I am sorry."

He turned away, and Makaria saw the look on his face, full of remorse. These were the hardest moments for him, when he came not even of his own volition, but of the Fates', and was condemned by his fellow immortal. Thanatos picked up his pace and walked towards Makaria, grabbing her hand and pulling them towards the next job. The last thing that they heard before disappearing from the wood was Aphrodite's voice, full of malice.

"No one will ever love you, Thanatos!"

Makaria cringed at the words, knowing how hard they hit Thanatos—no matter what he wanted to portray. He said nothing as they sped unseen through the heavens, touching down on a small, unknown hillside. The hill was dotted with Cyprus trees and large boulders, but no footpath in sight. Makaria surveyed the surrounding land but saw no one dead or dying. In fact, there was not a soul to be seen. She turned around and opened her mouth to ask Thanatos why he had brought them there but stopped short.

He was sitting on a boulder with his head in his hands, muttering something to himself. Makaria's breath caught in her chest as she took a few, cautionary steps forward. There was no mistaking the sorrow that bent his back, and it made her chest tighten. She had never seen him like this, openly upset. As she approached him, she reached a hand out to touch him, but stopped when he spoke.

"I just need a minute." His voice was thick with tears, and Makaria nearly threw herself at him. It was one thing to deal with a moody or angry Thanatos, but she had never seen him cry. She decided in that instant that it was the worst thing she had ever been witness to, in either her mortal or immortal life.

"Thanatos..." she trailed off as she walked around the stone, getting on her knees in front of him. He stiffened as he sensed her presence but said nothing. Makaria grabbed his wrists and tugged his hands away from his face, bending her head so he was forced to look at her. His eyes were watery, but his face was still dry.

I hope your bed of roses turns to thorns! Makaria found herself cursing Aphrodite with everything she could come up with.

"A minute, please." Thanatos pulled his hands from Makaria's grip and looked away but made no other effort to move or get her to leave him. Makaria was quiet for a few seconds, taking him in, before she shook her head.

"No."

Thanatos's eyes snapped to hers as his brow furrowed. "No? You can't give me a fucking minute here—"

"No." Makaria's voice was louder this time. Thanatos scoffed, his elbows going to rest on his knees as he leaned towards her.

"I know you're worried about your damn lessons, and I'll get to it—"

"Stop talking," Makaria cut him off for a second time. Thanatos didn't know what was more surprising—the determination in her voice or the fact that he followed the demand almost instantaneously. He looked at her with a raised brow as Makaria let out a long breath, scooting forward slightly on her knees until she was firmly between his legs.

"Listen to me. I don't know why you showed up today acting like yesterday didn't happen," Thanatos opened his mouth, but Makaria glared at him, and he shut it again. "But it did. I certainly didn't have a single regret about kissing you, Thanatos. I'll be honest," she swallowed thickly as she pushed down her own nerves, "I was rather looking forward to doing it again. Then you show up today like nothing occurred between us, back to your monosyllabic grunting! You weren't even acting like we were friends anymore. It was like I was nothing to you again." Makaria trailed off as she let some of her own insecurities bubble up to the surface. Thanatos's face looked pained.

"You were *never* 'nothing' to me."

Makaria paused for a second, surveying his expression, and continued. "You have a weird way of showing it."

"I…" Thanatos made an exasperated sound and looked away, but Makaria waited patiently for him to find his words. She didn't know the last time someone had poked at Thanatos's feelings, but she was fairly certain that it had been a long time. When he finally spoke, his voice was as quiet and tired as Makaria had ever heard it. "You heard Aphrodite."

Her heart broke.

"Thanatos…" she sighed gently, cupping his jaw with her hand. "You listen to me." Makaria forced him to make eye contact with her. "Who do you trust more, me or Aphrodite?" Thanatos's expression morphed from one of sadness to one of almost outrage.

"You, of course." His voice didn't waver, but Makaria knew that his admission had just as much to do with how much he didn't like Aphrodite as it pertained to how much he did like her.

"Then you'll simply have to believe me when I say she's wrong." Makaria shrugged as if he was the easiest thing in the world, like believing that the sky was blue. Thanatos shook his head.

"You're new to this. You don't know me. You don't—"

"Stop." Makaria trailed her hand down Thanatos's jawline until she gently gripped his chin, her breathing growing shaky. They stared at one another for a few, tense moments, and they could feel their power reaching for one another again. It happened every time that they got close; this current between them rose from its ever-present place in the background to the foreground around them. Makaria reached for every last ounce of courage that she had within her. When they spoke, their own thoughts betrayed their hidden meanings right below the surface.

"You…you have to trust me."

I think I love you.

"Okay."

I think I love you, too.

Makaria felt heat growing between her legs, that same rising pressure that seemed to overtake them every time they got this close to one another. As she stared into Thanatos's eyes, she could see that he didn't believe her, and her sympathy crossed over into frustration.

Makaria shifted, sitting back on her knees and trailing her hands down Thanatos's legs to his knees. The tension between them shifted immediately, as if the atmosphere had gone up twenty degrees. It was as though a fire had been lit next to him, and Thanatos felt sweat appear on his forehead like he was sitting in the blazing sun. He felt the warmth from Makaria's hands as she made soft circles on his legs, and he cursed himself as he grew impossibly hard underneath his chiton. He had no idea how a woman could make him go from so morose to so impossibly turned on with just a few simple touches, but Makaria had managed it, and he dared not move a muscle.

"I suppose I'll have to convince you then." She smiled at him, and Thanatos thought that his heart was going to beat right out of his chest.

"You d-don't…" he stuttered, feeling like a torch. He wasn't exactly celibate, but immortal and mortal women alike weren't exactly lining up to go to bed with the God of death. He didn't know the last time someone had touched him like this.

And this is Makaria, *of all the goddesses.* Even his thoughts almost sang her name.

"Do you not want me to?" Makaria's hands stopped moving.

"No, it's not that." Thanatos's voice was clipped as every muscle in his body seemed to tense.

"Do you not want it…to be me?" Makaria's earlier confidence almost disappeared entirely, and Thanatos could see it on her face. He shook his head so hard that he nearly fell off the edge of the boulder.

"No! No, absolutely not, if anyone… I mean if anyone was

going to... then you, yeah... but like... you don't have to." Thanatos struggled to get the words out and ran his hand through his hair awkwardly. Makaria felt her heart settle, and some of her previous confidence returned, the sight of Thanatos so befuddled and on edge making her feel almost drunk with power—and she had barely touched him.

"Well, then it's a good thing I want to." Makaria winked at him and closed the gap between them, kissing him softly before Thanatos could say anything stupid in retort. She broke the kiss, and Thanatos made a soft noise of complaint that only stoked Makaria's ego a bit further. She trailed her lips down his neck and across his shoulder while pushing the hem of his chiton up his legs. As soon as it was rucked up around his waist, she pulled away from him with a wicked smile that Thanatos had never seen before.

He had never seen any part of Makaria like this before. He wasn't complaining.

Makaria bit her lip at the sight of him, already hard in front of her. She leaned forward and cupped his balls in one hand, feeling his whole body jerk underneath her as Thanatos let out a sharp curse. Makaria chuckled quietly, flicking her tongue out and licking the head of his dick to taste him. Thanatos's entire body trembled underneath her, and she had hardly touched him.

"I haven't done this in a while," Makaria mused, beginning to stroke him slowly, tightening her grip ever so slightly. Thanatos's hips rose up sharply, and she let out a shocked, happy noise at how quickly he responded to her touch. "You'll just have to tell me what you like." Makaria looked up at Thanatos as she continued to pump her fist around him, only to see his head thrown back as he gripped the rock beneath him for dear life.

"A-anything, *ohhhh*," Thanatos cut himself off with a moan as Makaria chose that moment to swallow the head of his cock. "Anything!" he managed to shout out.

Makaria flattened her tongue against the underside of him, hollowing her cheeks out as she sucked more of him into her mouth. Makaria bottomed out, nearly at the root of him, when there was a high-pitched, scratching sound, which she realized was the sound of his claws burying themselves into the boulder.

In one quick movement, she pulled off his dick, and Thanatos nearly shouted at the loss of sensation. He looked down at her in desperation. He didn't care that she had hardly gotten started. He wasn't going to last long.

"Grab my hair, Thanatos," she whispered sweetly, going up on her knees to kiss him. He tasted himself on her lips and nearly tossed Makaria to the ground to get inside of her but found himself relishing the loss of control.

His hands flew to the back of her head, tangling in that long, white hair that had been driving him mad ever since he'd met her. He wrapped it around his fist and let Makaria drop back down between his legs.

She licked a hot, wet stripe up his shaft before swallowing him down again. Makaria gripped his thighs tighter, finding a rhythm as she took him deeper with each bob of her head. She was nearly gagging on him, but her senses were overwhelmed with nothing but *Thanatos, Thanatos, Thanatos.* The groaning, panting curses that spilled out of his mouth only lead her on. She released her grip on his thigh and gently squeezed the base of his cock, making him shout.

"Makaria, pull o-off. I'm c-close." He tugged on her hair with remarkable tenderness for the moment, but she refused. Makaria was a woman possessed, the feeling of Thanatos— angry, stoic Thanatos—falling apart under her was intoxicating. It was too good to pass up, and she wanted to taste every part of him. She twisted her wrist and swallowed him down again, her nose nearly pressed against his body as she felt his whole body seize. Thanatos came with a shout, a shockwave of his power exploding from his every pore as she swallowed his release.

Makaria pulled back with a gasp, catching her breath briefly before cleaning him up with her tongue. It only lasted for a second before there were strong hands underneath her arms, pulling her off him as Thanatos sank down to the ground and tugged her to his side. Makaria could only giggle as she looked at Thanatos's utterly wrecked expression as he pushed his chiton back down over his waist.

Makaria placed her head on his shoulder and squeezed his hand, and Thanatos leaned over and left a lingering kiss on her forehead. The atmosphere between them had shifted once again, going from desperate and aroused to tender and quiet in just a few moments.

"Do you believe me?" Makaria's voice surprisingly held no jest as she asked him, looking up at Thanatos. He met her stare and nodded, a small, relaxed smile appearing on his face. He pushed some of her hair off her forehead, some unknown emotion dancing in his eyes.

"I do, Makaria. I do."

18

It was cool inside the palace of Corinth. The heavily mosaicked walls and carefully constructed hallways were designed to optimize the breeze, making it temperate even at midday. Sisyphus, the king of Corinth, was nearly comatose as he slept in a pile of cushions, relishing in the wealth that brought him such a sanctuary.

Yet, there could be no fortune as great as Sisyphus's that was not acquired through foul means. The great ruler had married a nymph, which garnered him the ability to connect more easily with the immortals of the world, and he had abused those favors. Sisyphus was about to learn that when men tried to politic like the gods, they only ever ended up winning an audience with Thanatos.

Deep in the Underworld, the God of death himself was preoccupied. It was the first time in his long existence that something had pulled his constant attention away from work — Makaria. He had not neglected a single shade nor missed a solitary death, but he let his power roam the earth freely as he walked Makaria through the empty halls of his home. It was the first time that she had ever been there, and Thanatos found himself almost embarrassed to show it to her.

I'll never admit it, but maybe Nyx was right about decorating the place a little. Makaria didn't seem to care in the slightest, poking fun at him for the abysmal lack of decor and pointing out the things that she did like. Thanatos, however, was very careful to steer her away from the great doors that led into his receiving hall. Neither he nor Makaria had discussed what happened between them any further, and it felt too sudden, too presumptuous to reveal the empty consort's throne to her. Its very existence seemed to beckon to her, and Thanatos knew that he wouldn't be able to give her a tour of the room without revealing his hopes to see her sitting on it one day. He held Makaria's hand and tugged her along, picking up his pace as they walked past the entrance.

"What's in there?" Makaria pointed to the doors, and Thanatos cursed under his breath.

"Oh, nothing. It's a receiving hall."

"It's nothing or it's a receiving hall?" Makaria turned and looked at him with a brow raised, officially intrigued. Thanatos opened his mouth to answer when a massive gust of wind swept through the hall, effectively cutting him off. Makaria and Thanatos both ducked, holding onto hems and belts as it died down. Thanatos pulled his scythe out of thin air, his shoulders pulled back and his entire body primed for an assault. Makaria spared no thought to the intruder, her mouth going dry at the sight of Thanatos in a battle stance. The wind picked up again, this time only around their ankles, carrying the smell of smoke and iron, almost like blood. The scent made Makaria shiver, but it seemed to relax Thanatos, who lowered his weapon.

"Hephaestus!" he called out to the ether as if in welcome. "What brings you here? I don't know if you've ever been a guest in my home." A sudden pillar of dark red smoke funneled down from the ceiling, disappearing as quickly as it came and leaving Hephaestus standing in its wake.

"Thanatos." He smiled warmly, or at least, displayed what

appeared to be a warm expression. His face was partially obscured by a Corinthian helmet, which Makaria knew was rumored he never took off. The helmet hung low over his brow, only revealing his eyes, mouth, and a great, black beard. She noticed that the metal seemed to almost emulate power of its own, which she expected from Hephaestus. He wasn't quite as tall as Thanatos, but he came the closest of all the gods that Makaria had met, and his stance was wider. He had a barrel chest and arms the size of her legs, wearing only a leather apron and dirty trousers. It was an unusual uniform to say the least.

Thanatos didn't have any particular kinship with Hephaestus. He had no quibble with him, either, which meant that Hephaestus was the closest thing to a friend that Thanatos had in the pantheon.

"What can I do for you?" Thanatos held out his hand as the gods embraced. Makaria kept her mouth shut, her eyes dancing between the two immortals. Thanatos was tall and sleek, with sharp lines and a cold power radiating from him. Hephaestus was almost his opposite, broad and built, and looked like he had a forge in his chest instead of a heart.

"It looks like I can do something for *you*." Hephaestus's voice sounded like smoke. He pulled a set of thick chains from the folds of his himation, their joints still glowing like they had just been pulled out of the fire. Thanatos looked like he was about to salivate as he accepted the chains.

"These are..." He raised a brow as he studied Hephaestus, as if he was suddenly realizing that the gift might come with conditions.

"You're to be sent to Sisyphus, the king of..."

"Corinth," Thanatos deadpanned. He sensed Olympian interference from a mile away. Hephaestus shrugged.

"That's about all I know. Zeus is fed up with him and managed to get the Fates to cut the king's string. He's pulled a trick or two on immortals in the past, so Zeus asked me to make it so you could deliver him without issue."

Thanatos's hands tightened around the chains. "Does he think that a mere mortal could evade death?" His power flared, and even Makaria took a small step back as she watched his eyes flash. Hephaestus seemed completely unbothered.

"I don't know. I don't care. The requests come in; I make it. That is the extent of my involvement." He crossed his arms over his wide chest as if he was daring Thanatos to retort. Thanatos only let out a low growl, shoving the chains through the belt on his waist. No sooner did he do so than Sisyphus's name appeared written on his arm. Hephaestus's expression shifted slightly to one of smugness, before he tossed a sly wink at Makaria—the first time he acknowledged her—and vanished.

"Damn Olympians," Thanatos cursed. He let out a long sigh and turned to Makaria. "Let me handle this one. It's going to be rife with politicking, I can tell, and we're done for the day. You can go back to Hecate's, and I'll see you tomorrow?" Makaria couldn't help but smile at how Thanatos's mood had shifted. They both knew very well they would see each other tomorrow, yet, he asked. She knew that he was asking if he would see her on a more *personal* note, rather than their prior professional forced proximity.

Makaria chewed on her lip and blurted out her response before she lost the courage. "What if I...stayed here?" Thanatos froze so completely, Makaria wondered if he was briefly paralyzed, causing her to backtrack. They both started speaking at the same time.

"I'm sorry, that was rude of me to ask—"

"I would love if you did—"

The pair stopped, laughing awkwardly, and Makaria gave him a small smile.

"No, really. I shouldn't have asked. I don't want you to feel like I've invoked Xenia or anything." She waved her hand in the air idly as if to downplay the magnitude of what she had said. Thanatos looked concerned and shook his head, his hands going out to grip her arms.

"It was my fault. I was just...surprised." He let out a long breath. "I don't think anyone has ever asked to stay here. Please stay." His smile was bashful, and Makaria felt her heart flutter at the sight of a coy Thanatos. It was a rare expression from him that she didn't take for granted.

"I will." She winked at him, nodding towards the door. "I'll make myself at home. Go on and deal with Sisyphus. I'll be here when you get back."

Thanatos felt his chest fill with emotion. He could almost feel his walls crumbling viscerally. He was too overcome with his affection for Makaria to even realize that there were tears in his eyes. Makaria, on the other hand, realized that this closeness was something Thanatos had never experienced and felt a sense of sadness and anger consume her at the idea. She went up on her tiptoes and caressed his cheek, pressing a soft kiss to his lips.

"Go on," she said again, shaking him from his stupor.

His expression was adoring as he slowly melted away from his mortal form, going slowly like he wasn't ready to leave her presence. Makaria stood in the hallway for a few minutes after he had gone, then she set off to explore the rest of the estate. She trailed her fingers along the stonework, elaborate mosaics of filigree and coins appearing behind her wherever she touched the wall.

▸▸▸

THANATOS SWEPT through the palace of Corinth without any pretense. The mortal occupants inside were too intoxicated to distinguish his cool, sweeping power from the breeze they were accustomed to. He wanted to complete the job—send Sisyphus to the Underworld—and go back home, back to Makaria. It was a novel sensation that Thanatos was too wrapped up to even contemplate how unprecedented it was.

The throne room was full of people, and not a single one noticed Thanatos as he drifted among them. He kept himself out of sight, but it was strange to him that not a single person picked up the presence of death amongst their gaiety. There was a party in full swing, Thanatos could sense Dionysus's influence in every cup of wine. It didn't take him long to find Sisyphus, who was still lounging over a daybed. Thanatos looked down at his arm, confirming the name was still there, and raised his scythe. As soon as he was ready to release his arm and deliver the cutting blow, Sisyphus's eyes flew open.

"Stop!" the king called out sharply and raised his arm over his head as if to block the blow. Thanatos stiffened, not out of obedience to the mortal, but in surprise.

"Interesting. You can see me?" Thanatos turned his head to the side. He could already sense that Sisyphus's soul was wicked; his legacy was full of murder, assault, and theft. It was the kind of history that made Thanatos's empathy run dry and guaranteed the avenging angel came out to play. Thanatos felt his power ripple over his body, his teeth elongating as he flexed his claws. To his credit, Sisyphus only blanched for a moment before regaining his composure.

"Yes, great one, God of death…"

Thanatos looked surprised. "I must say, of all of those who bargain with death, you are one of the first to attempt to use accolades to sway me. Alas," his smile was cruel as he leaned over Sisyphus's body, "I have my orders. You've made a lot of very powerful immortal people mad, Sisyphus. I would be impressed if you hadn't squandered their gifts and favor to terrorize and brutalize."

Thanatos's voice dropped to a snarl, and Sisyphus's face

filled with fear. Thanatos pulled the chains from his person with his opposite hand, ready to bind the king's shade as soon as it was cut free from his body. His thoughts were already drifting back towards Makaria, waiting for him—waiting for him in his *home*—that he had one foot out the palace door.

Sisyphus sat up and pointed at the chains, squawking. "I have never seen anything more finely made! Tell me, how do they work?"

Thanatos sighed, his anger shifting to annoyance and impatience. "I don't know. It's not my job to know." He raised the scythe again, and Sisyphus slid off the cushions and knelt at Thanatos's feet.

"Please, God of death, I know the judgement that awaits me in the Underworld. There are gods who will call for their justice even if they must pull it from my shade, and who will Hades be to deny them…"

"Do you have a point?" Thanatos hissed, spinning his finger in a circle, encouraging Sisyphus to make his statement. Sisyphus was crafty; he had to be in order to have played the gods' game as a mortal for so long. He could see that Thanatos was distracted; there were other places that he wanted to be. Sisyphus didn't know why Thanatos was acting that way, but he knew that it was different from the famed stories of Thanatos's dedication to his job.

"Yes." Sisyphus clasped his hands together and begged. "Please, let me bind myself. I shall go willingly to the Underworld, my shade intact, and I will seek council with each god I have wronged for my sins."

Thanatos mulled over the option for a minute and then realized in shock that he was allowing someone to bargain with him. For once, Thanatos almost laughed.

It's been eons since I have been so preoccupied. Although, I suppose that Zeus would want him alive—wait. Thanatos looked down at the prostrate king and realized that his shade wasn't outside of his body. Thanatos's job was to deliver the final blow, to cut the soul from the mortal realm, but he didn't kill anyone. If Sisyphus's soul was still very much inside his body, and his name was still written on Thanatos's arm, then the Fates had struck an odd bargain indeed.

"It seems like you are to be brought to the Underworld alive." There was a flicker of hope that crossed Sisyphus's face, but Thanatos shook his head. "Do not find comfort in this. The blade of death is sharp and quick, but if the Olympians want to do it themselves, no mortal will suffer as much as you." Sisyphus now looked ready to faint, but he nodded his head pleadingly.

"I beg you, let me bind my own hands in fealty to show the gods that I know I am deserving of my penance..."

"Please stop talking," Thanatos groaned, holding on tightly to one end of the chain. "These games between god and man are impossible to decipher, and I despise being brought in as a messenger." He tossed the other end of the shackle to Sisyphus. "If you must." Thanatos watched as Sisyphus began wrapping the shackle around one wrist before his thoughts turned back to Makaria. He wondered where she was in his home or if she was comfortable.

When was the last time I had the kitchen stocked? There's probably no wine or nectar. I'm sure she can manage to conjure it with her power—

"Wretched mortal!" Thanatos was hauled from his thoughts as he felt binding black magic simmer across his skin. It made him nauseous as he dropped to his knees, feeling his power bottle up inside of him like a sealed amphora. He struggled to see straight, but when he raised his arms in front of him, he realized that the chains had been wrapped around his arms.

"Sisyphus!" Thanatos growled, but his power only flickered in his eyes. The king was laughing, falling backwards over the daybed, before he jumped to his feet and applauded himself. Thanatos's glamor was broken as he was stuffed into his mortal form, abruptly becoming visible to everyone in the throne room. Sisyphus had managed to bind Thanatos with the chains in the few seconds that he took his eyes off the king.

"You would add the God of death to the list of those who want your flesh?" Thanatos spat, his fury palpable through the bindings. Sisyphus shuddered for only a second before he burst into laughter again, yanking on the loose end of the chain. Thanatos fell forward, knocking his chin on the tiled floor.

"Do you see? Do you not see that I am the king who has conquered death? I am the mortal made immortal!" Sisyphus called out to the party, and his guests cheered raucously.

"Your suffering will be for the ages," Thanatos shook his head, some of his wits coming back to him as the initial shock wore off. Hephaestus had made chains that would not only bind a mortal, but a god. Thanatos pushed himself back up to his knees, his chin flecked with ichor.

Leave it to Hephaestus to fucking overachieve.

Thanatos knew that there was no way to keep Death from his job, and one way or another, he would be free of the bindings eventually. He just lacked a tactical plan at the moment. Sisyphus had been in the middle of a diatribe about his own greatness before he tossed a cup at Thanatos's feet.

"You there!" He pointed to some of his soldiers. "We shall throw the God of death in a pen fit for an immortal..." Sisyphus hiccupped and could barely speak through his own laughter. "Take him to the kitchen and lock the god in the cabinet!"

Thanatos rolled his eyes, giving Sisyphus an unamused glare. He bristled against the disrespect of being shoved in a cabinet—a cabinet, of all places!—while the soldiers hauled him off towards the kitchens.

For Fate's sake, I better get out of here before any of the fucking gods get wind of this.

Thanatos was pouting by the time the cabinet door was

locked in his face, trying to decide who would be the worst person to discover him.

Definitely Hermes. If he finds me here, I'll have to kill him myself.

The locked door muffled the sounds of the party in the throne room, and Thanatos settled in to wait.

19

Makaria knew something was wrong. She had waited for Thanatos all night, and he had never returned. When she saw the first light of dawn and felt Nyx and Erebus returning to the Underworld, her patience wore out. She'd been working with Thanatos long enough now to know that something as simple as retrieving a shade could turn into a greater ordeal. Especially if there were other gods involved, and those gods included Zeus, who had bargained with the Fates to pull some strings. Or rather cut them. She hadn't expected him to return to his home by any specific time, but when she saw the sun rising, her heart sank.

Thanatos was never late.

Makaria shut the door behind her and started off in the direction of Hecate's home, wondering for a brief moment if immortals needed to lock their doors. She still got caught up in some of the minor intricacies of her temporary mortality. There was a soft murmur of power through the meadows as Nyx and Erebus settled in their rightful places, yet it felt hollow to Makaria. She was deeply attuned to Thanatos's magic, and the Underworld without his presence was off-putting.

Oh my gods. Makaria nearly stopped in her tracks as the

realization overtook her. *I can't feel his power at all.* Makaria hadn't realized that since the moment she became a goddess, her abilities had been tied to Thanatos. Her understanding of the way that her power worked, how the magic was channel, all of it came from a knowing that she thought she had learned through observation. She understood now that as much as she had watched Thanatos, she had felt him even more. The absence of his influence in the Underworld was magnified in her chest, making her whole body feel concave as she nearly bowed under the weight of that knowledge. There were ways that Makaria and Thanatos were linked that they likely didn't even understand themselves.

In essence, their powers were shared. The strength of death didn't dilute itself. There was only one source. At their core and in their hearts, Thanatos and Makaria were two halves of the same soul.

It took a wicked, crippling feeling of absence to make Makaria realize it. She started running, the ground shrinking beneath her feet as her influence whisked her forward. A nearly manic wildness was overtaking her, as if the loss of Thanatos's presence was draining her sanity with every passing minute.

Please, let him not feel this too.

Makaria was soaked with sweat and worry, concerned that wherever Thanatos was, he was being tortured in the same way. Her head was pounding by the time she arrived at Hecate's, and it felt like there was a deadly pulling sensation on her heart. Hecate sensed Makaria's anguish and met her in the courtyard, catching the young goddess as she fell into her arms. She nearly exploded in a barrage of tears and shouts, trying to speak clearly.

"Thanatos, his power, didn't come back, last night…" Makaria was gasping for breath, but Hecate was nodding her head rapidly, trying to soothe her.

"I know, I know." She shook Makaria gently to get her to

snap out of it. "Listen to me! We're aware that something has happened. Nyx is inside. We were waiting on you."

Makaria stopped moving, looking up at Hecate with wide eyes.

"What have you heard?"

"Inside, inside," Hecate repeated, wrapping an arm around Makaria's waist and escorting her into the kitchen. Nyx was standing near the hearth, a deadly calm blanketing her expression. Makaria didn't need to be an established immortal to know that blank look was containing multitudes of primordial rage. Hecate helped Makaria sit down and squatted down to her level.

"Tell us what you know, Makaria."

"I don't know—"

"Where were you last night?" Nyx cut Makaria off, her eyes glowing and a black cloud of smoke rising up around her legs. Hecate glared at Nyx's attitude towards Makaria, but everyone understood that her clipped tone wasn't personal. Makaria sucked in a deep breath and released it, wringing her hands in her lap as she looked between the two goddesses.

"I was at Thanatos's home. He told me to come back to Hecate's for the night and I…" Makaria paused as fresh tears welled in her eyes. "I suggested that maybe I stay with him." Hecate looked pleasantly surprised at this admission while Nyx remained remarkably impassive. "Oh, wait, well, before that, Hephaestus arrived. He gave Thanatos a set of chains that Zeus commissioned and said he had to use them on a king named Sisyphus."

"That slimy bastard!" Aeëtes's voice interrupted them from the hallway, where he had been eavesdropping.

"Darling, shut up," Hecate yelled over her shoulder, squeezing Makaria's hands and encouraging her to continue.

"Yes." Makaria nodded, her breath somewhat returning to normal. "He was on his way to go retrieve Sisyphus…"

"Did Sisyphus's name appear on his arm?" Nyx interrupted

harshly and Makaria nodded. She couldn't help but glare a little at the primordial. Everyone had clearly established that Thanatos was missing, which must be painful for a mother, but her ire was wrongly directed at Makaria.

"It did. He noticed that too, grabbed the chains, and told me he'd return to me after taking care of Sisyphus."

"Why didn't you go with him?" Nyx's tone was getting increasingly more accusatory.

"Watch it," Hecate pointed a finger at Nyx. "I sense your strife, but the minute you turn on another woman in my house, I will kick you out. Your powers be damned."

Makaria stiffened, expecting the goddesses to launch themselves at one another. Nyx was immobile for a few seconds and then nodded, bowing her head gracefully in Makaria's direction.

"I apologize, young goddess. I am not myself with the loss of Thanatos's presence in the Underworld."

Makaria perked up at that, her eyes getting bigger. "You feel it too?" Her question was pleading. It was Nyx's turn to look surprised, and she tilted her head as if she was examining Makaria.

"I feel it because I'm his mother." Nyx didn't elaborate, continuing to stare at Makaria until she started to squirm under the silent gaze. "If you feel it, then it would be—"

"Because you matter so much to him." Hecate smiled a little too widely, stopping Nyx from finishing her sentence. Makaria was about to ask her to elaborate when Nyx resumed her line of questioning, albeit without the condemnation.

"Why didn't you go with Thanatos?"

"Because," Makaria sighed heavily, feeling guilty regardless, "we knew that it wasn't a blessed death, and it could be a mess with other gods involved. Thanatos wanted to get in, avoid the politicking, and get out. I told him I'd wait for him."

Nyx and Hecate looked at each other and exchanged a glance, one that Makaria knew conveyed an entire conversation that they didn't need to have out loud. She watched as Nyx stood up straighter, the black clouds of her power spreading out farther from around her legs. When she spoke, her voice was infused with her magic, and Makaria watched as it caused stars to appear in the kitchen ceiling.

"Makaria, you need to go to the mortal world and start covering for Thanatos. Death itself has stopped. You should be able to spread your power out to usher shades to Charon, like Thanatos does, and make your way to Sisyphus's palace. If that was where Thanatos was sent, then that horrible mortal king will have an answer."

Makaria felt her blood run cold. "I-I can't... I can't possibly... I can't cover for him! Why can't you?"

"My power may be great," Nyx was melancholic, "but even I don't possess the power of death. You're the only other one who does. It has to be you."

Makaria looked terrified. "Then...can you go look for him? Why do I have to do it all?" Makaria was desperate to help and wanted to find Thanatos more than anything, but she was overwhelmed that the responsibilities of replacing and finding Thanatos now rested on her shoulders.

"My abilities are...too great." Nyx's sounded apologetic, and her face looked pained. It was the most dejected that Makaria had ever seen the ancient goddess look. "There is refuge and peace to be found in my darkness, but...they are hidden there. All the powers of night and its blackness aren't useful when you need to *find* something. Even your son." Nyx's voice cracked.

Makaria's heart twisted as she saw a mother's grief contorting the primordial's face. If Nyx tempered her power and appeared in her mortal form, she would retain some of her strength, but not all. If she unleashed herself and returned to the mortal world at her full capacity, it would blanket Greece in nightfall—rather counterintuitive to finding someone.

How awful it must be, to be the most powerful one of all of us but you can't use that power when your son goes missing.

"I'll… I'll go," Makaria wiped at her tears and stood.

Hecate embraced her, and Nyx crossed the kitchen, wrapping her arms around them both. There was no time to waste, and they escorted Makaria to the edge of the courtyard.

"We'll send Hermes to you if we hear of anything that might help," Hecate hugged Makaria quickly and turned around to go back inside, leaving Nyx and Makaria alone.

"When I gave you this chance," Nyx looked at Makaria with pleading eyes, "I did it for Thanatos, just as much as I did it for you. He needs you now. The world needs you." Makaria tried not to pass out at that reminder. "I have faith in you, Goddess of blessed death." Nyx uttered Makaria's title like it was a prayer, bending down and kissing her brow. "May the gods fear you."

※※※

WHEN MAKARIA LANDED in the mortal world, her senses were nearly overcome. She had appeared at the edge of Corinth, knowing that her main priority was getting to the palace. While Nyx had instructed her to cover for Thanatos first and search for him second, for the benefit of them all, Makaria was doubtful of her own abilities. Between her insecurity and the growing ache in her chest from the absence of Thanatos's power, Makaria had promptly reprioritized those responsibilities on her way to Greece. That plan was abandoned as soon as she took in the chaos before her.

Corinth was on fire.

Everywhere that she looked, Makaria could see swaths of flame and pillars of smoke rising from far-off burn sites. She started running towards the city and quickly fell into its dirty streets, every new scene in front of her looking like it was ripped from the end of the world.

It was nearly impossible to breathe. The air was choked with ash and blood. Mobs of people were running around like wild animals, shrieking and crying out with desperation. Makaria watched in utter horror as one man pulled a sword from his belt and beheaded his neighbor for no reason that she could obtain. The nightmare went on as she witnessed the beheaded corpse rise, pick up its head, and begin screaming in the streets. Only then did Makaria realize that nearly half of the people scattering through the mud and the alleys were dead.

They sported egregious injuries and missing limbs, more than one of them carrying their own head. She tried to piece together what was happening until she watched another seemingly random murder a few feet from where she stood. As the body fell, Makaria acted on instinct, pulling the sickle from her belt and searching for its shade. The shade didn't appear, and the man continued to writhe in pain as he bled out in an endless loop in the dirt.

Only then did she truly understand what was happening.

They can't die. No one can die! Makaria fought the urge to pass out, trying to quell the nausea churning in her stomach. A crying woman, who ran past Makaria chasing a hog, caught her attention.

"Please! We're hungry, we're hungry!" The woman cried out to no one in particular, and Makaria understood the extent of the problem. *There's no death.* Nothing *can die, not even animals. Everyone will starve. The dead lay dying, in an endless loop.*

Her thoughts began to spin out of control, fear taking over every part of her being as she tried to comprehend that what was playing out in Corinth was happening all over Greece. Makaria felt her hands grow clammy, and her fingers started to shake. She had to grip the alley wall behind her for support.

Everything was closing in on her as her vision condensed to a single, solitary point. The colors, the screams, the horrendous smells, the consistent purgatory of the ever-dying threatened to drag Makaria down with them. She felt her nerves building and building, something simmering inside of her like a pot about to boil over.

Beneath her fear and hidden underneath her anxiety, there was power—*her* power—and Makaria fought against the panic that threatened to drown her with every passing second.

I am the Goddess of blessed death. I am the Goddess of blessed death. My fear does not control me.

Makaria reached deep down inside of herself to that well that contained the full extent of her immortal power. Most of it was still untouched, not yet unlocked, and it coiled in her belly. Makaria needed every last bit of strength that she could get. She knew that she couldn't replace Thanatos. She couldn't begin to tackle the horrors that now plagued Greece, but she could pause them. She could stop time. Thanatos could do it, and their power had something shared, something cosmic that bound them together. Makaria let out a loud shout, sliding down the wall, crying out to the heavens like she was in labor. If she could only just call on this one ability…

Then she saw Thanatos's face. It was as clear in her mind as the city before her, and it consumed all of her attention. She felt a warm sensation pour over her body, like sliding into a bath, causing the frigid grip of her anxiety to melt away.

Makaria thought of Thanatos and of how he needed her, wherever he was. It sent a surge of strength through her bones, and she threw her hands out in front of her with a shout more reminiscent of a battle cry. A fresh wave of her and Thanatos's essence blanketed Corinth. Makaria could feel it going further and further until it covered all of Greece. She stood slowly on shaky legs, trying to catch her breath.

The deepest part of her power remained locked away, but as she looked around…she realized she had done it.

She had stopped time. The horrors were frozen in midair around her like a mosaic of the upmost cruelty, but it had stopped. There were no screams, and the pain inflicted on the mortal realm was held at bay. Makaria could hardly believe it. She leaned back against the alley wall and started to laugh, feeling confused and unsure but equally proud of herself.

There was space for her to breathe.

Makaria released a long sigh and fixed her hair, wiping sweat off her forehead. She let herself collect her composure for a few more seconds, not that time mattered per se, then she set off for the palace.

She set off to find Thanatos.

20

The streets were eerie as Makaria crept through them, trying to keep her eyes downcast. Although time had stopped and every person she passed was as immobile as statuary, the scenes that unfolded before her were still horrendous. Parts of the city had become free for all, with violent men and criminals striking at one another in a crazed jest. Every other corner revealed people crouched low to the ground, hiding under baskets or barrels. There were still clouds of smoke in the air that Makaria had to walk through, even though the flames had subsided. She was getting more accustomed to death and all of its faces, but there were some things that she never wanted to become desensitized to.

Luckily, as the road got nicer beneath her feet, she knew she was getting closer to the palace. She dared to flick her gaze upward and let out a small, barely relieved sigh—the richer, more spacious homes closer to the royal estate showed less signs of violence. There were still citizens hanging out of their front gates, yelling in confusion at one another, but the wild blood lust of actions without alleged consequences had remained in the lower parts of the city.

The palace itself was a monstrosity, with brightly colored

statues that lined the path up towards the front door. Makaria slipped right through the gates in her mortal form, a small smile finally appearing on her face. Even though there was almost nowhere that was off limits to her as a goddess, it was still amusing to sneak past a guarded gate with none the wiser. Makaria passed lines of torches and busts on her way up to the front door of the palace, each one gaudier than the last. The front steps of the building were occupied, and Makaria could see two women fighting with one another. There was a cup of wine that was frozen midair, where one of the women was clearly throwing her drink at her opponent. There were several servants in various form of intoxication—apparent from their posture and their expressions—and even a pair of lovers caught in an amorous moment, which was poorly hidden by the column they tried to take refuge behind.

 Makaria felt her lip curl as she pushed open the doors and stepped inside, gleaning everything that she needed to know about Sisyphus by the company that he kept. The inside of the palace was no better than the outside, with massive tapestries adorning the walls with shining golden thread. Makaria eyed massive, open dishes of incensed oil that she knew likely smelled egregiously cloying and sweet. The absence of the scent in the air made her doubly grateful that everything was at a standstill.

 It wasn't hard to find the throne room. There was another set of doors at the end of the entry hallway, Sisyphus's name proudly painted on them. Makaria fought the urge to roll her eyes, even though no one could see her. Her initial panic had ebbed away, and although balance still needed to be restored to the entire world outside, the fact that she managed to halt it settled her frayed nerves. She would be able to find Thanatos, and they'd tackle the rest afterwards. Besides, the more she took in from the appalling setting around her, her attitude shifted more to discontent and to a more urgent desire to find Thanatos.

When Makaria pushed open the doors to the throne room, she was greeted with a scene of Dionysian proportions. Her revulsion was written across her brow as she took it all in, from the women haphazardly pulled into men's laps, the spilled puddles of wine covering the floor, and the drunken soldiers wrestling or throwing spears at one another. It was easy enough to find Sisyphus, who was sitting on a massive daybed in the middle of the room. He was buoyed up by cushions, covered in the finest of fabrics and woven together with the upmost artisan skill. Makaria wanted to rip them open with her bare hands just for spite. Sisyphus's face was frozen in an expression of manic, undiluted joy. It was not a sense of freedom and happiness that a child or a lover would wear. It was a look that was twisted and perverse. Makaria accidentally conjured the sickle, gripping it tight in her hand, and she allowed herself to briefly entertain the consequences of killing him herself.

This truly is a man who thinks that he has beaten the gods.

Thanatos was nowhere to be seen in the throne room, which was to be expected. If you managed to imprison a god, it was simply good sense not to leave him out in the open, but it disappointed Makaria nonetheless. She waved her fingers idly in front of Sisyphus's face, debating if she could attempt to unfreeze him and him alone in order to ask him questions about Thanatos.

But if I accidentally start time again for everyone... then the whole world plunges back into chaos.

Makaria was toying with all her options, of which there were precious few, when there was a soft breeze that enveloped the throne room. She stood up taller and stepped away from Sisyphus, brandishing the sickle out in front of her. There was no reason that the wind should be moving of its own accord.

"Oh, put that down, sweetheart." A cheery, almost jovial

voice filled the throne room. "I'm the most harmless one there is."

Makaria let out a grunt of disagreement, but she lowered the weapon anyway as Hermes stepped into the throne room. He didn't have a hair out of place and Makaria couldn't help but notice that he looked like he rather fit into the chaos that surrounded them.

"I thought the other gods weren't supposed to bother me when I was working," Makaria remarked drolly. Thanatos and Makaria's ability to stop time didn't affect the gods, although there was an unspoken rule that they weren't to be disturbed when immortals sensed what was happening.

Hermes shook his shoulders like he was a peacock ruffling his feathers, stepping graciously over someone's drunken body on the floor. He walked towards Makaria with a hand dramatically outstretched as if he was going to invite her to dance.

"Ah, you're new, so I'll forgive you. Breaking the rules is what I do best, sweetheart." Hermes's eyes were full of a glowing gold light as he grinned at her.

"Look, the other Underworld gods seem to tolerate you…"

"They adore me."

"They tolerate you." Makaria pointed a finger at him and continued. "But I can't indulge in whatever this is that you do." She waved a hand at him, and Hermes's face contorted in mock offense. "I have to find Thanatos, and you have really, really picked a bad time."

"I'll have you know that this is the first time a woman has ever complained about my timing."

Hermes literally lifted up his nose in Makaria's direction, and she blushed slightly. While she had slowly become more comfortable with her position as an immortal, she still got a little embarrassed when she felt out of her depth. Playing word games with Hermes was definitely one of those times.

"Anyway," Hermes clapped his hands, going on, "I'm here to help. I heard that Thanatos was missing and figured you could use a hand. Since, you know, if Nyx got involved, it would be a whole *eternal darkness* thing." He made a funny face at Makaria in emphasis before snapping out of it and changing topic at rapid speed. "I don't know why people don't think I'm helpful. Here I am, taking time out of my busy schedule, showing up in this overstated palace to assist and… What do you think?" Hermes turned to look at her as if he had just posed the philosophical question of the century. Makaria blinked her eyes rapidly and then motioned to the tableau of insanity they were in the middle of.

"I don't think working out your perception issues is helping."

"Ouch," Hermes winced, shaking his head and *tsk*ing. "You'll fit right in with the Underworld crowd, however." Makaria couldn't tell if Hermes meant it as a compliment or an insult, but it warmed her chest regardless to hear him say it so casually, like he believed it.

"I know that Thanatos was sent here to fetch Sisyphus, but I don't know what happened."

Makaria filled Hermes in on everything that had happened, including the far-too-delicate hold that she had on time. By the time she had finished, Makaria was beginning to get anxious again. "I don't know where to even start looking. If those chains bind his powers, we can't sense him at all."

Hermes's eyes lit up at that, and he let out a giddy chuckle, rubbing his hands together like he was plotting. "Maybe you can't…but I can."

"How in the name of the gods is that possible?" Makaria half-groaned, wanting to find Thanatos but finding it hard to believe that Hermes would have an advantage no one else did.

"If you weren't so pretty, you'd be a real drag to be around, you know that?" Hermes scoffed.

"Well, that was offensive."

"I offend everybody." Hermes shrugged easily, off topic. "I

offend myself. You're beautiful, sweet one, but goodness, you're killing my mood right now."

"I feel awful this is effecting you so harshly," Makaria deadpanned, and Hermes was set off in another peal of laughter.

"You sounded just like Hecate! That was amazing. Do it again."

Makaria gritted her teeth together, poking him in the chest with the rounded end of the sickle. "Tell me how you can find Thanatos, or I'll get Hecate to curse the parts of you that you're probably overly proud of."

Hermes nearly paled, gasping dramatically and taking a step backwards from Makaria.

"That was terrifying. Good job! You'll be a fully-fledged goddess of death in no time, and that's just it, my darling. That's what *you* are, but messages are kind of my thing. If Thanatos is calling out to anyone, I'll pick up on it, whether he's got power or not. The gods and men all send messages." Hermes looked at Makaria expectantly, but she only stared at him and pinched the bridge of her nose.

"Feel free to get excited any minute now." Hermes pouted, crossing his arms over his chest. "I did just solve your problem."

"Hermes," Makaria rubbed at her temples, "why have we been talking this whole time if you could do that?"

"Well, I for one always like trying to make new friends but—"

"*Do it!*" Makaria snapped, looking around in awe as if there were witnesses to the conversation. Hermes sucked his teeth for a second before closing his eyes, mumbling under his breath as a soft, golden wave of power started dripping off him.

"It's not like he's going anywhere... Let's see... No, no, no..."

Makaria felt herself growing anxious as Hermes's power

increased. His eyes stayed shut as he seemed to be rattling through options he saw in his mind. "Still not there… here… oh… wait… *oh*."

Hermes's eyes popped open, and he smiled, a massive, open-mouthed grin nearly splitting his face in two. He looked like he was so excited that he was about to start vibrating.

"Did you find him?" Makaria felt her stomach jump, dangerous hope flooding her veins and making her almost woozy.

"Oh, boy, did I!" Hermes did a little jump and started running towards a side door on the far wall. He looked over his shoulder and yelled back at Makaria, who stared after him, bewildered. "Well, come on then! You were the one he was calling out for, after all." Hermes disappeared down another hallway. Makaria flushed, unable to stop some of Hermes's wild giddiness from affecting her as she thought about Thanatos calling out to her, and quickly followed him.

The rest of the palace was dimly lit, presumedly because the entire palace staff and the rest of its occupants were in the throne room. The halls were a maze of archways and doors, and Makaria pretty quickly gave up trying to keep track of where they were. She followed Hermes and his nearly iridescent trail of gold, sparkling power. As she was getting ready to ask him where they were going, he abruptly stopped, nearly tripping over his own feet. Hermes placed his hand on a rather inconspicuous door before turning to look at Makaria with glee in his eyes.

"This is it!" He wiggled his fingers in jest. Hermes leaned against the door, shoved it open with his shoulder, and disappeared inside. Makaria went running in after him, assuming that they had stumbled upon a massive, hidden cell…only to realize they were in a kitchen. Hermes was standing in the middle of the room, staring at her, rocking up onto his toes repeatedly.

"Hermes…" Makaria grunted, "why are we in a kitchen?"

"I'm *so* glad you asked." Hermes was nearly bouncing with excitement, and Makaria thought that the god had gone mad. He stepped towards a long, low row of cabinets against the wall, bending at the waist to grab a cabinet door but not opening it.

"Makaria, without any further ado, I give you…" Hermes snorted as if he couldn't talk fast enough, "…the terrifying, the almighty, God of death."

Makaria looked at him with a furious scowl, ready to fight him that he had led her on a chase through the palace. Hermes flung the cabinet door open and jumped back, grabbing Makaria's shoulders as they both peered in.

As he had promised, there was Thanatos.

Sitting in the cabinet.

Hermes started laughing so hard that he fell over, landing on his backside and nearly rolling back and forth. Makaria's first instinct was a rush of relief like she had never known before, but only a second later, she found herself covering her mouth with her hand and trying to hide her laughter.

Gods were already large, and Thanatos was the tallest of the lot. Inside the cabinet, Thanatos's knees were wedged up to his chest while his hands wrapped around his shins. His head was tucked forward, and his shoulders were up near his ears, cramped into a kitchen cabinet that was likely only supposed to fit a few bags of grain. Hephaestus's chains were still looped around his wrist, and the one end had fallen out onto the floor.

Makaria stared at him with a mixture of alleviation and happiness, but Thanatos's expression showed no reprieve. His mouth was pulled into a thin line, and his brow was furrowed, and Makaria could see as he flexed his fingers repeatedly.

He looked positively murderous as he closed his eyes and took a long breath. Makaria, however, knew that expression.

Thanatos was pouting, in all of his terrifying glory. Which, at the moment, had to be believed rather than seen.

"Hi." Makaria walked a few paces forward and bent down,

her hair spilling off her shoulder and blocking Hermes from Thanatos's view. The illusion of a private moment seemed to lessen his ire, and his eyes softened for a fraction of a second.

"Hello," his voice was low, if not a little strained. "I'm glad to see you."

Makaria pursed her lips together, and a tiny giggle escaped. "You're in a cabinet," she whispered dramatically, and Thanatos nodded his head solemnly as if he was coming to terms with bad news.

"I am."

"Thanatos is in a cabinet!" Hermes leapt to his feet, shoving forward and poking his head next to Makaria's. Thanatos carried on like he wasn't there.

"I'm glad you found me." He was tender when he addressed the goddess.

"*Thanatos is in a cabinet!*" Hermes stood up and started rubbing his temples as if he was struggling to soak in the magnitude of the moment all at once.

"The world needs you something awful right now," Makaria informed him gently like she was discussing the weather.

"Do you need me?" Thanatos dared to ask her, feeling surprisingly confident for an immortal god crammed into carpentry.

"Thanatosisinacabinet," Hermes breathed out all of the words at once, finally leaning back against the wall and sliding down it. He made an imaginary toast to no one in particular. "I will remember this moment until the day I die."

"All that you should remember is I'll be the one who's there when you do!" Thanatos yelled over Makaria's shoulder in Hermes's direction, but that only caused the trickster to start laughing anew.

Makaria felt her blood pounding in her veins, but she looked down at Thanatos and was overcome with the affection she saw in his eyes. He was used to being the capable one, the god who was the most in control. There was something vulnerable about his inquisition as to whether she needed him now, in one of the most ridiculous, powerless positions that any god had been placed in.

"I do." Makaria winked at him and promptly tugged the chains right off Thanatos's wrist. Thanatos let out a groan as his power flooded back over him, and the illicit sounding moan caused a rush of heat between Makaria's legs. She held out her hand and helped him out of the tiny space. He unfurled in front of her, stretching out his arms and rotating his shoulders. Makaria couldn't help but stare as the process emphasized how broad he was.

"Hermes." Thanatos demanded the god's attention, his voice reverberating in such a way that Makaria knew without a doubt he had his power back. Hermes jumped up to his feet, barely stifling his laughter and looking at Thanatos with an eager expression.

"What can I do for you, God of the crawlspace? Shall I send out a message about your forwarding address or—*hmph!*" Hermes's eyes got wide as indignation crossed over his face, his lips staying firmly closed as he could only make various humming noises in Thanatos's and Makaria's direction.

"Did you…" Makaria smirked and looked from Hermes to Thanatos.

"Did I send Hermes's gift of speech to Charon? Absolutely." Thanatos grabbed Makaria's hand and led her out of the kitchen, pausing next to Hermes, who was still making muffled, squawking noises. Thanatos winked at the messenger god.

"You'll get your voice back, Hermes. Charon will have it waiting for you." Thanatos tugged Makaria out of the kitchen and down the hall, pulling her in close to his body as they left the palace. Before they made it to the front doors, Thanatos's mood shifted.

"Is it... bad?" he sighed. Makaria knew what he was talking about.

"It is," she tried to break it to him gently, "but it's stopped for now."

"I can tell." Thanatos looked up at the ceiling of the palace hall like he was searching the heavens. "You did a good job, Makaria."

Makaria shook her head, the images of Greece on fire flickering through her mind. "No, I couldn't help anyone. It was horrible. All I could do…"

"You stopped their pain," Thanatos cut her off, cupping her cheek and running his thumb soothingly across her skin. "No one is denying that you've made great progress, but you're still not even a fully-fledged immortal. You couldn't have stepped in as Death. You did the next best thing you could, and you made sure *everyone on earth* stopped hurting."

"Well," Makaria leaned into his touch, "it sounds a lot more impressive when you put it like that."

Thanatos bent down, barely grazing her lips in the softest of kisses. He pulled away far too quickly for Makaria's liking, igniting heat in her belly.

"You are impressive. Now," Thanatos smiled, "I'll admit, I'm about to show off." He kissed Makaria on the forehead once and vanished, power exploding in every direction. If his power wasn't so familiar to Makaria, it would've knocked her over.

Flecks and pieces of Thanatos's magic started to blanket the world, and Makaria could sense balance being restored. She released a long, happy sigh, and started walking down the steps of the palace to wait for Thanatos to return to her.

21

It didn't take as much time as one would expect for Thanatos to right the balance in the world. He released his power and let it sweep over every mile of the mortal realm, taking every creature and soul swiftly and gently with it. The only person who was truly put out was Charon, who was working overtime to transport shades across Styx. Thanatos dropped in briefly to visit him on his way home, still letting his influence spread over Greece to finish the job, and only got a glare from his brother.

Thanatos *should* have been in a horrible mood, but he couldn't bring himself to it. Balance was restored promptly, and the events that transpired would soon be only a story for the poets. There was still a twinge of embarrassment that had taken root in Thanatos's core, which was to be expected when he was temporarily sidelined by a mortal, of all things, but it couldn't sprout. There was only one thing on his mind as he hurtled through the meadows of the Underworld, and that was that someone was waiting for him.

Makaria was at home, his home, waiting for him.

It was a completely new sensation to Thanatos, and it felt like he had been drugged. The feeling was nothing compared to the chained, hollow feeling of his brief captivity, but instead, it pushed him to new heights. He could barely contain it as he materialized on his own front steps, pushing the door open to the large estate. He could sense Makaria inside the walls, and the sensation was driving him to a different kind of madness. As soon as he stepped inside, the phenomenon only escalated, and Thanatos felt like the ground had dropped out beneath him.

Everything about the main hall had been changed. The drab stone and wood walls had been transformed, covered in tile and tapestries. The imagery in all of the small stones told the story of death, Thanatos's story, through the pictures of sickle, scythe, and coin. There was not a single starving or crying human, not one mutilated beast of burden or desperate, pleading human. Instead, there were only soft, sleepy smiles or accepting, empty expressions on the faces of those who were being carried off by a great pair of wings. The basins in the hallway flickered with firelight, illuminating the scene around him, causing the scenes to feel almost alive. There was power thrumming through the mosaic, as if it was breathing, and no one could look upon it and claim that it was the work of a mortal man.

Waves of emotion ran over Thanatos until his knees buckled, his legs collapsing under the weight of his feelings. His chest twisted so violently that he wondered briefly if immortals could have a heart attack.

The space took his breath away. There were lit incense sticks in the alcoves, and the entire hall smelled like lavender and frankincense. Each of the individual improvements on their own would've been enough to evoke an emotional reaction from Thanatos, but all together... He was overwhelmed with the realization that his house—for the first time in eons—felt like a *home*.

"Thanatos?" Makaria's voice was whisper soft, but it cut through the pulsing sound of Thanatos's heartbeat echoing in his head. He jumped to his feet and pulled her to his chest before he could even get a good look at Makaria's face, holding her tightly to him like she might evaporate at any moment.

She let out a soft laugh, wrapping her arms around his neck and tilting her head to kiss his cheek.

"I take it that you don't mind I did a little redecorating?" Her voice sent shivers down his spine, and Thanatos shook his head. He pulled back to get a better look at her face without loosening her grip.

"You could burn this house to the ground because you liked it better that way, and I'd agree with you," Thanatos murmured on an exhale, his thumb now stroking small circles on her cheek.

Makaria felt her breath catch in her throat, her eyes going wide at the admission. They were more than friends—this much was apparent—but their attraction for one another still carried a heavy amount of trepidation. Thanatos kept his thoughts close to his chest, and his admission was one of the heavier claims he had made.

"Do you want this?" He gave her hips a small squeeze for emphasis as if there was any doubt to what he was referring. Makaria felt her chest tighten at the raw vulnerability in his eyes.

"Yes," she nodded her head quickly. His relief was immediately obvious. "Thanatos—" Makaria started to say something but was cut off with a kiss, Thanatos lips just grazing over hers. He pulled back slightly, and Makaria felt herself leaning towards him, chasing after more of his touch.

"Then… please, please don't say anything else," Thanatos pleaded, sounding almost desperate.

The atmosphere between them had shifted immediately, both of them remembering where they had been heading before they were interrupted by Hephaestus. It was a potent, heady feeling that pushed them both to the brink while they warred with themselves that this was a fleeting sensation.

Something about every interaction felt limited, sacred, as if it was something to be enjoyed all at once before it was gone forever—and they had already wasted too much time. There was no time now for them to discuss what had happened or what would happen next. There was only this very moment. Thanatos tightened his grip on Makaria and pulled her closer to him until there was no space between them. She cried out as she felt his arousal, hard against her as her hips canted towards him of their own accord.

Thanatos was trailing kisses down her jaw, his hand moving through the folds of her peplos as he tugged it off her shoulder, leaving her naked to the waist. Makaria let out a soft gasp as the cool air hit her skin, her breasts pebbling and hardening to stiff peaks. Thanatos let out a ravaged groan at the sight, pushing Makaria up against the tiled mosaic and dropping to his knees.

"Fuck, these are perfect," he said, sounding reverent, before nipping her breast sharply and sucking it into his mouth.

Makaria tossed her head back and cried out, her hands scrambling for purchase as she gripped Thanatos's hair. He bit down and tugged on her nipple, causing her to pull his hair, both of them gasping for air as the touches overwhelmed them.

He didn't know how far she wanted to go, and doubts began to creep into the very edges of his mind as he switched to her other breast and gave it the same attention. Makaria was lost under the sensation of his biting teeth and warm tongue, chasing away any sting, the toying line between pain and pleasure blurring underneath his touches. Their power was beginning to mix with each other again, like warm flames licking up their bodies.

"Please, Thanatos." Makaria gripped his hair harder and pulled him off her, chests heaving like they couldn't get enough air in their lungs. "I want you."

"Are you... Are you sure?" The desire was apparent in

Thanatos's eyes, but Makaria's heart sank when she saw how much he questioned her even after she had voiced her enthusiastic consent. Makaria realized that it was going to take a little more convincing on her part to get over the eons of silent conditioning that had made Thanatos doubt how attractive he was.

"I wouldn't be here if this wasn't what I wanted," Makaria whispered, leaning forward and pressing her lips to the crease in his brow. "I want *you*, Thanatos."

He visibly shuddered at her words, and Makaria was torn between being desperately turned-on at the sight of the immortal on his knees and the sadness that the simple fact she wanted Thanatos felt so foreign to him. She pushed herself off the wall and slid her hands down to Thanatos's shoulders. With a firm push, she knocked him backwards so he was sitting on the floor, and she straddled his waist in a quick movement. Before Thanatos even realized what had happened, Makaria was grinding against him and desperately pulling the edge of her hem.

Thanatos let out a low growl as he felt himself get impossibly harder at the feel of Makaria rocking over him, pulling at her skirts. He got impatient and grabbed a hold of the offending garment, ripping it in half in one tear. It hung around Makaria's legs in tatters, and she laughed.

"Impatient?" she cooed sweetly, bracing her knees on either side of his body while she attempted to remain in control. Thanatos's head only dropped back as he groaned again, feeling Makaria's hand slid up his thigh and begin to tortuously stroke his cock.

"You're running out of time before I destroy the illusion of control you have here." Thanatos already sounded wrecked, his hips thrusting to meet each twisting stroke of Makaria's palm. She was only able to let out a breathy giggle in response, the empty feeling between her legs increasing to a pulsing, wet sensation that was threatening her very sanity. Makaria released him and pushed Thanatos's chiton up to his chest, revealing all of him to her.

She barely stifled a moan at the sight, his erection heavy between his legs and the dark hair that trailed down his body. Makaria felt another wave of arousal run through her body as she pushed up and aligned herself over him. Slowly, treacherously slowly, Makaria guided Thanatos inside of her. The pace was killing them both. Thanatos's entire body tensed underneath her like granite while Makaria felt her own arousal drip down her thighs.

"For the love of the *fucking* gods, Makaria." Thanatos's head dropped back as he braced himself on his elbows. He said her name like he wasn't sure if it was a blessing or a curse. Makaria only whimpered in response, freezing just as she was about to take all of him.

"You're the tallest man I've ever met and that's *proportional*," her voice was breathy, her arousal drowning out all the bite in her tone. Thanatos chuckled at that, a thoroughly satisfied male sound, then he picked his head up. She felt like divinity, and even partially nestled inside of the goddess, Thanatos knew he was addicted.

"Why didn't you say so, darling?" he crooned, pushing off his elbows and leaning towards her. "Let me help." Thanatos sucked her breast into his mouth again, laving his tongue against her until he felt Makaria shudder. He felt her tightening around his erection, and he fought back an intense urge to flip them over and take her like a beast. He violently discarded that thought as he prioritized the woman atop him, one hand dropping to her center and stroking her clit in slow circles.

"*Fuck—*" Makaria cried out, her body flooding with arousal until she seated herself fully on Thanatos's dick, taking him to the hilt. Thanatos nearly shouted but kept up his pace as he touched her, his other hand supporting his weight. Makaria was blind with lust, but she cupped one hand on Thanatos's jaw and forced him to look at her when she began to move. She rose and fell against him in an intoxicating rhythm, grinding against his pelvis each time he disappeared inside her, nearly trapping his hand between their bodies.

Time was lost, and neither of them were aware of how long they stayed in that torturous pleasure that overwhelmed them both nearly to the point of pain. Makaria had never felt like this being on top of a man, so drunk with power but devastated with the delicious drag of him inside her. Nothing had ever felt so full, so *right*, and she became so overwhelmed with the feeling that she picked up her pace chasing her high.

Thanatos was hanging on by a mere thread. His body was coated in sweat as he braced himself against her movements, feeling like his shade was going to leave his body every time she took all of him. No one had ever wanted him like this, *ever*, someone who demanded he look her in the eye as she circled her hips on top of him and rode Thanatos like she owned him. He didn't care if this was fleeting; he'd take every second that she gave him.

"Makaria," Thanatos choked the words out, and it was a warning. Makaria whimpered, torn between the cresting wave of her release and the desire to stay in that moment. He increased the pace and pressure of his thumb on her clit, his hips rising to meet her as he thrusted from beneath her. Thanatos leaned back a bit more, meeting Makaria's gaze with a teasing expression. His words were a low, gravelly sound that went straight down Makaria's spine and electrified her.

"Look down, sweet goddess. See how well you're taking it. How does it feel knowing that you're full of me?" Makaria let out a strangled whimper, and Thanatos felt her contract around him. He grunted, his words becoming even more strangled as he spoke. "Come for me, I want to hear what you sound like when you're *fucked by Death*." Thanatos growled the last words so violently, they were barely intelligible, but Makaria felt her whole body careening over the edge. She shook and fell against his chest as her arousal rocked through her, leaving her a shuddering dead weight on top of him. Thanatos came with a shout as soon as he felt her orgasm contracting around him, his own strength finally giving out as he laid back against the floor.

With the last of his strength, he gently pulled Makaria off him so she was nestled into his side. They lay there for a few moments, catching their breath, barely able to hear themselves over their own heartbeats. Makaria felt Thanatos shift and picked up her head to see him looking down at her. Part of her afterglow was shattered when she saw the vulnerability that had returned to his eyes. She kissed his chest, tossing a leg over his waist.

"Come on then," she goaded, her voice hoarse. "On your side."

Thanatos raised an eyebrow at Makaria but did what she said, only to feel her arms go around his neck as her leg at his waist tightened. She tucked her head behind his, kissing the shell of his ear. Thanatos didn't move a muscle, and Makaria waited for him to relax into the embrace, knowing that no one had tried to cuddle the god of death before. It took a few more minutes until she felt him loosen him, wrapping his hand around hers in front of his chest.

They were nestled together in a sweaty mess, cuddled in a heap of limbs in the middle of the hallway. It was a rather ridiculous sight to an outsider, especially with Makaria's shredded garment falling around her as she held onto Thanatos like a pack. As their heartbeats evened out and they caught their breaths, they fell asleep before they could move. Under the firelight dancing off the tiled mosaics, on the hard stone floor, neither Thanatos nor Makaria had ever been more comfortable.

22

When Makaria woke, she was expecting—at most—a pleasant ache between her legs or a sore back from spending the night on the floor, wrapped around a massive god.

Instead, she was loathe to find a crushing absence, a cold chill that only Death could leave behind. Makaria woke the next morning to discover that Death had left her behind.

※※※

When Thanatos woke, it was to an all over more pleasant sensation. It was robbed from him by the blade of his insecurities, sharper than any scythe or sickle. The warm, close embrace of Makaria at his back now felt mocking, and although it felt like leaving a limb behind, he detangled himself from her. Thanatos had never known the morning after embrace of a lover, the soft, unguarded touches of a partner who had bared themselves entirely the night before—leaving only quiet laughter and exploratory touches by the daylight the next morn.

Without that context or a memory to pull from, Thanatos left. He dared himself to look back, condemning himself to an image that would haunt him for all eternity—Makaria, curled up on herself and asleep in the hall, alone. He couldn't breathe over the strength of his own instincts, which threatened to override him like the need to breathe. Everything in his body protested against leaving her there, alone and unprotected, but his mind all too brutally reminded him that she would want nothing to do with him when she woke.

He snapped his fingers, and a blanket wrapped around her tiny frame. It was a cruel replacement, but the memories that did occupy Thanatos's mind were worse.

The cold, cruel laugh of a nymph as he reached for her at first light. The sharp sting of a slap on the wrist as she pushed him away. The rejection that overwhelmed him and flooded his senses with an icy shock.

A dare. It had been a dare.

The drunken nymph, sent from a wild Olympian party, had agreed to report back in the early reign of Helios how the death god felt. Was it like lying with a man? Did taking death inside you feel cold? Would she die? Thanatos had walled up his heart that day while every detail of his affairs and intimacy was dissected as hungover conversation like a party favor.

"That is what awaits you in the morning," Thanatos reminded himself under his breath. Makaria's pleas and assurances from the night before had been drowned in his shame.

Thanatos took himself across the plains of the Underworld, leaving the last remaining pieces of his heart scattered across the sky, until he arrived at the one god's house who might be able to staunch the bleeding.

Hades.

Convinced that there was nothing waiting for him in his own home, Thanatos slipped inside the walls of Hades's. He knew that the god would sense his arrival but had the good sense to wait in the receiving hall, acting like a proper guest as if there was formality between them. Hades's great room looked nothing like Thanatos's, aside from some of the same structural supports.

This was a room that was adorned for a god that people respected, covered in tribute. The burning basins of fire had flames that almost licked the ceiling, fueled with precious oils and ambers that created a fragranced burn. Everything was made of black stone, gleaming in the light and shining with cracks of mother of pearl in the onyx marble. It felt holier without the crowd of people that had been there for Orpheus and Eurydice's judgement day, like it had been reverted to a temple-like space.

Thanatos's eyes landed on the two thrones upon the raised dais. Hades's home had once been like his, with a second throne that sat unused and slightly off to the side, a sheet thrown over it. Now, both of the royal seats had been moved so they were side-by-side. The second one was now ringed with fresh blossoms around the base and pomegranate seeds and human skulls had been carved into the wood of the armrests.

Thanatos knew that Persephone had accepted Hades's offer of courtship, and furthermore was now his consort, yet seeing the empty thrones made his chest ache. It was the same pain that he felt when he saw Aeëtes looking at Hecate, in full necromancer form, and wasn't afraid of her. The creatures of the Underworld were pairing off one by one, and at the end of the day—at the end of their lives—there would just be Thanatos.

A part of his brain raged violently against him, shaking the bars of the cage he had put it in. It yelled and stampeded and screamed, furious that he hadn't believed Makaria's declarations of affection. He had been the one to abandon her. Every time those noises almost broke through, they were still throttled by the cruel laughter of the nymph and the echoes of a thousand years of angry rumors about Thanatos.

That was as true to Thanatos as the rules of the universe — the sky was blue; Apollo was a dick; he was the God of death, and no one would love him. It was like a block in his mind that he couldn't break through. It had never happened to him in all this time. How could he possibly start to believe that it was happening to him now? He couldn't, not when there were years of evidence to the contrary.

The loud slam of a door opening startled Thanatos, immediately followed by a resonant laughter.

"Thanatos, my friend, don't tell me after all these years you've gone soft? I can't remember ever being able to sneak up on you."

Thanatos turned around, unable to keep a small smile off his face, always pleased by Hades's goading sense of humor.

The God of the Underworld was dressed in his usual black, down to his sandals, his hair looking even longer then when Thanatos had last seen him. He was a broad man, who looked like he worked in the Underworld more than ruled it, but there was a dark power in his eyes that dared anyone to try and defy him. Underneath his exterior, which was as dark as the world he ruled, Thanatos knew that Hades had a heart that had been cracked open a mile wide by Persephone.

"Careful or I'll have to prove otherwise for the sake of it." Thanatos winked at Hades and opened his arms, the gods greeting one another with an embrace. Hades clapped him on the back a bit too forcefully, and he pulled away, his near permanent smirk lighting up his face.

"I wouldn't be mad if you did. I could use a good brawl." Hades rolled his shoulders back as if illustrating his pent-up energy. Thanatos cocked a brow at him.

"I would think with a new bride around, you're using your energy plenty."

Hades's smirk turned downright lecherous, licking his lip

as he grinned. "That is an entirely different kind of brawl, my friend."

There was warmth in Hades's eyes when he said it, which caused Thanatos's chest to constrict again. It flickered across his face, and Hades's expression sobered.

"What is it that you've come to talk to me about? Although I wouldn't mind a social visit, you're not one to make them."

"I've been known to stop by for sport on occasion."

Hades scoffed, rolling his eyes as he sat down on the dais steps, supporting his weight on his elbows. He looked like the picture of a god in repose, ironically lounging on the steps in front of his throne instead of *on* it. If Thanatos didn't know Hades personally, he'd assume it was some sort of a power move. Although everything the gods did was technically somewhat of a power move.

"In the last thousand years, I can't think of a single time you've come just to say hello," Hades teased him, aimlessly cracking his knuckles. Truly, if Thanatos didn't know Hades, he would've thought that everything was a threat. Thanatos pulled his scythe out of thin air, brandishing it with a wink in Hades's direction.

"I'm sure it's happened, no?"

Hades only threw his head back and laughed at the audacity, the gods threatening one another with violence because they couldn't remember the last time they had a social visit.

"All right, easy there." Hades held his hands up in mock surrender. "Is this a social visit then?"

Thanatos quieted, the mirth draining from his face as his expression turned solemn. Hades's eyes went wide at the sudden transformation, as if a curtain had fallen and revealed what was going through Thanatos's head.

"I take that as a no," Hades murmured, trying to keep his face as neutral as possible. He had never seen Thanatos anything other than murderous or content. He had never seen the god exhibit any extremes such as joy or sorrow. Thanatos stood before him now like a man without a rudder, with a haunting, searching sorrow in his eyes.

"No," Thanatos affirmed with a quiver in his voice.

Hades was silent, barely moving a muscle, as if he was watching a wounded animal. He rightfully assumed it was best to be quiet and wait for Thanatos to break the silence. It took a few agonizingly long minutes, where Hades almost broke to ask him what was wrong. Thanatos finally turned to face Hades with a disgruntled sigh, crossing his arms over his chest.

"I don't know what to do."

Hades waited and nodded for Thanatos to go on when he didn't elaborate. "I typically always have the answer, but you're going to need to give me a few more details." The slight jest got a tiny chuckle from Thanatos, who shook his head.

"You're worse than Hermes sometimes."

"I'm older. If anything, he got it from me."

"You really want to claim responsibility for Hermes?"

"Fuck no," Hades groaned, his head falling back before he snapped to attention. "Don't change the subject." He pointed a finger at the god. "If you need some time, that's fine. If you want to talk about it…then talk about it. I don't have all day." Hades's slipped a bit of a commanding edge into his tone. Not unkindly, only to urge Thanatos to speak.

"Yes, you're very busy with your consort waiting for you upstairs."

"As a matter of fact… Hey." Hades's voice dropped to a growl. "I mean it, Thanatos. Stop changing the subject."

Thanatos was quiet, all the humor draining from his face again like it flickered off. He turned away as if he couldn't look at Hades when he spoke.

"I think… I think I have feelings for Makaria."

Hades's expression didn't change. He didn't say a word. After a second, Thanatos turned back to Hades to see if he was even there. The god stared back at him.

"You can't be this thick," Hades deadpanned. "You're just

now admitting that you think you have feelings for her? I hate to be the one to tell you..." He paused. "Actually, no, I don't mind being the one to tell you this at all. You're way past feelings."

"What does that even mean?"

Hades rolled his eyes. "I only saw you look at her during the caucus with Orpheus and Eurydice, and you're in love with that goddess."

As soon as Hades said it, Thanatos pulled the scythe out again, brandishing it in Hades's direction. The god merely tossed Thanatos an amused look and waved his hand, causing the scythe to disappear. Thanatos grunted and curled his lip in response, knowing that Hades's power would have dominion in his own receiving hall.

"That accusation—"

"An accusation!" Hades was laughing. "I tell you that you're in love with the new death goddess and you're calling it an *accusation?* It's true; you don't know what to do, do you?"

Thanatos's eyes flared blue, and he waited a beat before shaking his head. Hades continued, unable to keep his droll attitude out of his voice.

"I'm not sure why you've come to me about this, Thanatos. If you *feel* something for Makaria, say something to *her.*"

Only then did his tone somber as if he was reflecting on a memory in which he had learned that the hard way. Thanatos shook his head again, frustrated, beginning to pace as if there was a piece to the puzzle that he couldn't get Hades to understand. Hades waited a few more moments for him, content to let Thanatos fret it out, until the anxious movement became too much.

"Thanatos." He stood up, going to put a hand on the god's shoulder to stop his erratic movements. "Come on, what's really going on?"

Thanatos sighed, a burdened, heavy sound, and looked at Hades with sad eyes. "I don't... I don't deserve that kind of love, Hades." He whispered it, full of pain, and Hades felt his breath catch in his throat at the raw, unbridled sadness that he sensed pouring out of the god. Hades also sensed how thoroughly Thanatos believed that statement, and instead of admonishing him, he waited for him to continue.

"No one will ever understand death the way that I do. They won't. Death… Death is the opposite of life. There isn't a shade in existence that would see that and know why death will always have to come first."

Hades let out a long breath and shook his head in admonishment. "Normally, I would agree with you." Thanatos head snapped up as he stared at Hades, almost a little in shock. "But you're not talking about any normal shade. You're talking about Makaria, a goddess of death. Thanatos…" Hades shook his head. "You can't be that stupid. She's an immortal of the Underworld and was deigned to work with you. It's like she was made for you. If she feels the same way…go for it, my old friend."

"It can't be. There can be no one who was *made* for this, designed for this kind of isolating existence."

"Maybe she wasn't. I don't think you were, either. Did you ever consider that you can be there for each other? 'In life and in death', as the humans vow?" Hades chuckled sardonically. Thanatos scoffed, burying his frustrations with anger.

"The world would have everyone believe that I am the one responsible for death. That I am the one who cuts their string, who gives the final blow, the one who decides and acts. I am none of those things. I am the end." Thanatos started pacing and let out a long, slow breath, his head hanging low.

"You are a new beginning, Thanatos," Hades reminded him sternly as if he was scolding a child. "We all know this." He fought the urge to go over and stop the frenetic pacing. "Do not even speak of yourself as they do. You are the end of nothing. Perhaps this is a beginning all its own, with you and Makaria in the role of death." Hades's tone dropped, a flicker of magic slipping into his voice. "Besides, do you really want to preach to me about the lies of Olympians and of reputations?" Hades cocked a brow in challenge, his bident appeared in his hand.

He let his power release around him for a brief moment, illuminating him in black flame and casting a shadow against the crown of bone and black gemstones that appeared on Hades's brow. Thanatos knew he was driving home a point about how often the name of Hades incurred images of the devil himself, instead of a fair god with an entire dominion to govern.

Thanatos made a noise that could barely be distinguished as a sniffle, picking his head up and rolling his shoulders. He shook his head as if he were shaking off his own feelings, bracing himself for the onslaught of his own stoicism. The silence stretched on between them.

"Whatever you've done, you can do undo it," Hades said rather nonchalantly, his weaponry disappearing and his power receding. Thanatos said nothing. "I'm pretty sure you can't fix anything from here."

Hades pushed him again, essentially kicking him out, and Thanatos got the hint. Hades knew that it was best to push Thanatos to action, where he would feel more in control—all of the gods of the Underworld were this way, especially the men. Hades wasn't above admitting they tended to be a fickle bunch.

Thanatos nodded in agreement, clapping his hand on Hades's shoulder in wordless agreement. They both bowed their heads once towards the other god, and Thanatos disappeared from the great hall altogether.

He had apologies to make.

23

There was an ache in Makaria's chest that she couldn't begin to explain. It was an ancient pain, something that had befallen the broken hearts of the world ever since the dawn of time. It was a slow, burning emptiness that simultaneously threatened to burn its host down to the ground or spur them forward in unnamed mania.

The greatest of heartbreaks come to those who were not expecting them. The individuals who put their feelings on the line and were met with rejection suffered an unrequited pain, a pain that their honesty and courage never deserved in response. It had happened since the earliest days of souls incarnate as they began stumbling around the new world, looking for their other half—mortals and immortals included.

Makaria sat up slowly, afraid to move. The air around her felt wrong. If she moved too quickly, she was sure that something would collapse. There had to be something inherently wrong for everything to have gone so sideways. Her brain seemed to have a delayed reaction, everything was taking a little bit longer to process. She kept waiting for the scene to change, but no, she was really here, waking up alone on a cold floor with a blanket wrapped around her that she didn't recognize.

Where did Thanatos go?

Even her thoughts sounded small inside her head as she grappled with all the different reasons for why he might've left. She had been slowly chipping away at her insecurities since she arrived in the land of the gods, proving to herself more than anyone else that she could be worthy of a job like this. There could be no other higher purpose, in her mind, helping usher shades to their next stage, their new beginning.

All of that progress shattered in an instant, splintering like shards of steel and jagged pieces of pottery. It left scraping claw marks across her heart, and Makaria couldn't catch her breath.

Did that mean nothing to him in the end? The worst doubt of all crept in—that Thanatos had never believed in her or cared about them together. *He was always just biding his time, waiting for my time to be up. After all, he'd be there when it was all over... Was he just getting used to how I felt? What my soul tasted like?*

It shouldn't make sense, the sudden voracious nature of Makaria's thoughts. Everything in her had shifted in a moment. This was the nature of the misplaced and the unsettled. Her whole life, she had been looking for her place among the dead. Now that she had been rejected by Death himself, an honor that every shade in existence received, every wicked thought and insecurity from her time as both a mortal and an immortal roared to life.

Makaria stood on shaky legs, her face ashen as she looked around the hall. The incense sticks still burned, and the basins were lit with their eternal flames. The light flickered around the walls from the warm glow, tossing fractals of color off the tiled mosaics that now painted the space. Makaria looked at them now with fresh eyes and thought she might be sick. She cast her eyes to the ground and ran out of the hall, her budding powder ebbing and flowing across her skin as it responded to her distress.

She ran until she could run no more, not paying attention to where she was. It didn't matter to her anymore. Even if she stumbled upon the worst of the Underworld's prisoners, she wasn't afraid to take their place. When Makaria finally sank down to her knees, it was in the soft, sandy soil next to the banks of Lethe. The river was immediately identifiable by its current; it was the slowest moving of all the Underworld's rivers—so slow, it looked stagnant to a mortal eye.

Time stopped and started in a small circle around Makaria, her adolescent powers acting defiantly in response to her internal suffering. She didn't know how long she had been sitting on the side of the river when a gentle hand appeared on her shoulder and squeezed. Makaria was startled, jolting away in response before looking up at her visitor.

"Nyx," she breathed, sounding reverent. In all her years of devotion to the goddess, there had never been a more welcome visit from the primordial. Nyx's brow was furrowed in concern. Her face remained gentle as she dropped her hand from Makaria's shoulder and sat down. The two of them said nothing else, Makaria's head dropping down to rest against Nyx. Nyx slid her arms around Makaria and pulled the young immortal into her side, embracing her in such a way that only a mother could.

It snapped any last tether that Makaria had to reality. Her own mother hadn't been the nurturing sort, dedicating all of her time to other priestesses in her care, so the affection was years overdue and sorely needed. Makaria started to cry, fisting her hands in Nyx's tunic while she said nothing, stroking Makaria's hair and giving her space to unleash. Makaria's power shot out around them, spiking at random intervals, releasing in small waves as she sobbed. Nyx reigned it in, gently coaxing the nearly sentient magic to a standstill, helping guide Makaria to a sense of stoicism. It wasn't quite peace, but it would do. When Nyx finally spoke, it was with the utmost gentleness.

"Now, child, I *know* that you aren't this upset over a man. Even an immortal one."

Makaria snapped her head up, her mouth dropping open as she stared at Nyx.

"That's incredibly dismissive," she spat, hiding her sore heart behind petulance. Nyx merely shrugged.

"You aren't though," Nyx pushed, "or Hecate would've sensed your distress, not me. What is this really about?"

Makaria froze. Of all the things that she expected Nyx to say, this was not one of them, and it was the least welcome. She was upset about Thanatos, of course, but it was a symptom of a deeper ache. When she had woken up alone that morning, it was a cruel mimicry of every morning she had spent in solitary in the mortal world. Her sense of worth and self-assurance, the idea that she deserved and had a space in this world, had shattered again. This time, it had broken on an immortal scale, and she wasn't sure if she could handle it.

"I want to give up my immortality." Makaria's voice was nearly unintelligible as she said it. The admission felt wrong even as she forced her lips to make the words, like there was a greater part of her, buried deeply, that knew it wasn't what she wanted. Nyx's face contorted, and Makaria avoided eye contact as she felt the borderline fury rolling off of the primordial.

"You want to *give up* your chance at making your immortality permanent?" Nyx sounded like she was spitting metal. Makaria nodded. Nyx caught her face lightly, tilting Makaria's chin until she was forced to look at her.

"You have to say it. Out loud."

"I… I want to give up my immortality." Anyone could hear that Makaria's voice was shaky and unsure.

"Try again." Nyx was firm. "Your fate has not been spun.

You don't have your immortality yet, and you are insistent on coming to me as though you're already a failure."

Makaria wrestled out of Nyx's grip, growing more flustered. "I want to give up my…" She struggled over the words, unable to force herself to say *'I want to give up my chance.'* Makaria knew how fatalist it sounded, and she was filled with self-loathing.

"That's what I thought." Nyx sucked her teeth as her expression gentled. "What's upset you? The real answer, mind you."

Makaria stiffened. "Well, Thanatos…" Her words trailed off. Everything sounded wrong in her head. She could hardly express herself without feeling ashamed.

Nyx could see Makaria's mind turning and interrupted her. "Thanatos was only ever a tutor for you. He does not decide your place in this world." Makaria sniffled, her shoulders bristling as she looked away from Nyx. "Neither do I. Only you can do that."

"How can you be so sure? Everyone's blind faith in me has been crippling, don't you see that?"

"We see parts of you that *you* don't," Nyx argued. "Makaria…" She started to speak and then stopped, as if she was reconsidering what she was about to say. Makaria waited while Nyx seemed to be visibly weighing her options. When she spoke again, it was barely a whisper, with a reverent tone that the most ancient of primordials hardly ever took. "The secret is this: there is no greater force that decides you are worthy. A partner doesn't determine your worthiness. Your parents don't determine it. The only person who decides what your place is in this world is *you*."

Nyx's voice had slowly grown in its ferocity, and she was gripping Makaria's hands, which had started to shake. "I'm sure that my son has done something that was incredibly stupid, probably because he was afraid."

"He—"

Nyx held up a hand. "This doesn't concern him. He certainly is not excused, but he has other people who will smack some sense into him other than his mother." Her somber attitude broke, and she gave Makaria a small, conspiratorial smile.

"I feel foolish," Makaria admitted, chewing on a fingernail. "I shouldn't let everything get to me so strongly."

"A wide heart is full of empathy. The strongest lovers are the best fighters. Don't judge yourself for how you feel, child, but certainly don't let it rule you."

"You make it sound so easy." Makaria couldn't keep a bit of flippant attitude out of her voice. Nyx shrugged, ignoring the sarcasm.

"It's the hardest thing you'll ever do. You'll spend your whole life working on mastering it." Nyx caught Makaria's side eyed glance. "Your whole *immortal* life."

"Oh, really?" Makaria felt her temper rising slightly. "I don't see you struggling with it." Nyx let out a quick bark of a laugh before she quickly covered her mouth with her hand.

"I'm sorry." She was smiling. "You'd laugh too if you knew how wrong that was."

"It's true. I worshipped you my whole life and—"

"From the mortal realm. You didn't have a god's perspective. Erebus and I got into a fight during the Titan Wars, and the other Olympians were worried I'd end the world."

Makaria's eyes went wide at how casual Nyx made it sound, like she wasn't talking about threatening all life on earth.

"Would you have done it?"

Nyx shrugged. "Probably not. The point is, I didn't, even though giving into my emotions certainly would've felt better at the time. That's the piece you need to understand, young goddess. There are bigger things at play when you're immortal. Your feelings affect the lives of others, of innocents. The only way to prove your worthiness is to prove it to yourself. If you're able to stand on your own two legs and know who you are, you'll be immovable. You'll have your bad days, of course, but you won't… Oh, I don't know, threaten to eat the sun and drink the stars." Nyx winked at Makaria, and she finally cracked a small smile.

She felt sheepish but didn't feel like her heart was hemorrhaging anymore.

I don't know what will come of Thanatos and me, but I can decide what becomes of me. As soon as she said the words to herself, the pain in her chest lessened. Nyx saw the shift on Makaria's face and pulled her into a hug.

"Now," Nyx whispered, "do you want to give up your chance at immortality prematurely?"

"No." Makaria was quiet, but she sounded resolute. She didn't know how to prove to *herself* that she was worthy, once and for all, but she still had months to figure it out.

"That's more like it." Nyx helped Makaria to her feet and hugged her once more, kissing her brow. "That's the woman that I remember. The woman who deserves to be immortal."

"I'll do it." Makaria's voice was a little bit louder, even stronger.

"I know you will. I wouldn't have chosen you if I had the slightest doubt." Nyx motioned towards the horizon, an unspoken offer to escort Makaria back to Hecate's house—she certainly wasn't going back to Thanatos's. As they started to walk towards the familiar, infamous kitchen, Nyx couldn't help but probe a little further.

"Now… What exactly did Thanatos do that upset you so?"

Makaria blushed, not wanting to get into an account of her sexual exploits with Nyx's son. "Well, we spent the night together…" Makaria glanced up at Nyx's face cautiously, only to find it was impassive. "…and he wasn't there this morning when I woke up."

Nyx stopped walking and snapped her head towards Makaria, her expression cold. "He did *what*?"

Makaria couldn't help but feel somewhat justified, her brows rising as she held up her hands as if to say *'I can't believe it either.'* She could almost hear Nyx's jaw grinding as dark power slipped down her arms.

"I will end his shade myself so he knows what it feels like," she muttered. "I did not spend one-thousand years raising an immortal teenager so he could act like—" Nyx was cut off as the ground started to shake beneath them. The goddesses were caught by surprise, both of them falling to their knees as the Underworld trembled. There was no telltale signature to the disturbance, neither Nyx nor Makaria could sense whose power was causing the chaos. The earthquake lessened but didn't stop entirely, allowing them to slowly rise to their feet.

Nyx's magic had activated in an instant, her eyes glowing white as stars started dripping from her hair. Makaria's immature power answered too, although the sight was a little less impressive than Nyx's demonstration. Her body glowed like an angel, some of her now signature white hair standing on end. Makaria assumed that Nyx had caused the disturbance and was shaken by the surprise intensity of her own response.

"I'm mad at him too, but you don't need—"

"That wasn't me." Nyx shook her head. There was dread in her voice, something that Makaria had never heard before. It sent a chill down her spine. "That's not a god. It's…"

Beside them, there was a sudden swell as the river began to overflow, the noticeably slow current becoming ragingly rapid.

"Fuck!" Nyx cursed, her voice dropping to almost a growl.

"What is it?" Makaria looked pale, which was impressive for an immortal whose power expressed itself in an already white, glowing aura. The ground hadn't stopped shaking.

"That's a stampede," Nyx whispered. "The Underworld has been overwhelmed. Styx must be overflowing, which means that shades are trying to swim across…"

"Has that ever happened?!" Makaria gasped. Her mind began reeling with the idea of so many desperate souls on the banks of Styx that they decided to try and swim across it. By doing that, they risked their spirit being drowned by those without fare who had been abandoned. It would be a watery death, erasing their memory forever.

Nyx picked up her hem and began running towards the far-off dock, her maternal instinct kicking into overdrive when she thought of Charon, alone at the entrance to the Underworld. Makaria started running after her, and Nyx's response to the goddess was breathy and almost frightened.

"It happens when an act of the gods threatens all of Greece."

Makaria's heart stopped.

III

24

Outside of Athens, the small town of Eleusis was throwing a party large enough to rival not only its metropolitan neighbor, but all of Greece. Eleusis was home to Dionysus's largest temple, and he shared the city with Demeter. Oftentimes, it felt like Mt. Olympus wasn't big enough for the two personalities, and Eleusis wasn't either. That evening, however, there was no doubt as to who the reigning deity of the city was—it was the third day of Dionysia. The streets were running with wine, and it was almost impossible to find water anywhere in the town.

There were three massive theaters scattered throughout Eleusis's limits, which sat vacant for most of the year. Demeter threatened to have them torn down every spring and every harvest, but they were empty threats. Every god knew what happened when they went after one another's sacred places, especially after Hera. It had taken hundreds of years for her comeuppance, but it was thorough when it occurred, and not a single god took her side.

The theaters still stood, and they were packed to the brim, full of drunken revelers. Each theatre held the population of Eleusis three times over, but they were full of travelers who had come for the festivities. Dionysus didn't inspire great loyalty, not as much as some of the other Olympians, but when the festivals in your honor became wine-addled orgies, people were more apt to attend.

Dionysus himself was seated in the front row, in a place of honor, watching one of the plays that had been dedicated in his honor. It should have been of no surprise that while he claimed a scholarly affection for the tragedies, it was the comedies that were his favorite. It was there, in his favorite theatre—humbly named the Theatre of Dionysus—where the god was presiding over his court. The space was a traditional amphitheater with a large wall that served as the back of the stage, featuring two-levels of several cut-out doorways and windows. There were drunken partygoers, currently hanging from them, some standing straight up and toasting the crowd, while others were hanging perilously by their knees.

The front row had been removed entirely to make way for Dionysus's entourage and had been replaced with a long banquet table. For three days, the table magically refilled with food and wine, and anyone who could approach Dionysus himself and prove entertaining enough could eat there until the festival ended.

Being the final day of the festivities meant the table was packed to the brim, people elbowing each other and tossing cups over other worshippers' heads to make space. The truth of the matter was that Dionysus agreed to let everyone sit at the table because he found it more amusing to watch drunk mortals brawl than listen to their second-rate diatribes.

The floor was sticky with wine and smushed food, occasionally decorated with the odd lost sandal. The air was thick with the smell of incense and alcohol, roasted meat, and rather unpleasantly, sweat. Dionysus was almost as red as the wine he drank. He was presently occupied by watching twins fist-fighting over a small sliver of space adjacent to him.

The rest of the amphitheater was just as rowdy, with

several different groups of musicians playing discordant songs, each of them trying to play the loudest. There was no shortage of people climbing on top of each other, in both drunken and amorous fashion. The last time he counted, a few hours prior, Dionysus had noted no less than four different orgies scattered amongst the crowd.

It was only a matter of time until the party descended—or ascended, depending on your point of view—to nothing but a massive, sexually-charged romp. If it wasn't there already. This was Dionysia, the pinnacle of excess, that pushed mortals who tried to keep up with Dionysus and his eternal entourage to the brink. There was not a single soul, god or man, that had their wits about them in the theatre or in all of Eleusis.

It was into this chaos that Apollo descended.

The god had been licking his wounds ever since Thanatos had scared him away from the clearing with Marsyas, waiting for the right time to get vengeance. In true narcissistic fashion, Apollo had created a web of half-lies and scapegoats. It was Marsyas's fault that Apollo had to prove his superiority against the fawn. It was Pan's fault for not keeping the fawns in line. Pan himself, the son of Hermes, was a minor deity who belonged to Dionysus. He was seated at the right hand of the god in question as Apollo materialized on the grand stage in front of them.

There was a half-assed monologue underway—people stopped paying attention to the theatre itself halfway through day two of the festival—and the actor fell backwards and gasped at the burning, golden apparition.

Apollo landed with force, getting a sick satisfaction from feeling the stones crack beneath his feet. He was dressed in a blood-red linen shirt, covered with a bronze breastplate and greaves, but no helmet. Apollo's face was murderous, and his eyes glowed with fury, his hand gripping his infamous Golden Bow at his side.

"Dionysus." Apollo grinned, looking like the image of heavenly perfection.

Dionysus jumped to his feet, knocking the banquet table over in progress. People, food, and drink went scattering everywhere, a great crashing noise drowning out the screams in the theatre.

"How dare you bring a weapon into a festival! You carry that disgusting thing around like a child." Dionysus's face was ruddy, his cheeks inflamed. His voice sounded almost sick, like it was coated in vinegar and oil.

"It matters to me more than you care for you children!" Apollo sneered, jumping down from the stage and stalking towards the god. He waved his hand around dramatically when he spoke, almost as if he were the one performing. "You lead them here like lambs to a slaughter!"

"A slaughter!" Dionysus scoffed, ramming his finger in Apollo's chest as his power started to overtake the theatre. "You are making dangerous declarations, Apollo. This is not one of your songs. You are not welcome here."

Dionysus and Apollo squared off, posturing as they stepped as close as they could to one another. They were two drastically different images—Dionysus, who was double the size of the sun god but drunk and out of shape, and Apollo, leaner than Dionysus but the picture of athleticism. Vines had started to rapidly grow over all the walls of the theatre, edging closer to the gods as Dionysus's power manifested violently—something it was not known for.

"You should have told your precious worshippers," Apollo turned to Pan and spit, "to save it for the Festival. If they hadn't been drunk as their father the day they were born…"

Pan jumped to his feet. "You can't seriously be using *drunk* as an accusation! You fool," his lip curled, "everyone's always *fucking* drunk." Pan was painted as a frivolous creature, but few knew how deeply he loved those he chose to.

Apollo tossed his head back, his hair shining like a mocking halo, laughing. It was a cruel sound. The immortals tensed as Apollo straightened up, sneering at Pan.

"Everyone's always *fucking* drunk, and we always *fucking* fight about it. That's what we *fucking* do."

"H-he has a point." A man poked his head up from underneath the overturned table, holding an amphora with two hands, clearly inebriated. Dionysus rolled his eyes and snapped his fingers, and the worshipper fell into an intoxicated sleep.

"You have no business here, Apollo," Dionysus growled again, his voice shaking the theatre with its timbre. "Get out of here before I decide to do something drastic."

Apollo seemed to consider this for a minute, a sardonic smile slowly making its way across his face. He took a few steps back from Dionysus and nodded contritely as if he was accepting defeat. Everyone watched with a cautious eye as Apollo gracefully jumped back on the stage, stepping over drunken bodies. He reached center stage and turned, facing Dionysus and Pan once more. The wind began to pick up as Apollo started to glow again, levitating a few feet in the air.

"I'll depart," Apollo bowed his head, milking every second for all its worth, "but I'd never be so dishonorable to not leave you with tribute."

Before anyone could react, Apollo pulled his arm back and aimed his bow, an arrow appearing magically in his hands as he strung it. The crowd had only started screaming when the first arrow flew into the chaotic masses. Dionysus let out a bellowing war cry, his power surging forward all at once as he flung himself towards the god. Apollo merely rose higher, and Dionysus went sliding across the stage, just missing grabbing a hold of Apollo's feet.

Two more arrows were fired into the crowd.

Pan was right behind Dionysus, a dagger in his hand. He shouted in frustration as he saw Dionysus fall, and the drunk god made no move to stand. He had passed out, intoxicated, where he fell.

Pan leapt onto the stage, holding the blade out in front of him as he circled Apollo from below. He couldn't defeat Apollo in combat, but the plan was to keep him distracted from firing at the party. The entire amphitheater had exploded into chaos.

The theatre was large enough that some couples didn't realize what was happening and were still having sex in the rafters. Torches had been overturned, and fires were spreading onto anything flammable, heating the stone. People were shouting, unaware of their surroundings, unable to determine what was a drunken illusion and what was reality. They couldn't tell if the arrows had found a singular target, but Pan did not want to find out.

"You know," he yelled up towards Apollo, "for someone who's so worried about their appearance, I don't think that anyone likes you."

Apollo knew that Pan was goading him, but nonetheless, he fought the temptation to drop to the stage and go to blows. He scoffed, notching another gleaming arrow. "You can do better than that, son of the Trickster!" The arrow flew into the crowd, but Pan didn't follow it, keeping his expression trained on Apollo. He heard mortal screams behind him but didn't falter.

Pan's expression turned wicked. "Artemis has the twin to that bow, does she not?"

Apollo twisted his head and stared at the fawn, his jaw clenching as his body went rigid. The god didn't react well to anyone bringing up Artemis in conversation, and Pan knew it. Better yet, he was prepared to exploit it. Apollo dropped slightly, his concentration broken as he focused on Pan.

"Careful..." his voice was a growl, inaudible to the mortals that surrounded them. Pan only tilted his head, but even the small movement conjured images of his father. Apollo fell a little closer.

Pan flipped the dagger effortlessly between his fingers, his eyes turning black as he met Apollo's gaze.

"Answer me one thing, Apollo. For all the arrows you've

got… all of Olympus is dying to know… you ever aim one at Artemis's quiver?" Pan's salacious tone left no room for argument.

Apollo nearly boiled over with rage and fell to the stage, lurching for Pan with his hands outstretched as if to choke him. Pan lithely hopped out of the way, skirting to one side as Apollo fell to his knees where the fawn had been standing not a second prior.

Apollo let out a furious battle cry, turning around and throwing himself again in Pan's direction. The fawn side-stepped him for a second time, his hooves making a tapping noise on the stone that infuriated Apollo. Pan giggled like a child, mocking in a singsong voice as he gracefully swept away from Apollo's grasp at every turn. He led him around the stage, hopping just out of reach. Apollo shouted again, his cherubic face now flushed and sweaty.

"Let me put that in simpler words because I'm dying to know." Pan gave Apollo a short bow, winking as he stood. "Do you fuck your sister?"

Apollo made a bellowing sound like a bull, diving for Pan's legs this time instead of his head. The fawn escaped him again, barely, and laughed while he did it. While he had been goading Apollo and distracting him from firing more arrows into the crowd, the masses had time to evacuate, even if it was in a panic. The amphitheater was now empty, save for those drunkenly passed out on the floor, still including Dionysus himself. The benches were strewn with litter, half-eaten plates, and empty cups. It looked like it had been ripped apart by wild animals, which was partially true.

Pan knew the nymphs and the dryads would've taken to the streets, alerting the trees and the wind to Apollo's deceit. There had been a limited window for Apollo to interfere before alliances were called in, and it became an Olympian matter—and Pan had successfully wasted the rest of his time.

Pan looked out into the crowd and saw that it was nearly

empty, and he turned away from Apollo and jumped off the stage. He hopped onto the overturned table, holding his arms out like he was holding court. The sun god walked to the edge of the stage, aiming his bow at Pan's heart. The fawn seemed unaffected.

"I wish I could say that it's been fun, Apollo," he smirked, "but I only lie when it's entertaining. You are the furthest thing from entertaining that there is, which makes you a rather shit god of the arts, doesn't it?"

Apollo spat on the ground at Pan's feet. "Give me one reason to not send this arrow right through you, god of the wild."

There was a flicker of worry on Pan's face, then he heard a commotion in the street outside and felt a rush of power wash over the auditorium. Power truly felt like a wave. Apollo sensed it and sneered, cursing violently before gathering up his magic around him in a golden cloud, preparing to exit.

"Because you," Pan yelled at the disappearing god, "are terrified of Poseidon!"

It was not an exaggeration that the alliances and family trees of the gods got messy. Pan preferred to keep some of his ties a secret and only openly associated himself with Hermes and Dionysus. However, he was often in the company of Aegipan, the goat-fish god, who resided in Poseidon's oceans. Pan was almost doubled over in laughter as water started trickling through the cracks in the theatre's stone, washing away some of the debauchery.

Apollo had almost vanished from sight, but as the last of his essence ebbed away on the tide of Poseidon's presence, a dark laugh cut through the cleansing influence.

"Did you ever stop to ask yourself, you stupid goat, what I was even aiming at?"

A gold cloud of powder shifted and undulated at center stage, Apollo's voice full of victory and deception. Pan stiffened, his blood running cold as he shouted back at the amorphous god. Panic was threatening to take over as he realized what Apollo had done.

"You're mad!" Pan screamed, turning on his hoof and running up the aisles of the theatre. He turned when he reached the top of the amphitheater, screaming at the sky; he knew Apollo could hear them. "The gods will exile you for this, you pompous *fool*. All of Greece will suffer if you fired plague arrows into a crowd at Dionysia!"

The gold power ebbed away, and Apollo did not respond.

"Please tell me that I misheard you or you're playing an awful, awful trick." Poseidon's deep brogue startled Pan, who turned around and found himself face to face with the god. Poseidon had arrived prepared, in gleaming armor made of coral and mother-of-pearl, his trident in hand. Pan had the decency to look sheepish as he stared at the ground.

"To be fair, I kept him from firing more arrows into the crowd?" Pan grimaced, knowing that Apollo had played him.

Poseidon growled, his voice as deep as the sea. "You gave the crowd time to *evacuate* after Apollo had already fired his arrows. Which means you *spread the plague!*"

"How was I supposed to know that they were plague arrows?" Pan squeaked in his own defense, taking a step back from Poseidon as the god's grip on his trident tightened.

"Because that's what Apollo does!" Poseidon spat angrily before pinching his nose with his thumb and forefinger. "Never mind, we don't have time. We have to tell the others."

Poseidon flicked his fingers, and a fresh wave of water poured over the entire amphitheater, magically avoiding the sleeping drunkards. He turned to leave, and Pan followed close behind him, listening to Poseidon mutter angrily under his breath the whole time.

"You and Aegipan only have one man and one goat between you, and I'd do well to remember that!"

25

Everything was a blur as Makaria and Nyx set off for the banks of Styx. They could sense the tension in the air increasing as they got closer, as the ground continued to shake. The soil seemed to ebb and flow like oceanic tides, trembling with the overabundance of souls that were flooding the entrance to the Underworld. The goddesses rounded the top of a small hill on the opposite bank of Styx, the chaos unfolding before them like a historian's painting of a massacre. Charon's infamous dock came into view, and Makaria couldn't help but gasp at the sight that unfolded before her.

She couldn't see the boatman at all. The river was crowded, full of souls, swimming or standing shoulder to shoulder, all of them crying out with twisted visages. Their screams were silent as the water sucked them under, the shades of the other abandoned dead grabbing them and hauling them down to their depths. As more and more heads disappeared under the water, Makaria watched on in horror as none of the other spirits seemed to notice or care. They kept jumping into the water as soon as there was space, turning the river into a massive sea of tangled limbs fighting against one another.

Charon's boat was stuck in the middle of the gruesome mass, stuck on the shoulders of wailing spirits. Ghostly hands and arms hung off the sides as apparitions tried to claw their way inside. Those who had a precious seat inside shoved them away and tried to beat back the hands that reached for them. Only then could she finally identify Charon, who was standing at the rear of the boat, yelling something in the language of the dead. Makaria, who wouldn't be fluent until her full powers manifested, only caught every other word.

"Please...stop, there will be enough... Don't... I am trying to *help*!"

Her heart wrenched as she heard Charon's distressed pleas. Even now, overwhelmed as people tugged on every inch of him that they could grab, he was attempting to remain calm. He showed no anger for the overwhelmed ghosts of the dead. He did not raise a single hand against them. She couldn't even sense any of his power; he must be keeping it contained in order to ensure none of the spirits were inappropriately harmed.

Nyx was standing next to Makaria, taking in the same horrendous upheaval to the balance of life and death. Makaria could feel Nyx's power rising up to the surface next to her. Goosebumps traveled down her arms at the proximity of it. But Nyx, too, was attempting to keep it together—all the Underworld gods knew that this was no mere fault of the mortals. This kind of disturbance could only be caused by a god, and the fault was not the recently departed's. Makaria scanned her eyes over the river, and her desperation increased as she saw the banks of Styx.

The dock looked like it had been ripped in half by a titan. Splintered boards were sticking up in the air like jagged fingers, like a giant was reaching up from the depths to drag them all to oblivion. The bodies of the deceased were standing shoulder to shoulder on the sand, packed so tightly next to one another that Makaria couldn't see the ground beneath their feet. As more and more shades kept spilling in from the open-mouthed cave at their backs, the crowd swelled even further and pushed those nearest to the water into its depths. Her entire body went cold.

Oh dear gods, they aren't jumping in the river because they want to attempt to swim it... They're being pushed in as the beach becomes more crowded.

It was a heinous sight, and with each passing minute, more shades were tossed into the water haphazardly. The scene spreading out before her became a mockery of the balance of life and death, the sanctity of the Underworld was being threatened.

"What do we do?" Makaria gasped, looking up at Nyx. The primordial's face was filled with concern, but she shook her head solemnly.

"I can only do what I can to those who have reached the opposite shore. These are citizens of the Underworld. They are governed first by Thanatos, then Charon, and finally, Hades."

Makaria felt her temper rising as she looked back out over the carnage at the foot of the hill. She turned to Nyx, her eyes furious. "I don't understand," she hissed. "You're the most powerful being in *existence*, and you can't do anything to help?"

Nyx's head moved slowly as she turned to face Makaria, her face turning from desperation to one devoid of expression. It was the face of the woman who had birthed Death himself from her womb, and Makaria swallowed thickly and took a step back.

"I am power." Nyx's voice had dropped an octave, trembling with the weight of her abilities. "I am not all things to all people. My powers were crafted before the dawn of time with a specific purpose. Do you think that ending the world in a crushing wave of obsidian darkness, blacker than anything you've ever seen, would help?" Nyx's words were cruel, but they were calculating, and Makaria's cheeks blushed with shame. Her eyes were downcast, and she shook her head. Nyx seemed to soften at that and let out a long breath.

"That is my son down there, Makaria. Thanatos, his brother, is undoubtedly struggling to hold the entire world together in the mortal realm. Do you think that a mother would hold back her own power if it would help her children?"

"No," Makaria breathed the word, full of regret.

"My powers have a very specific purpose. So do yours. Which of us do you think is better suited to this task?"

Makaria's mind went blank as she looked out over the sea of souls, a harsh wind rising from the crowd and sweeping their horrid cries over the hilltop. Her hands started to shake, but as she watched more spirits fall into the crushing waters of Styx, she felt her coin purse manifest at her waist. There was a ripple of power over her skin as her body was wrapped up in an ethereal light; it decorated her form like the folds of a peplos, illuminating every inch of her with a calming presence. At the very essence of it overlooking the carnage, the souls closest to where Nyx and Makaria were standing let out sighs of relief.

The power of blessed death, as infantile as it might be and not even yet at its full strength, soothed them like a balm to a burn.

"I... I would only add to the numbers on the river," Makaria's voice shook with nerves. As soon as she said it, there was a great rip of power that tore the ground beneath them. A dark, cavernous crack split the earth, ripping through the horizon until it stopped just short of Makaria's feet. She turned her back on the river and looked for the cause of the massive manifestation of magic, and her mouth fell open at the sight.

Hades had arrived.

The dark king of the Underworld was in a chariot pulled by black steeds. The horses had red eyes and were stomping their hooves as they ran, shaking their heads and shrieking as they shook the ground. Behind them, Hades held onto the reigns with one hand, his other arm outstretched as he pointed his bident towards the river. The god was in his fullest immortal expression, his black hair and beard almost glowing as the aura around him pulsed with power. His magic manifested as black flames, licking up his massive body swathed in a chlamys the color of pitch.

Makaria shuddered at the sight. If Hades's power wasn't so distinct and overwhelming, she'd hardly recognize him from the god she saw overseeing the council of Orpheus and Eurydice.

The cavern in the ground stitched itself together in front of the horses' pace, only ever a few feet in front of them. It looked like the chasm was racing to mend itself in the presence of the Underworld's monarch. Makaria saw a flutter of movement in the chariot and looked again, and her shock doubled.

There, standing next to Hades, was Persephone—and this was *not* the Persephone that Makaria had shared wine with. This was the queen of the Underworld, standing at the right hand of her consort. She was dressed almost identically to Hades, in the same black garments, although hers hung from her body in a himation. Her eyes were wholly black as her power ebbed and flowed in rhythm with Hades's, both of them now virtually consumed in their own flames. She had one hand placed on Hades's back, the other holding a four-tipped torch. Her face was pulled into an expression that was so coated in fury, Makaria didn't know which of the deities looked more ferocious.

"The dread queen." Nyx's voice broke through Makaria's thoughts although she hardly whispered it aloud. "I was wondering when Persephone would let that out."

A great baying sound pulled Makaria's attention back to the rapidly approaching chariot. Cerberus was racing alongside the horses, darting gracefully around their thunderous gait, alternating between a snarl and a happy, lolling tongue. It was as though the beast was all too excited to be on the war path but kept remembering he had to look fierce.

"Don't worry about the numbers on the river," Nyx commanded her, nodding in respect to Hades and Persephone. "That is not your job. Go to Greece. Help my son." The smallest ache slipped into Nyx's voice. Makaria knew that she held more concern for mortals than most, but in that moment, her position as a mother trumped all else.

Makaria said nothing and turned towards the mouth of hell, a slight trepidation in her step as it dawned on her that this was not the reunion with Thanatos that she intended to have. Her own thoughts reprimanded her swifter than any other god could.

How dare you let the fate of innocent souls and your own purpose be clouded by a trivial matter. Go now.

Makaria didn't look back at Nyx as she spread her arms out and gave in to every last bit of her power that she could access.

⊱⊱⊱

MAKARIA DIDN'T HAVE any memory of the trip to the mortal world, only that she felt a rush of euphoria before she felt her feet settling on the ground. She could sense more of her power flooding her veins, although there was still a core of it, deep within her, that she knew was still untouched.

As her vision came to, she was met with a sight that looked even more appalling than the one she had left behind. Makaria had appeared near the center of Athens, and the city was burning. All around her were the cries of the dead and dying as everything around them looked to be in chaos. She could hear the sounds of a battle happening somewhere in the distance, the echoes of swords clanging together, and the screams of men having their legacies cut short.

Inside the city walls, however, it was not war that ravaged the citizens, but sickness. There were grotesque bodies leaning up against walls and hunched together, the cries of mothers as their children wept inside stone houses. Try as she might, Makaria couldn't get a singular idea of what exactly the people were suffering from. One man ran past her in a final burst of phrenetic energy before he collapsed a few paces past her, covered in what appeared to be burns. Another woman had a sick, wet cough, that speckled her own chiton with blood as she choked for air.

There was no order to be found amongst the sickness, not even the uniformity of maladies. Makaria thought that her heart had already been broken beyond its mortal capacity, but the sights and sounds around her proved her wrong as it splintered further. She forced herself to look around at the hellish afflictions before her, to command her body into action. The majority of the dead had not died, their shades hanging onto their immovable bodies, crying out for relief. In these moments, however long they lasted, there was only suffering — stuck between two worlds, neither living nor dead, endlessly staring at their own mortality.

Makaria did her best to focus, but the sight filled her with agony, and it was hard to distinguish the deaths that were meant for her. The sheer number of shades that were crying out to her, from all over Greece, seemed to wash over her senses and threaten to drown her. She felt panic begin rolling in her stomach and took a long breath, wrestling with it in an attempt to push it down. She glanced around at the spirits in her immediate vicinity, looking past them when she saw that none were marked with glimmers of her power. None of them called back to her, and she forced herself to move her feet.

As she walked past those souls, each step splintered her heart further. The shades recognized her as a goddess of death and wept. They pleaded as she stepped past them, begging for the release only death could bring, for its peace and serenity.

Makaria started to cry as she walked down the street, ash beginning to fall from the sky as the barren landscape cracked beneath her feet. She reached the city center as the panic in her stomach exploded throughout the rest of her body. Makaria fell to her knees. She let her head fall back, and she screamed at the sky.

"How?" Her voice cracked as desperation flooded her cries. "How am I supposed to help when I am so limited? So small?"

A gust of wind swept through the city, nearly tossing Makaria on her back. She wavered but immediately jumped to her feet, recognizing the presence of another god, and not just any god, but Thanatos.

He landed a few paces from her with a force that shook the city. His body was glowing with fierce power, each muscle locked into a battle stance that had been honed over a thousand years. His grip on the scythe in his hand was so tight, the weapon's handle had splintered, but the cracks glowed with his blue power. Makaria could tell that Thanatos was barely keeping himself together; his whole body thrummed with force. She felt his power all around them in the air, but the casualties still covered Greece from end to end. It was a scale that she had never seen or heard of before, and it looked like no extension of Thanatos's power could cover it.

When Thanatos turned his head and saw her, she felt it. She could see it in his eyes, even as he pulsated with strength and power.

The God of death was tired.

26

The silence that stretched between them was not silence at all. The world around them had descended into madness. Makaria pushed aside any lingering resentment or embarrassment that she had as she looked at Thanatos's weary face. She could see into parts of him that no one else had ever accessed before; she knew what it was like to work with the dead. He was suffering now, in what must have felt like an eternal loop of failure.

"Thanatos," she whispered, almost reverently. He tilted his head, a weakness etched onto his face that she had never seen before. The tension between them was palpable, but Makaria cut through it as the desperation in his eyes broke her further. She thought that there was nothing else within her that was capable of shattering, and every minute in this mortal world, turned into a pit of hell, was proving her wrong.

"Makaria," Thanatos groaned, his knees wobbling despite his posture as the picture of strength.

Nothing else mattered to Makaria, and she ran to him, throwing her arms around his as she launched herself at Thanatos. He let out a sharp cry that sounded like it was a mix between relief and pain, sinking to his knees as he hugged

Makaria in his arms. He dropped his scythe as his arm went around her back, the other cradling her head. There were a million things unspoken between them, but none of it mattered now, there was just the ache that only a death god could understand.

Makaria held onto Thanatos for as long as she dared, but the scenery around them was too horrific to get lost in him. She gently pulled back from him and cupped his jaw, running her fingers through his hair as she looked into his tired eyes.

"What's happening? Can't you stop time?" she pleaded.

"I can't." Thanatos's eyes fluttered closed. He sounded tortured. "I've tried, but this disaster was caused by a god and the Fates have allowed it. Those influences are keeping me from freezing time."

Makaria's brow furrowed, and she shook her head in confusion. "I don't understand. There was a god's weapon with Sisyphus and…"

"It's not linear," Thanatos cut her off. "The chaos and the games of the gods don't always make sense. Not even to me." His voice turned resolute as he slowly got to his feet, Makaria detangling herself from him.

"I came to help, but I don't know what to do." Makaria felt her voice shake with more unshed tears, and she cursed herself, hating how weak her voice sounded when they needed all of the strength that they could get. Thanatos slipped a finger under her chin, tilting her gaze up to his.

"You came." He sounded reverent.

"Of course." Makaria was unamused. "We have quite the conversation ahead of us, but nothing…nothing gets in the way of what I am." She felt her power escalate in its intensity. "Of what we are."

Those words destroyed Thanatos and rebuilt him a mere second later; it ripped through his defenses and choked his doubt. Everything that he had built up in his mind—that no one would be able to do this job like he could and that no one, not even Makaria, could love death incarnate—was eradicated with those four words.

They were the same. The heady acknowledgement of that hung between them, each second more perilous than the last. Makaria seemed to realize what she had said almost a full minute later, sucking in a short breath and covering her mouth with one hand. She turned and tried to glance away from Thanatos, but his hand shot out and gently rested on her shoulder. The feeling of his warm skin on hers almost overwhelmed her, even though it was the simplest of touches, and she balked at the devastating degree to which they had been so obtuse.

"What *we* are," Thanatos repeated the words slowly as if he was savoring every second it took him to say them. Makaria nodded, standing up taller. She let out a small, pleasantly surprised gasp when the sickle appeared in her hand. The smallest trickle of power rushed over her, a small taste of a little more of her abilities rising to the surface. Thanatos must have sensed it too, and he smiled.

"We'll talk," Thanatos promised, another rush of the sounds of war breaking over the city walls and catching his attention. He cursed. "We'll talk about what happened—"

"You mean when you left the morning after the best sex I've ever had without a word?" Makaria couldn't help but bite back a little, wanting him to feel the weight of how that had made her feel. Thanatos flinched like he had been hit.

"Yes, about when I left... Wait..." He smirked. "The best you've ever had?"

"You want to focus on that so I can stroke your ego *now*, of all times?" Makaria sucked on her tooth and made a scoffing sound in astonishment. The ease between them was already returning; even with everything that had happened, it was too familiar to be in Thanatos's presence. It felt too good, and he felt the same. After lifetimes, both mortal and immortal, of trying to find their places in the world, the other person was too much of a safe harbor for them to ignore. Their power was reaching out to one another again, coaxing and alluring, eager to get to work side-by-side.

"No, no, not now," Thanatos picked up his scythe, "but I will never forget that you said it." He winked at her before sobering, taking a few steps backward as he shook out his shoulders. He leveled his gaze at Makaria.

"I need you." The words were quiet, but full of strength as Thanatos said them. They were a little fucked up, and they both knew it. There should be more screaming and yelling; it should be impossible for them to simply fall back into each other without talking about it, without more time. As Makaria studied Thanatos, the sky red behind him, she realized that she didn't care—and neither did he. There wasn't an ounce of reservation in his statement as he acknowledged her. The need that he had for her wasn't just one of lust, as he had proven, but one of totality.

They needed each other. Their power was cut from the same cloth. There were dark parts of their hearts that only they didn't turn away from. She would probably toss a few harsh words his way later to make him grovel, but as she stared at him in the chaos, Makaria realized that she was still very much in love. Thanatos already was.

This went unspoken between them, but not unknown. It seemed to click into place as their magic sang. Thanatos lit up with dark blue flames that caressed his legs while Makaria glowed with a heavenly aura around her that made her look more angel than goddess. Understanding flowed between them like water, as if their consciousness reached out to the other's and pulled them into the knowledge of their affections, insecurities be damned. Makaria felt another wave of her power dance over her skin, and she flipped the sickle in her hands.

"I don't need you." There was a surprising amount of affection in her voice as she said it, and Thanatos understood. It filled him with warmth. He understood what she was truly saying.

He had abandoned all pretenses, accepting that needing her help was not a weakness. Thanatos knew that he was lovable, and she loved him.

Makaria had tossed aside her insecurities, letting the dark flames of the Underworld burn away any need that she had for anyone else's approval. Makaria knew that he loved her, and she loved herself.

Thanatos winked at her, and his head dropped back, his arms slowly flexing as his biceps curled. He let out a massive, whooping battle cry, and Makaria could hear the sounds of pottery breaking as it ripped through the air. His claws extended, sharp, vicious, and black, clicking against the handle of his scythe. He grew even larger as he stood in front of her, power cresting and ebbing like the flames it embodied. When he raised his head, she could see it—he was transforming once more, and the last of his shreds of control were gone. He grinned, but it was wild and unhinged, and she could see that his teeth had sharpened into fangs. As Makaria opened her mouth to respond, there was another sudden surge of power.

Thanatos let out a scream of satisfaction as two behemoth black wings ripped free from his back. Makaria's mouth fell open. They were glorious, each one nearly as long as Thanatos was tall, stretching out on either side of him. The wings were covered in luxurious feathers as dark as the night sky, looking as soft as they did strong. Thanatos shook his wings out, ripples of power flinging from them as they moved. He turned his head to Makaria and smiled, all of the former exhaustion wiped from his face. If she had been mortal, Makaria would have gone to her knees before him. If it weren't for the apocalyptic dystopia they currently stood in, the immortal Makaria would've probably gone to her knees too.

This was the angel of death.

The god who stood before her now looked truly wicked. His face was frightening, and his power was almost absolute. He had wings and fangs and claws, and he looked back at

Makaria with an expression that was more beast than man or god. This creature had been created for one purpose and one alone, and that was death.

Makaria wasn't frightened.

Thanatos held a hand out for her, and she stepped towards him, sliding hers into his grasp. As his hand closed around hers, Makaria could tell that he was still being careful to not scrape her with his talons.

"This is who I am." Thanatos's voice had changed. It was now even deeper and darker, a low sound that Makaria knew mortals couldn't hear. "This is what I am. Does it frighten you?" Thanatos tilted his head and asked her point blank. Makaria forced herself to wait before responding, searching every part of her heart. She found not a single reservation residing there.

"No." Her answer was clear, and Thanatos's smile widened. He released her hand and stepped back, surveying the scene around them like a general at war. He turned back to Makaria. "Do your job, Blessed Death." It was a command as much as it was an encouragement. Makaria nodded back once in agreement. Thanatos ruffled his wings and with a swift kick up from the ground, shot off into the sky. A wave of his power ricocheted off the surfaces around them, and Makaria saw several shades get cut from their bodies and disappear to the Underworld in response.

Thanatos looked like the true harbinger of death, his silhouette striking and terrifying against the blood red sky. Makaria looked on for a moment longer, unable to turn away, until the sickle in her hand turned cold. It froze over in an instant, so cold that it almost burned, bringing her attention to it.

There was someone calling for her.

Her nearly sentient powers had been elusive with her again, but now they roared to life. It was an echo of Thanatos's strength, but it did not reflect that she was weaker. Her power was like the moon and his was like the sun, both playing off of one another and reflecting their radiance to the other. Makaria was overwhelmed with the voices that called out to her, and unlike earlier, she could see the shades that were marked blessed.

They cried out to her. Their distress gripped her, and Makaria took off at a run. She moved through the city at lightning speed, her white hair glowing in the dark chaos like a beacon. It trailed down her back and flicked across her face as she ran, moving as swift as Artemis through the forest. She held the sickle in one hand and deftly freed souls from their torment, their cries morphing into ones of relief as she moved through the city like a benevolent scourge.

She could sense Thanatos flying above her, commanding the shades of the dead from his vantage point in the sky as Makaria swept through those on the ground. She didn't know how much time had passed as they worked together, flares of their magic encouraging each other. They moved in a dance of brutal mimicry, sweeping through the city and the sky as one entity. Everywhere that Makaria's feet touched the ground, a coin appeared in her footstep.

Her power picked them up on the wind and sent them off with the shades of the blessed while Thanatos snapped his fingers and sent the additional tokens straight to Charon. In a time like this, every exception must be made, including those of burial rites—although the fare of passage across Styx could never be waved.

As Makaria finally reached the city gate, she was gasping for breath. She braced her hands on her knees and sucked in lungfuls of air, trying to rally. After a minute, she looked out upon the new hell that greeted her.

While a plague was ravaging Athens, war had come to its doorstep. Humans were panicky creatures, and unsure of what to do about the sudden, disastrous illnesses, armies and battalions had fallen on one another in revenge. They blamed other gods and their devotees that people had worshipped too much or not enough. It made a bad situation even worse.

Makaria felt Thanatos land behind her. A moment later, his hand was on her back, and he nodded out towards the carnage that raged on before them.

"Can you go on?" His voice sounded ragged again, and Makaria looked up at him in confusion. Thanatos's face was solemn with fatigue again, and his wings seemed to be shaking in exhaustion.

"How… How much time has passed?" Makaria was still trying to catch her breath. Thanatos ran a hand over his face.

"It's been three days."

"*What?*" Makaria shrieked, but it came out more as a choking, gasping sound. She could have sworn that their sweep through Athens had taken an hour, maybe two.

"This is what happens when you give yourself entirely over to the call," Thanatos informed her delicately. "It's also why we typically are granted the ability to stop time because we can lose track of it if we aren't careful. Death never stops."

"And in a situation like this…" Makaria's mind whirled as she tried to comprehend death and all its intricacies.

"Yes." Thanatos tugged Makaria closer. She sank into his embrace, feeling exhausted and overstimulated all at once. They allowed themselves a few moments of respite before Makaria pulled out of the embrace. The sun had gone down in the mortal realm, and while the plague still ravaged Greece, the human battles had ceased for the night.

"We have to get answers," she said, resolved. "This cannot continue." Thanatos seemed reluctant, but not disagreeing.

"This will continue," he warned her. Makaria looked back over the city behind them, shaking her head in disbelief.

"It's not stopping, Thanatos. I don't think we made any measurable progress in *three days*. We have to see what's happening in the Underworld."

Thanatos let out a melancholic sigh, but he nodded and held out his hand for her.

"I know." Makaria kissed his cheek sweetly as she accepted the small embrace. "It hurts me to walk away from this too, but it's the only way we can get to the bottom of this. We need to find out what's caused this and—"

"Strike at the head." Thanatos finished her sentence, his power shifting to carry them to the Underworld. He looked around the grief-stricken atmosphere as they faded away.

"I will bring death to whomever is responsible for this. The Fates be damned."

27

Thanatos and Makaria arrived in the Underworld and were greeted by the sounds of an immortal argument. Hades, Persephone, Nyx, Erebus, and Hecate were all standing on the hilltop near Styx, and powers and tempers were flaring. Makaria had never felt so much strength in one place before, and it almost sent her reeling. Thanatos wrapped an arm around her waist and guided her towards the group.

"Thanatos." Nyx's hand covered his heart as she crossed the gap between them, hugging her son tightly before doing the same to Makaria. "I'm glad you've come." Her voice was tense. Makaria got the distinct sense that Nyx was hedging her bets that whatever the argument was about, she was assuming that they would side with her. She escorted them the short distance back to the group, where they were greeted with a myriad of acknowledgements and short nods. Makaria found herself in between Thanatos and Hecate, with Hades on Thanatos's other side.

The gods were quiet, looking at each other with tense expressions. There was a camaraderie amongst the gods of the Underworld that the Olympians didn't have. Otherwise, they would've already descended into a war of their own. Instead, they found themselves trapped in an argument on the hillside.

"Go on." Erebus looked at Hades, apparently encouraging him to catch Thanatos and Makaria up to speed. Hades pinched his nose between his thumb and forefinger while Persephone moved closer to him and scowled at Erebus.

"This is Apollo's fault," Hades uttered simply. Makaria's eyes went wide as her breath caught in her throat. She could feel Thanatos go rigid next to her, his temper flaring at the mention of the god's name.

"Of course it is," Thanatos growled as his power spiked. "He's been insufferable since the Dionysia festivities began."

"Before that." Hecate scoffed, her arms crossing over her chest. "*Fucking* sun gods."

"Apollo used the Golden Bow."

"Fuck," Thanatos muttered, rubbing a hand over his tired eyes. Makaria didn't understand what it meant, but Thanatos's reaction told her everything she needed to know.

"He fired plague arrows into the crowds of Dionysia," Hades continued recounting stoically. "Pan called Poseidon because, well, never mind. That's not important. Poseidon was the first one at the scene. He showed up not long after he arrived at Styx to tell us."

"What does that mean?" Makaria couldn't keep herself from asking. She still felt too in the dark when it came to some of the matters of the gods.

"The Golden Bow was given to Apollo, and the bow's twin, made of silver, belongs to Artemis." Persephone leaned forward, filling in Makaria. "While Artemis's silver bow is said to kill without pain, Apollo's is the opposite. Whatever the intention he imbues behind it, it is designed to maximize strife. The plague strikes each mortal man differently, and as you already know, that chaos has pushed humans to war in their confusion."

"How do we stop it?" Makaria turned to look at Thanatos,

searching his face for answers. He shook his head slowly, but it was Erebus who answered her.

"We don't. Once an arrow has been unleashed, it will run its course unless the same magic user, Apollo, or the magic's twin, Artemis and her silver bow, stops it."

"Is that why we can't stop time?" Makaria chewed on her lip as a sense of desperation washed over her.

"Yes." Erebus sounded like he was ready to go to war. His eyes glowed like lit embers. He seemed to be the one who was having the hardest time containing his powers. "Anything that would get in the way of the curse is inhibited."

Makaria let out a short breath through her nose as she grappled with the truth of what lay before them. Thanatos was still tense next to her, staring at the ground as if he was running through a million different scenarios. She watched as he tried to solve a seemingly unsolvable problem, and her heart went out to her lover. The rage that had been contained inside of her broke like a seal.

"Who the fuck gave Apollo that kind of power?" Makaria snapped accusingly, staring at the circle of gods and looking at each of them in turn. As soon as she said it, she almost wished that she could take it back. The arguably most powerful gods in existence were all part of the Underworld, and she had no business accusing them. There was a dreadfully long minute of silence before Hades burst out laughing.

His dark curls shook and fell in his face as he knelt over at the waist, triggering the same reaction from the rest of the gods. Makaria stepped a little closer to Thanatos, a small, awkward smile on her face. She could sense that he was chuckling under his breath, trying to hide his laughter, and she gave him a sharp elbow to the ribs.

"She's not wrong." Hades was the first to regain some of his composure. He looked at Makaria, a warm smile on his face that was almost in drastic opposition to the severity of his presence. "Zeus gave it to him, and yes, we all put up a fuss about it."

"What has caused the strife between you?" Thanatos asked, looking between his friends and his family. Hecate stepped forward, her lips pulled into a thin line.

"Hades wants to, and let me make sure I quote you effectively," she tossed a glare Hades's way that only Hecate could get away with, "*Rise the scourges of hell and invade Mt. Olympus until every last ally of Apollo, mortal or immortal, is beneath my heel, in my realm where they belong.*" Hecate snorted. "Did I get that right?" Hades only growled in response, but Persephone rubbed small circles on his chest, and he seemed to back down.

"Some of us think that a full-out war between the gods," Nyx calmly interjected, "would probably make the situation worse."

"A war between heaven and hell," Makaria murmured under her breath, feeling almost nauseous with the severity of the conversations she found herself having these days. Thanatos must have heard her, and he leaned down and whispered in her ear.

"That's a shitty heaven."

Makaria snorted, and the other gods turned to look at her, but she waved them off as they continued to argue.

"Stop." Thanatos held his hand up, and Makaria was surprised to see how quickly they all listened. "I would agree that we can't go knocking on Olympus's gate, but someone needs to die. I'll admit my biases." Thanatos crossed his arms over his chest. "This is about Apollo. Either we get him to reverse it, or we null his power." Thanatos turned to look at Makaria, as if he knew that she was about to ask what he meant. "That means I get to kill him."

"I thought you didn't kill people. The Fates did." Makaria teased him, and Thanatos winked at her.

"You're getting caught up on a technicality."

"She does that," Nyx chimed in, not unkindly.

"This is very sweet," Persephone waved her fingers in Thanatos and Makaria's direction, "but we need a plan."

"Where is Apollo?" Thanatos asked.

"We don't know." Hades was grinding his teeth together with such force, Makaria thought he might break his own jaw. "Poseidon is out searching with everything at his disposal, the rivers, the streams, everyone."

"He'll find him." Thanatos calmed slightly. "Apollo can't avoid water. In the meantime, we'll go back. Keep working." Some of the exhaustion returned to his voice, and Makaria was embarrassed at her hesitation.

"You can't keep up at this pace," Nyx interjected.

"It can't kill me," Thanatos snapped, his temper wearing thin again.

"No, it can't, but think of Makaria. She's not a true immortal yet, so she can't go on forever like you can. Besides, it can't kill you, but it can make you tired. It can ruin you. What if you made a mistake?" Nyx knew that she was pushing a very sensitive wound but did it anyway. Thanatos almost snarled at his mother.

"I would never."

"You don't know that. We haven't seen anything on this scale that requires death to work so tirelessly."

"It's true," Hecate chimed in. "And…I'm sorry to say, but it's not even working. You are both running yourselves into the ground, and it's hardly making a dent."

As much as Thanatos and Makaria were loath to admit it, the gods were right. Makaria stepped closer to Thanatos, and he grabbed her hand, his thumb rubbing small circles. The gods were quiet until Hades stepped forward, snapping his fingers twice.

A rush of power left him, and Makaria could see the dark wave of influence go rushing down the hillside. He looked at Thanatos carefully, as if he was evaluating him.

"Do you trust me?" Hades's voice was somber. Thanatos

looked caught off guard, but he only hesitated for a second before nodding. "Do you?" Hades looked at Makaria.

"If Thanatos does."

Hades nodded, finding this answer acceptable. "We're going to have to get a little…creative," he chewed on the word, "but I have an idea."

There was a sudden burst of cold air, and six wraiths appeared behind Hades. Makaria let out a small shriek and jumped backwards, Thanatos wrapping his arms around her and pulling her back to his chest. The creatures floated off the ground, their faces obscured by long, black cloaks that hung in tatters. Their very essence was cold, but it was devoid of any particular sense of malice.

"The 'god of riches' can be interpreted loosely." Hades had started to grin deviously. "If you consider your power to be a treasure to you, Thanatos, I can store part of it in the wraiths. They can be like living containers, if you will. It won't work in perpetuity because they can't hold power for long, but they can sweep over the mortal realm and attempt to keep up while you rest."

Makaria seemed to get more confused every day with the rules of the gods, but that was apparently part of it. The gods bent things to their will every day. Thanatos agreed eagerly.

"Let's do it."

The immortals of the Underworld came to agree on a loose plan. Thanatos would allow Hades to send the wraiths out in his place while he and Makaria slipped off to his home for whatever break they could manage. Poseidon would hopefully find Apollo before much longer. When he did, there would be a hunting party that Artemis herself couldn't rival.

Makaria watched as Thanatos very literally handed over a semblance of his power to Hades; it was a dark, glowing sphere in his hand. Makaria, not being fully immortal, wasn't able to contribute in the same way. It seemed painless, and the wraiths absorbed the magic and disappeared as soon as they had come.

The other gods began to filter away, and a new wave of exhaustion rolled over Makaria. Thanatos was right there as her knees buckled, his arm going around her waist. He kissed her brow gently.

"Let's go, please," Makaria murmured. Thanatos's response sent pleasant shivers down her spine.

"If there's any peace to be found tonight, I'll find it next to you." She felt his power cover her like a warm blanket. "I'll take you home."

Makaria could barely hear Persephone tossing a salacious, playful whistle over her shoulder as the two gods of death disappeared together.

※※※

When they arrived at Thanatos's home, Makaria realized that they were in his bedroom. The space was palatial in size although it was almost entirely empty. There was a massive pallet bed in the very center, low to the ground and covered in a myriad of luxurious cushions. There was a tall, marble column at each corner that went up towards the ceiling, and a leopard's pelt was tossed across the end.

"I think you're the first person to ever be in here." Thanatos voice was a low, sultry murmur behind her. Makaria leaned back into him as she felt his hands on her shoulders before he started trailing down her arms.

"I love what you've done with the place," she commented drolly, noting the absence of additional furniture or decoration. She felt Thanatos shrug and shivered as his lips kissed the base of her neck.

"You can do whatever you'd like to it. I admired the changes you made downstairs."

"Mm," Makaria murmured before turning around in Thanatos's hold so they were face to face. "About that night…"

"I'm sorry." The words tumbled out of him before she could say anything else. Makaria dipped her head slightly before leaning forward and placing it on his chest.

"I know."

It might have been too soon. It was probably more than a little fucked up, but Makaria didn't have it in her to care anymore. Everything had changed in Athens for them. Words wouldn't do it justice. It would only cheapen what their magic had said to each other, how they had wormed their way into the core of the other person's being.

They stood there for another minute before Makaria picked her head up. She stood up on her tiptoes and cupped Thanatos's jaw, kissing him with a feral need she didn't know existed inside her. Thanatos was gasping for air when he pulled back, his hands frozen on her waist.

"You're going to need to stop that if you want to get any actual sleep." His voice was tense with need. Makaria turned around to face the bed as if she was weighing her options. Thanatos thought that she was indicating she'd rather sleep until she ground her ass against him. Makaria's hands went up into his hair as she pressed herself closer to his body, sending him over the edge as his erection stiffened under her ministrations.

"Bed." Thanatos bent down and murmured the directive in her ear, biting it gently as he did so. Makaria's body was shaking with want, the close proximity forcing their baser instincts to the surface. It didn't matter how tired they had been or that the world was ending all around them. Their time felt more precious than ever, and this was the only way they would spend it. Makaria moved on command, her body responding almost before her mind did. She knelt down to the mattress that was nearly on the floor, and Thanatos almost snarled.

"I want you naked for me."

Makaria paused for a second, keeping her eyes straight ahead before she undid the ties at her shoulders. Her peplos fell down around her ankles, and she stepped out of it and onto the mattress. Thanatos let out a groan as he stared at her naked body in the low light of the room, her power still giving off a subtle glow around her. It illuminated her skin and made her look like moonlight.

"I want to sink my teeth into every inch of you." Makaria jumped as his voice was suddenly closer, his massive body moving dangerously silently for a god so huge. "How do you want it, my love?"

She flinched again as she felt Thanatos's hand come around her waist, the other drawing small designs across her belly. His fingers slowly trailed upwards until they were circling her breasts, cupping them in his hands. She sucked in a sharp breath, feeling arousal flooding between her legs.

"Do you like being touched here?" Thanatos pressed against her back. He was naked too, and Makaria squirmed at the feeling of his hard-on pressed against her. The entire sensation of his body, corded with muscle and tense with arousal, was a pulsing heat against every inch of her.

"Yes," Makaria whimpered, her head falling back against his shoulder.

"Good," Thanatos chuckled darkly, his hands groping her breasts. She shifted, trying to get more, more, *more*, and he had barely touched her. He pinched her nipples between his deft fingers, eliciting more wanton sounds from her with each caress.

"Please." Makaria was begging now, and she didn't care.

"How do you want it?" Thanatos asked again, the obvious arousal in his voice only matched by the strength of his affection. He continued his assault on her breasts as one hand trailed down her body, slipping through her wetness as he explored her. "Oh, my," Thanatos grunted, "what a needy little goddess."

Makaria circled her waist and ground her ass against his erection, and Thanatos cursed.

"What a needy god." Makaria sing-songed in retort, but her breath hitched a second later as Thanatos slipped a finger inside of her. He slowly started to work her over with a devastating rhythm, until Makaria was practically riding his wrist. Each undulation rocked her against his dick, overwhelming Thanatos as his hard cock was trapped in between their bodies.

"Don't make me ask a third time," Thanatos warned, sliding a second finger in.

"—hard!" Makaria gasped at the intrusion, crying out a second later when he pulled his hand away. "You mother—"

"Get on your hands and knees," Thanatos grunted, taking a step back from Makaria and trying to catch his breath. He was harder than he'd ever been in his life, and he hadn't even been inside her. Makaria nearly fell into position, dropping down onto the mattress. She arched her back, her legs sliding further open as she practically mewled into the sheets.

"Please," she begged again. Her whole body felt as tight as a bowstring. Thanatos got down on his knees behind her, his hands stroking down her sides before palming her ass. He traced one hand down to her clitoris, giving it the lightest of touches that had Makaria squirming as he gathered her wetness on his fingers. He dragged his finger up until he was gently probing her backside. She stiffened for only a second until Thanatos was whispering in her ear, his entire body bent over hers.

"One day," he was purring, "I'll take you here. I promise, goddess, I'll be the one you call blessed."

Makaria let out a wanton moan, dropping her head and biting the sheets. Thanatos straightened up, one hand gripping her waist as the other firmly grasped his cock. He worked himself over a few times, desperately trying to not come over her back, although he nearly did at the thought and stored that away for later. He slicked himself down with Makaria's wetness and guided himself forward until the head of his dick probed her entrance.

"I can take it," Makaria was almost crying as her body vibrated with the need of him. Thanatos pushed forward ever so slightly, just barely breaching her as he let go of himself and slid his other hand to her clit.

"Mmm." Thanatos sounded like he was weighing his options. "I don't know if you can." He made slow circles on the sensitive nub. Makaria's legs shook, and Thanatos used his knee to knock her legs a little wider. Makaria went down on her forearms, the sudden, subtle friction of the sheets against her stiff nipples driving her to mania. "You needed a little help last time, lover." He was toying with her, his voice simultaneously full of dark command and affection. Makaria nearly screamed in frustration before she pushed back up on her hands and knees.

In one rocking motion, she thrust herself onto Thanatos's cock, taking all of him inside of her at once. He let out a shout, falling forward as his hand moved from her waist to catch his weight. He was pressed against her now, her entire body flush against his. All he could focus on was the tight, hot heat that enveloped him, and Makaria nearly wept with relief as her walls spasmed around him.

That was all that it took, and Thanatos began rocking his hips against hers, thrusting wildly. They gave themselves over to every primal instinct that inhibited their darker hearts, content to fuck one another to death if that was what it took to get the edge off—even though neither of them had ever felt more alive.

"Such a good girl," Thanatos growled in her ear, "taking all of me like that."

Makaria glowed brighter at that, her bright essence swallowed by the dark tendrils of Thanatos's power. Every inch of Makaria was filled with him, claiming her, and Thanatos poured each bit of his soul into her. He took her the way he wanted to on the floor of his hallway, rutting like wild animals. They were perfectly in sync as they rocked against each other, panting and crying out when the pleasure became almost too much.

Makaria's orgasm took hold of her, and she collapsed on the mattress, all of her strength drained from her body. Thanatos finished with a shout that shook the walls, barely able to keep from falling on top of Makaria. He pulled out with a groan, Makaria whimpering at the loss as his release dripped down her legs. Thanatos fell down on the bed next to her.

Makaria cracked one eye open, her face pleasantly flushed, and was met with a warm, sated smile from Thanatos. He looked gentle, almost coy, a far cry from the god that had just nearly fucked her senseless.

"My turn," Thanatos murmured softly, pulling Makaria into his body.

This time, he cradled her to his chest, holding her against him like she was precious. Makaria fell asleep surrounded by the infamous Thanatos, the scourge of the gods, purring like a kitten in her ear.

28

When Makaria woke, this time it was to soft kisses as Thanatos trailed his lips across the contours of her face. She smiled without opening her eyes.

"This is a vast improvement to the last time I woke up after having sex with you."

"Oof," Thanatos made a mocking sound as if he had been wounded, "I deserved that one." He whispered the words against her hairline, his arms tightening around her.

"Why are you waking me up?" Makaria groaned sleepily against Thanatos's chest.

"Poseidon found Apollo." Thanatos yawned, sounding exceedingly casual. Makaria's eyes flew open, and she pushed away from Thanatos as she stumbled to her feet. She found her clothes at the edge of the bed, tying the garment around her body with frightening speed.

"Thanatos!" Makaria turned around and saw him still lounging on the bed, one arm bent behind his head. The sheets were rucked around his waist, and she couldn't help but drink in the sight of him. "I'm sorry," Makaria crossed her arms. "Does that not feel like relevant information to you?"

Thanatos chuckled darkly, and in a blink, he appeared in front of her, dressed and armed with his scythe. He pointed to her sandals on the ground a few feet away. Makaria didn't even remember when she took her shoes off last night.

"I'm waiting on you," he winked at her devilishly. "Do you want to get going, or…"

"Just you wait until I get all my powers," Makaria grumbled as she hopped around, slipping her sandals on. She rejoined Thanatos, and he put an arm around her shoulders, getting ready to whisk them to the banks of Styx.

"I can't wait."

For the first time, Makaria realized that she wasn't filled with anxiety at the idea of her worthiness. She didn't flinch when Thanatos agreed with her. They disappeared on the winds, and in a blink, rematerialized on the riverbanks. The same gathering of the gods awaited them, with the addition of Poseidon. Thanatos tilted his head in greeting at the sea god, who gave him a singular nod in return.

Poseidon struck an imposing figure, broad-chested like his brothers with a reddish tint to his hair. His beard was longer than Hades's, and the cuffs on his wrist and his breastplate were made of polished coral. It was impossible to strike a more imposing figure than Hades in the Underworld, but Makaria was sure that Poseidon, on his own turf, would rival his brother.

"I found him." Poseidon was curt and to the point. "One of the river nymphs tracked him down to the Forest of Chaidou."

Hades cursed under his breath, and Persephone's lip curled. She was still in her dread form, and Makaria only then noticed the crown of perfectly petrified roses in her hair, studded with thorns.

"What's the problem?" Makaria looked to Thanatos, finding his expression tense.

"He's hiding out with Artemis," Hecate hissed. A flicker of power ran over the goddess, and she reappeared dressed for war. Her signature bracelets were wrapped around her wrists, in the shape of dog heads with open jaws, making it look like her hands emerged from their mouths.

"When was the last time anyone went hunting?" Nyx stretched her neck from side to side, swords appearing in her hands. The blades glowed with such a strong aura that the edges were blurred. It took Makaria a minute to realize that they weren't made of metal, but of pure starlight. She felt Thanatos's power emerging, running over her skin in waves that warmed her in ways that weren't entirely appropriate for the setting. There was a soft breeze, and she heard his wings reappearing from where he stood behind her.

One by one, all the gods shifted into their immortal forms, weapons appearing in their grips like extensions of their bodies. Poseidon elected to not participate, fairly pointing out that since he wasn't a god of the Underworld, it would make alliances messier if they weren't able to capture Apollo swiftly. They said their goodbyes, and the god vanished.

Hades evaluated the immortals as they stood in a circle, looking every inch the lord and master of the Underworld. He had pulled his hair back and tied it with leather, obsidian hoplite armor covering his black tunic. His bident glowed like the metal was about to melt, but it never did. With a nod towards the rest of the group, Hades put on a Corinthian helmet.

"It's time."

Persephone stood next to him and looked straight ahead. There was nothing frivolous about her as she stared into the void, her eyes black. She looked like a snake, all coiled muscle and deadly, graceful accuracy.

Hecate had a wicked smile on her face, like she had been waiting for the opportunity. Red glimmers of power danced over her skin, her peplos cut at the knees. She wore shin guards that glowed with runes, as if lit from within.

Erebus seemed to be trembling in place, itching for a fight.

His entire body was tight with anticipation, smoky shadows rolling over his skin. He licked his lips and cracked his knuckles. Makaria realized there were no weapons on his person, and he didn't need them. Those shadows were sentient and did as commanded.

Nyx held her swords of starlight and flipped one over in her hand as if she was testing the weight of it. Makaria watched in awe as Nyx's himation came alive. The constellations of Leo, Scorpius, Draco, and Canis Major started blinking to life, moving around her skirts like it was the night sky.

Makaria turned around to look at Thanatos, still soaking in every bit of him in his full strength as the angel of death. He looked ready to kill, but he caught Makaria staring and gave her a subtle wink. Makaria looked down and realized that her sickle was hanging from her waist, and her own aura was pulsing with a power that she didn't recognize. She felt like she was about to crawl out of her skin, her magic rippling under the surface like it was ready to crack her open to get out.

Hades turned around and the gods fell in formation behind him, Makaria moving instinctively next to Thanatos. They fell into a V-shape with Hades at the helm. Hades barked a command in a language that Makaria didn't recognize, and there was a great commotion that sounded like a dreadful chorus of moans of the dead. Makaria turned to see where the sound was coming from, and nearly fell backwards into Thanatos.

At Hades command, the wraiths had returned. This time, they were all riding black steeds. The beasts were the same ones that Makaria had seen pulling his chariot earlier, and she knew that they were creatures forged from hellfire. A second later, a great snarling sound ripped through the groans of the wraiths, and Cerberus pushed his way through the legs of the steeds. He stood nearly as tall as Makaria, and a pack of lesser hellhounds followed him. Cerberus took his rightful place behind his master, and the gods spread out.

"Stay close to me," Thanatos leaned down and whispered to Makaria. "We're all a little…unpredictable like this."

"No one would hurt me, would they?" Makaria looked up in horror. Thanatos shook his head.

"Never intentionally," a Corinthian helmet similar to Hades's flickered into place on Thanatos's head, "but the gods of the Underworld are about to abandon their humanity for the hunt." He didn't elaborate, and Makaria understood.

Hades raised a hand and flicked it towards the cavernous mouth of the Underworld's entrance.

The gods were on the move.

▶▶▶

Thanatos's power wrapped around Makaria and helped buoy her as the rulers of the Underworld emerged from the mouth of hell. They took to the sky at a breakneck pace, racing through the heavens on their way to the Forest of Chaidou. Makaria did her best to avoid glimpsing down at the mortal world below, knowing that she would still only see chaos and destruction ripping it apart.

She had never felt power like this before. There was such an influx in the skies, she thought that the heavens themselves might rip under the pressure. Hades was at the front of the war party, flanked by Persephone on one side and his guard of wraiths and hellhounds on the other. Cerberus surged forward with a haunted baying howl, breaking in front of Hades and picking up his pace. Each of the dog's jaws snapped in a different direction. He had found the scent.

Thanatos had fallen in behind Hades, his great wings extending from his back. Only their eyes were visible from their helmets, shining with the black and blue power of the Underworld. Even the stars seemed to move out of the way.

Nyx and Hecate followed behind, the goddesses grinning at one another like they were going to a party instead of a god-hunt. Hecate let out an undulating cry that ripped the sky open, and Makaria watched in fascinated horror as the moon disappeared inside the tear. The stars shined brighter in response, and Nyx laughed darkly in encouragement. Hecate raised a brow at her as if to say *'your turn'*, and Nyx's whole body rolled. She shrieked, and the constellations ripped free from her skirts.

They expanded in the sky, their massive, celestial forms becoming more solid as they raced alongside the troupe. Makaria looked at them all—the lion, the scorpion, the dragon, and the dog, as their growls and howls joined in the dread symphony. The entire world shook with great tremors of power, the horrors of the Underworld blanketing the heavens. They pulled the moon from the sky, brought the constellations to life, and rode with wraiths. From horizon to horizon, the earth was blanketed with the powers of hell. The few mortals who were distracted enough from the sickness on earth to look up at the sky thought that the world was ending.

Black ghosts with no faces lined the clouds, on horses with glowing red eyes. The gods of the Underworld ripped through the sky with their presence, dressed for war. They raced across the skies, the hooves of the horses shaking the stars as the roars of beasts cried out with the call for blood.

This was no battle, not a casual hunting party.

This was a wild hunt from hell.

Every immortal in the heavens looked like a bringer of the apocalypse.

Cerberus howled again as they spread out across the sky over the forest. They had arrived. Hades raised one fist in the air, and every creature went deathly quiet, from the hellhounds to the dragon made of stars. The immortals spread out across the acreage, splitting up and swimming through the nighttime clouds as they set up a perimeter around the wood. Thanatos still held Makaria close to him as they swooped over the treetops, moving out towards their edge of the forest.

"Are you okay?" Thanatos asked her gently, his voice quiet and tense. Makaria nodded in response, not wanting to make any additional noise. Thanatos's eyes crinkled, and she knew he was smiling at her underneath the massive helmet.

"Do you guys get together and do this often?" Makaria jested, and Thanatos shook with silent laughter.

"*Thanatos.*" Makaria startled as she heard Hades's voice in her head. Thanatos turned his head in the direction of the last place he saw Hades, and Makaria realized that he had heard it too. "*Go to the mouth of the wood. The beasts will flush him out like an animal for slaughter. We will run him into your arms.*"

There was a ripple in Thanatos's power that somehow, Makaria knew meant that Thanatos was laughing silently in glee. They floated down through the trees, arriving on the inside of the forest border. The trees still encompassed them on all sides, but Makaria could sense the open meadow behind them just through the branches. Makaria gripped her sickle with one hand, a righteous fury settling into her veins as they waited.

This was the part of hunting that no one talked about. You didn't think about it until it was happening, and then it consumed you. There was more waiting during a hunt then there was hunting.

Makaria stepped closer to Thanatos, and he extended his arm and grabbed her hand. The sounds of the wood began to change. The soft, nighttime echoes of nocturnal birds and scurrying mammals faded away. In the distance, Makaria could hear the sounds of the hellhounds and the shrieks of the wraiths, chiming off in different sections of the forest.

They were growing closer.

The atmosphere around them thrummed with anticipation. The waiting was making Makaria begin to sweat, and she started to feel excitement pooling in her gut. Her energy shifted as her power spiked, feeling more bloodthirsty with each passing moment. The echoes of the dogs and the screams of the horses rang out through the night sky, even closer this time. Makaria felt her body fight the temptation to lurch forward and go after them.

Her fingers began to twitch. She started to lose her grip on reality as her vision condensed to a singular point, staring at the horizon. The sounds started to get louder, coming from both sides, and then a battle cry cut through the animalistic shouts.

"They've found him," Thanatos growled, his voice a low, gravelly rumble. Makaria felt every muscle in her body go tense. She let go of Thanatos's hand, brandishing the sickle. Next to her, Thanatos flipped the scythe in the air, and when he caught it, he now held one in each hand. The couple dropped into a crouch, mimicking each other's movements without thinking. They even started breathing in sync, two halves of the same whole. Their power came from the same, holy source. It surged inside Makaria, and she felt it knitting her even closer to Thanatos, filling her with strength.

A handful of the massive pine trees in front of them snapped in half, all of them toppling to the ground in one movement. Without thinking, Makaria launched herself into the air, brandishing her sickle high above her head. She had a terrifyingly striking silhouette against the dark wood, her white hair as bright as fire. As she swept through the air, she didn't notice that her eyes turned from gray to black and claws ripped through her fingertips.

The only thing that Makaria could see was Apollo.

He had emerged from the broken trees, breathing heavily. He was wearing a torn tunic and pteruges; it looked like he had abandoned his bronze breast plate and helmet in favor of speed. Apollo looked insane, his eyes wide and bloodshot as his face was split open in a manic grin. His whole body twitched as the thundering of hooves and the shouts of the other gods echoed from behind them.

Apollo looked up just in time to see Makaria baring down on him. She landed on a fallen tree trunk, further cracking it in half. Apollo pulled his bow from his back and strung it, aiming the arrow directly at Makaria's heart. She was unfazed at the sight of the weapon, flicking her wrist as the sickle morphed into a longer broad sword.

"Apollo!" Thanatos's voice shook the air.

Makaria and Apollo both turned to look at him, diving towards them from the sky. Without a word, Apollo's smile twisted from manic to cruel, and he released his arrow at Thanatos.

Makaria's world stopped.

Everything was ripped away from her. Nothing else mattered besides Thanatos. Makaria released a blood curdling scream and kicked off from the ground with a force that sent Apollo to his knees. Thanatos didn't change his descent or his path, intent on keeping Apollo's focus—and his weapons—on him instead of Makaria.

As the Goddess of blessed death screamed, a ferocious, burning fire ripped through her back. She pushed through the air as power pushed its way violently through her skin. Massive, serpentine wings erupted from Makaria's back, with thin, sinuous membranes that glowed like mother-of-pearl and equipped with deadly talons.

Makaria hardly noticed the change, leaping directly in front of the golden arrow's path. As her wings settled and her teeth sharpened into fangs to match her consort's, the cursed arrow of Apollo struck her through the heart.

The fully immortalized Goddess of blessed death started to

fall, her winged body blocking Thanatos's view of Apollo on the ground.

The last thing that Makaria saw was Thanatos ripping off his helmet midair, his face contorted in rage and pain.

Then everything went black.

29

Makaria's head was pounding. She slowly returned to consciousness but refused to open her eyes. The pain in her temples ebbed slightly, and she flexed her fingers and toes before wiggling her legs. Nothing seemed to be broken. The last thing she remembered was an intense fire in her back and Apollo's crazed eyes.

What the fuck happened?

"She wakes!"

"—wakes!"

"—wakes!"

A trio of voices startled her, jolting away from the sound as she blinked her eyes open. She was back in the Underworld—she could sense that much—but she was in a cavern that she didn't recognize. There were dripping stalagmites all around the perimeter as well as a small trickle of water running through the small space. The ceiling was low, but in the very center was a massive cauldron hanging over a green fire. The firelight was dim, but it illuminated a massive tapestry that spread across the walls.

Makaria couldn't make out what was on it, but it looked like all of the depictions on the banner were moving. She tried to follow it to find its edge until her eyes landed on a small loom in the corner. It was unassuming, but it glowed with golden thread. It hummed with a power so intense, she could hardly look at it for more than a second.

Oh my gods.

Makaria knew where she was. She sat up straighter as face dawned in recognition.

"She knows."

" — knows."

" — knows."

The disembodied voices were coming from everywhere all at once. Makaria stood up slowly, realizing that she couldn't stand up entirely without hitting her head. She watched with utter fascination as the Fates materialized in front of her. They were in their true forms—young women of unparalleled beauty, most notably with all of their eyes and teeth, contrary to the legend.

"Fates!" Makaria almost immediately dropped back down to her knees. "You honor me with your presence." She grappled to find a sense of composure. The Fates, so often on the receiving end of ire, were subject to flattery.

"I like her."

" —like her."

" —like her."

The sisters' triple voice echoed as they took in Makaria, studying her like she had answers to their questions written along her body. Clotho spoke first, without the sisters' echo.

"I have to admit, I was rooting for you from the start. Your thread changed so often, sometimes I thought it would shake itself free from the loom."

Makaria raised her head, her face still painted in an expression of shock. "My t-thread?"

"Yes." Clotho smiled at her. "We were so glad that Nyx took the path of making you immortal. I knew that you would do it from the start, but then again, did I?" This was apparently very funny to Clotho and her sisters, who giggled like they had a naughty secret. The joke was lost on Makaria, but that felt appropriate for a conversation with the Fates.

"Am I... Am I dead?" Makaria couldn't help but spit the question out, clapping her hand over her mouth as the query escaped. Clotho looked at her with warm eyes.

"You can speak freely here, child. And are you dead? That depends entirely on you."

"Me?" Makaria squeaked, pointing to her own chest. The Fates all nodded in sync, walking over and plucking a gold thread from the loom. As they brought it back over to Makaria, she could see that the thread was glowing so brightly, it looked white. Its essence was familiar to her, and Makaria realized that was because it was the story of her life—the Fates held her thread in their hands. To their point, however, it had not been cut.

The edges of the thread looked like they had been singed and cauterized, but not cut.

"When you jumped in front of Apollo, there was no fear in your heart." Atropos's voice sounded older although the triplets looked identical. "You had never been surer of yourself in that moment. You leapt without wings, somehow knowing that you would catch yourself."

Makaria fell backward, dropping into an awkward sitting position. She hadn't even fully realized what had happened, but the Fates were right. Makaria felt her power, the power that had been bubbling in the deepest part of her, surging to the surface as they waited for Apollo at the edge of the wood.

In that moment, Makaria had a mission. She had loved ones to defend, and she was more than capable. She had ridden alongside their hellish hunt and not felt fear, she had helped soothe the streets of Athens until she lost track of time. Makaria had dared to fall back into Thanatos's arms, recognizing their places alongside one another and choosing to forget the sins of their past.

She had done all of those things because she knew that she could. There had been anxieties, yes, but nothing stopped her from pushing forward. She had chosen herself. Makaria made herself worthy the minute that she and Thanatos stepped onto the streets of Athens together—it had simply taken her powers a little longer to catch up.

Of course, she wasn't in the streets of Athens anymore. She wasn't even in the forest. She had pulled her own wings from her back and flew straight into Apollo's arrow. Makaria sucked her teeth and made a *tsk* sound.

"Terrible luck with that arrow then, I guess…" her voice trailed off, looking between the sisters. She didn't know what they expected of her or where to go from here. Her heart ached when she thought of Thanatos. He would be fine against Apollo, but if she didn't return… It was his loneliness that consumed her. The idea that he would sink back into the hollows of history, sacrificing himself on the rumors and bad will of other immortals.

The sisters giggled again at Makaria. Lachesis held the thread out towards her. The goddess looked at her with wide eyes, not daring to move a muscle.

"The magic in that arrow is a god-killer," Lachesis murmured with a voice like silk. "I suppose it's a good thing you're a goddess."

Makaria's heart skipped a beat. She held out her hand cautiously, slowly reaching for the thread. The sisters nodded in encouragement.

"Go on." Clotho grinned.

"Why?" Makaria asked, brimming with curiosity.

The three sisters turned and looked towards the loom, where a thread had started to vibrate. It was silver.

"That's why." Lachesis grinned. Makaria didn't know what it meant, but again, she didn't feel like pushing her luck any further. Atropos winked at her when her fingers finally closed around the thread.

"Of course, sometimes we just play favorites."

"Honestly," Clotho nodded in agreement, "can you imagine if Thanatos gets any more morose? We have to work with him all the time, and he can be *such* a downer."

Makaria was only half paying attention, her gaze transfixed on her own golden thread of fate. It slipped through her fingers like imported silk, moving like water over her skin. A few seconds after she held it in her hands, it evaporated. The thread disappeared in a small cloud of golden, sparkling magic. Makaria let out a terrified squeak, looking at the Fates.

"I didn't do anything!" She held her hands up in surrender. The sisters only nodded solemnly, all of their heads moving in sync. The lower half of their bodies started to fade away.

"You can do everything now."

"—-everything now."

"—-everything now."

"You control your own fate."

"—own fate."

"—own fate."

Makaria watched, dumbfounded, as the Fates disappeared. Their voices echoed on the wind until Makaria was alone. She sat in silence, trying to absorb everything that the Fates had told her.

"Oh!" Clotho suddenly reappeared in front of Makaria, startling her. "I almost forgot. You're needed elsewhere." Clotho snapped her fingers, and before Makaria could respond, the earth tilted, and everything went black again.

ᚹᚹᚹ

EVERYTHING WAS WARM. So, so warm. Makaria found herself shimmying closer to the source of the heat, making her melt down to her bones in a thoroughly pleasant way.

"Makaria?" There was a choked gasp above her. Makaria blinked her eyes open, adjusting to the light. Compared to the firelight of the cave, it was too bright. It took a few seconds as she squinted against the harsh intrusion, then she saw a head silhouetted against the blue sky. She blinked again and refocused her vision until Thanatos's face came into view.

"Makaria?" he asked again, gently shaking her as his hand cupped her cheek. She immediately leaned into the embrace and made a satisfied sound. "Can you hear me?"

"Yes..." her voice was stunned but strong.

Makaria felt a ripple of energy run through her body as everything started coming back to her. They were still on the forest floor, but now she was in Thanatos's lap. She looked up at him, her brow furrowing at the sight of his panicked face. Makaria leaned up and kissed him softly, and she felt his whole body relax underneath her. She sat up straighter as Thanatos's hand went to her back to help her sit, and she took a good look around. She could see the rest of the Underworld immortals dotted around the tree line in various positions. They were watching intently but seemed keen on giving Thanatos space.

There was a muffled shouting noise that caught her attention. Makaria turned her head to the left and jumped to her feet. She moved so fast that she shook slightly, but Thanatos stood right behind her, a steady presence behind her.

Apollo was sitting on the ground, his hands bound behind his back and a gag in his mouth. The bonds wriggled across Apollo's arms. Makaria thought that they had tied him up with snakes until she realized that it was Erebus's shadows. Apollo's eyes were still murderous as he fought against the bonds. His vision narrowed as he let out what was undoubtedly a string of curses in Makaria's direction.

Makaria turned around and looked up at Thanatos. He

looked concerned, but mainly relieved. His eyes had lost some of their glow, and his claws had retracted, but his glorious wings were still spread wide. As Makaria turned back to Apollo, her balance felt off. She realized it was because *she* had wings too. They were different from Thanatos's; his were much larger and covered in feathers, while hers were sleeker and looked more like bat wings.

"What happened?" She shook her head in bewilderment, trying to catch up to a myriad of sensations at once.

"I could ask you the same question." Thanatos scoffed, a little disbelieving. "When you charged Apollo, I watched as you..." His voice hitched. "You changed into your immortal form, your *permanent* one. I thought that was the least of my surprises until you jumped in front of that arrow and your wings ripped from your back. I couldn't even react to that piece of information because this fucker," he kicked some dirt in Apollo's direction, "shot you in the heart."

"Well," Makaria cringed sheepishly, "technically, he shot you."

"About that," Thanatos slid a finger under her chin, "we're going to have a long discussion about the whole self-sacrificing routine. When I saw you fall, I... I thought I knew pain, but seeing you in that moment made me realize that I hadn't even tasted it. I won't ever watch you do it again. Do you understand me?" Makaria could only nod, and Thanatos pulled her tight and pressed a kiss to her forehead. He couldn't hold back some of his tears, and her eyes filled all the same.

"Ahem." Hades stepped towards them, emerging from the trees. "I don't mean to cut this short although I can't help but think there's a better place to do it, but we do have a god to handle." Hades was looking quite pleased with himself, carrying his helmet under his arm.

Thanatos gave Hades a curt nod. "It will be handled."

That seemed to be enough for Hades, who looked at the other deities and waved his finger in a small circle, signaling their departure. One by one, each of the immortals dissipated. The wraiths and the hellhounds turned to dust where they stood, vanishing back to the Underworld. Thanatos looked towards Apollo and then Makaria.

He slowly pulled the armor off his forearm, revealing the skin beneath it. Thanatos held his breath for a moment before dropping the metal piece and waiting. Makaria stared without blinking. They waited for the Fates, for the command to appear on Thanatos's skin.

Slowly, ever so slowly, the words appeared in blood.

'Apollo relinquishes the curse or he dies.'

Thanatos let out a relieved sigh, and Makaria did the same, her hand going to her chest.

"Makaria, look…" Thanatos pointed at her arm. She gasped as the same message appeared on her, written in bright, red words.

'Apollo relinquishes the curse or he dies.'

"Why?" Makaria's brow furrowed as she shifted her gaze from Thanatos to Apollo and back again. Thanatos was overwhelmed but slowly stared to smile.

"I think it means that…either of us can do this job."

"That doesn't make sense." Makaria started to rebuff Thanatos but stopped.

She thought back to the conversation she'd had with Hypnos, which felt like an eternity ago.

She remembered her and Thanatos joking about the death of Narcissus on the riverbank. Makaria started to laugh, sounding both amused and shocked.

"I think," she looked up at Thanatos mischievously, "that we can decide whatever we want when it comes to who's blessed." Thanatos thought for a second, and a devilish smirk appeared on his face.

"I wasn't sure the Fates would give us that one," he mused, "but that's true. Is someone blessed with goodness, or have they been blessed by evil?" Thanatos crossed his arms over his chest as if he was deep in thought. "That's a heavy question. The Fates have us debating morality now." He rolled his eyes although his tone was full of mirth. "I knew this was what getting a partner would do to me. I used to just show up and take the names, now I have—" He was cut off by another string of angry, muffled curses.

"Oh!" Makaria turned towards Apollo. "I forgot he was here, honestly."

"I did too, lover. Don't worry about him."

"You were getting a little caught up on the technicalities there, sweetheart." Makaria was in a rather pleasant state of shock, even with a raging Apollo squirming around at their feet. He screamed again, looking like his eyes were going to pop out of his head.

Thanatos looked down at Apollo, his expression hardening. "I need you to shake your head, yes or no. Will you rescind the curse willingly from the mortal realm?"

Apollo began shouting so violently that spit soaked the gag, dripping down his chin. He shook his head with force, screaming and muttering incoherently. Makaria felt a chill go down her spine at the realization of what they were going to have to do.

"Shall I?" Thanatos looked at Makaria, and she nodded. She would not look away, no matter what happened.

Thanatos pulled his scythe from his belt, and with no ceremony or final last words, raised it above his head. As he prepared to cut Apollo's shade from his body, Makaria caught a flicker of silver light at the corner of her vision. She turned her head, following the light, and watched as a tall, lean goddess stepped out from behind the trees. She was glowing with silver power, a matching silver bow at her shoulder, and her brunette hair tied in braids.

Artemis. Makaria's thoughts were jumbled, but she remembered the Fates and the glowing thread. Before she could think twice or react, Makaria whipped the sickle out of thin air. She cut down with striking speed and accuracy, striking at Apollo's shade.

Thanatos looked at her, stunned but impressed, and dropped the scythe. Makaria turned towards the forest, raising a brow in challenge. Artemis was hidden from Thanatos's view by a tree, but she stared directly back at Makaria. Her face was frozen in a calm fury.

"*God killer.*" Artemis's cold voice filled Makaria's mind. "*I will not rest until Olympus knows of you, Makaria, Goddess of blessed death, god killer, destroyer.*"

"*It has a nice ring to it.*" Makaria was laughing internally as she smiled towards the stoic hunter. "*Be sure to tell them where to find me.*" She watched as Artemis curled her lip in a snarl then leapt off into the trees and disappeared into the forest.

Makaria had only been a fully-fledge goddess for a few hours. She knew that Artemis would ruin her Olympian reputation before she even had a chance to form one. When she had seen Artemis on the edge of the clearing and saw Thanatos about to strike, that silver thread broke through her mind.

She couldn't let another god watch Thanatos and see only cruelty, ignoring the nuances of the tableau before them. There didn't need to be any more rumors about her angel of death.

Makaria knew herself better than anyone else, and she knew that she was worthy.

No reputation would ever matter to her beyond the one she held for herself. She had grabbed the sickle and finished Apollo, rather unceremoniously after all had been said and done, and made sure Artemis was watching. There would be no mistaking who had killed the sun god.

Thanatos put his hand on Makaria's shoulder. "What was that?" He looked off into the wood, but Artemis was long gone.

"Don't worry about it." Makaria smiled, wrapping her arm around Thanatos. "Should we do anything about him?" She nodded at Apollo.

"No." Thanatos shook his head, gently guiding Makaria as

they began walking out of the forest. "Artemis lives in the forest. She'll bury him."

They walked in silence until they reached the meadow surrounding the forest. As they emerged into the bright, morning sun, Makaria could sense on the air that Apollo's magic had been repealed. The balance had been restored to the world with one strike—which in the end, seemed a pretty fair deal.

"What are you thinking about?" Thanatos asked her softly, his expression content as he walked alongside her. Makaria looked up at him, her eyes full of adoration as she saw the joy etched into his features.

"I'm thinking…" she drew out her words, "that you should take me home."

"Home?" Thanatos repeated, a soft blush rising on his cheeks.

"Home." Makaria smiled, and Thanatos bent down and kissed her fiercely. When they broke apart, Makaria was giddy.

"Take me to *our* home."

The God of death swept his lover up into his arms, disappearing on the morning breeze and carrying them back to the Underworld. As they traveled through the heavens, their power coalescing with one another, the earth sensed the shift.

In Thanatos's receiving hall, the second throne shifted on the tides of new power. It moved forward on the dais so both thrones were side by side, never to be moved again.

30

After witnessing the chaos that a god could incur firsthand, Makaria wasn't surprised to see how swiftly the gods could sweep their messes under the rug. The rest of the Olympians had discussed the death of Apollo at length, but in the end, their own egos won out. Apollo would've let Greece burn, and if the humans were vanquished, who would worship them? Of course, many of them had borne witness to the assembled forces of the Underworld's dread hunt and weren't keen on declaring war. Poseidon had pulled the short straw of moderating that conversation and visited the Underworld to tell Hades that he owed him.

Hades laughed at this, only to have Persephone agree with Poseidon. The speed at which Hades caved would've been legendary if it were not already common knowledge that nothing happened these days without the dread queen's approval.

As soon as Apollo had been vanquished, his magic was eradicated. It shocked Makaria how quickly the world righted itself. They had passed through Athens on their way back to the Underworld. The city looked like nothing had happened.

Those that had died, however, had a choice. They had

become citizens of Hades as soon as they entered the Underworld, but he struck a bargain with the Fates. Anyone who had died as a result of Apollo's actions could choose to return to their mortal life. Makaria was surprised at how few spirits wanted to return, but Thanatos assured her that was normal. Dying was a traumatic process, and being reborn wasn't easy, either. Many people had been reunited with loved ones or had been renewed with purpose for their next incarnation and preferred to wait it out. Either way, the balance of life and death had been restored, and now there were two gods to see that it stayed that way.

Thanatos and Makaria unleashed their power, ushering shades to Styx in the background while they returned home. They didn't leave the estate for three days, which was the longest break that Thanatos had ever taken. It had only taken a special kind of motivation to keep him in bed.

Makaria rolled over, slipping an arm over Thanatos's waist as she laid her head on his chest. Her favorite spot was the hollow in between his neck and shoulder, where she found that she fit perfectly.

Thanatos let out a low grunt as he stretched his arms, shifting underneath her.

"It's time to get up, lover."

She could tell from his tone that he was smiling, but she kept her eyes closed, tightening her grip.

"No... It's so early."

"You don't even know what time it is. Besides, I thought you were becoming more of a morning person." Thanatos chuckled, tracing her cheek with his finger.

"I lied," Makaria snorted. "That was when I was trying to seduce you."

Thanatos laughed at that. "You were trying to seduce me?"

"For the love of the gods," Makaria scoffed, sitting up and looking down at him. "You can't be this obtuse, Thanatos. Yes!"

"For how long?" Thanatos cocked his head as if this was the first time he had entertained the possibility.

"I mean... I was into you as soon as I saw you at the Dionysian party on Olympus. Once I realized who you were, obviously, things got a little tricky, but I was still very much into you."

"You're kidding." Thanatos looked dumbfounded.

"How could you be this ancient and so thick?" Makaria scoffed playfully. "You realize now that I love you, right? Just making sure?"

Thanatos pulled her back down to him and kissed her fiercely, tangling his hands in her hair. He broke the kiss with a sigh. "Yes. It's one of my favorite things about you."

Makaria smiled. "Now I have to know... When did you realize that I liked you?"

Thanatos shrugged, "I'm not sure. I knew I loved you after that first night we were together, probably before. I think only then I realized you might be interested too."

Makaria shrieked, collapsing into amused shock. "It wasn't when I sucked your cock in a field?"

"Eh." Thanatos shrugged. "You never know."

"You... never... know." Makaria repeated his words back to him with an awestruck grin. "You surprise me, God of death."

"Come on." Thanatos kissed her nose. "We've got a job."

Makaria sat up a little straighter as he got out of bed, pulling on his clothes. It wasn't often that there was a shade that required their personal attention. Technically, they could let their powers run over the mortal world forever, and they wouldn't have to do a thing. Neither Makaria nor Thanatos liked the idea of being so disconnected, so they didn't do it often.

"Why didn't you say so," Makaria slumped back over her pillow and rolled over. "You can handle it."

Thanatos chuckled darkly. He bent down over the bed,

now fully dressed, and trailed his lips up her exposed back. "Please. I'll make it worth your while."

Makaria shivered and peeked at him. "Are you attempting to seduce *me* now?"

"No." Thanatos straightened up with a spark in his eye. "I think we've established now that the seduction has occurred. I am, however, explicitly attempting to bribe you with sexual favors."

Makaria burst out laughing and sat up, shaking her head at him as she navigated around the room and got dressed. Thanatos was waiting for her by the bedroom door, taking her hand as they exited.

The couple yawned in sync as they walked down the hallway, getting closer to the receiving hall. They looked at each other in amusement, poking their heads into the great room before they left. There was Hypnos and Hesperus, each sitting in one of Thanatos's thrones, while poppy petals fell gently from the ceiling. The estate had been dramatically transformed since Makaria's arrival, even though Thanatos had put his foot down about some of the changes—he was still the god of death, after all.

"Brother!" Hypnos clapped his hands as the couple stepped into the room. "I'm so glad you're here."

"In my house?" Thanatos cocked an eyebrow, his voice stern but without malice.

"To be fair," Hesperus pointed a finger at him, "you didn't use to spend a lot of time here."

"That's true," Makaria whispered. Thanatos feigned shock. "Whose side are you on?"

"The side of logic." Makaria shrugged, slipping up the dais and greeting Hypnos and Hesperus with hugs. Thanatos felt his heart warm at the sight. She had fallen in quickly with his entire family and had somehow managed to bring them all closer.

"I was just taking in the sights," Hypnos held his hands out and indicated the second throne, "and basking in my incredible foresight to get you two of these."

Thanatos grunted. "Aren't you due for a nap? Isn't there some insomniac scholar somewhere dying for your presence?"

"If they're dying, that's on you."

Thanatos growled in response as Hesperus and Makaria started laughing.

"Oh, give it up." Hesperus winked. "Everyone knows your 'moping death god' routine is over."

"It most certainly is not!" Thanatos crossed his arms over his chest and almost pouted in response.

"It is." Makaria grinned sweetly. "I do think I have to take some of the blame for that though."

"First Hades, now Thanatos," Hypnos hummed. "What is the Underworld coming to?"

"Where are you headed off to?" Hesperus cut off his partner before Thanatos could respond. The gods of death both opened their mouths to respond, and when realizing they didn't know, they looked over the words that reappeared on their arms.

"A man in Thebes named…Oedipus," Makaria answered. Thanatos's and Makaria's expressions both started contorting in horror as Oedipus's story flashed before their eyes. Thanatos opened his mouth to speak, but Makaria cut him off.

"No, no, no!" She pointed a finger at him. "That is *not* blessed. This one is all you."

"That man has been blessed with a curse! An oracle predicted all of this, certainly, that falls under the 'blessed with unfortunate information' territory."

"I'm not doing it!" Makaria argued. Yet, both of the gods started to leave the hall together, still going back and forth about who was responsible. Hypnos and Hesperus watched their retreating figures with affection, listening to the debate.

"There is nothing blessed about *sleeping with your—*"

"I disagree! It's been blessed by a lot of evil, clearly. You think that's normal…"

Their voices faded away as they disappeared to Thebes, still arguing but neither refusing to go. The lines would never become fully apparent as to who was responsible for what, but it didn't matter to Makaria and Thanatos. The rest of the gods certainly never cared. They had found something that worked for them, as imperfectly perfect as it was, and the rest of the world was all the better for it.

There were still days when Makaria doubted herself. Even being a goddess and a consort of Death himself couldn't eradicate that entirely. But those days were fewer and farther in between.

On occasion, Makaria would sense that Thanatos was pulling away—typically after a period of things going exceedingly *well* for them. He still grappled with the idea of receiving love and affection, to which Makaria responded by violently dragging him back from wherever he had gone to sulk, threatening to lock him in a cabinet. Thanatos would respond by locking them in their bedroom instead.

The burden and blessing of death was now shared. The woman who had become a goddess found life in death, and Death himself had found life doing the one thing he swore he'd never do.

Death and his consort were one.

EPILOGUE

Eurydice was dead. Death was supposed to be peaceful. If it wasn't, at the very least, it was supposed to be an ending. Death was finite. It was that finality that ushered in a sense of stoicism, even if peace was too great of an ask. All of Eurydice's problems started after she died—the first time *and* the second time.

Dying took a toll on a person. It was why you were only really supposed to do it once. She had never been an overachiever in life, but in death she was apparently determined to be an outlier.

In life—and in death—Eurydice was a nymph and a daughter of Apollo. She didn't know her father very well, and he hadn't ever made himself known to her. Most of Eurydice's life had been spent in the forests of Greece, spending time with the other creatures of the wood—her sisters, the tree nymphs; her cousins, the river nymphs; her friends, the fauns; and her best friend, Pan.

She had never stepped out of the woods until she had heard Orpheus's lyre. Eurydice had always loved music above all else, which was what brought her out of the trees and towards the poet. The rest of the story told itself.

Their love affair had burned like a flame. There were even times when Eurydice wondered if she had been bewitched, but everyone around the couple had been so encouraging.

"Oh, *he's so dreamy, Eurydice!*"
"*You're* so *lucky, Eurydice!*"
"*He loves you so much, Eurydice!*"

On her wedding day, Eurydice met her father for the first time. Apollo, having had a falling out with Orpheus and no paternal attachment to his daughter, decided to strike back at Orpheus through her. He had taken the form of a terrifying wolf, chasing her into the field where Asclepius's serpent had been hiding in the grass. The snake bit her, and Eurydice died.

The Underworld wasn't unpleasant. Everything happened so fast that Eurydice didn't have much time to let it sink in. The entire process had felt like an out of body experience because it was. Charon was perfectly polite to her. The judges —Rhadamanthus, Minos, and Aeacus—sent her to Asphodel. It wasn't until she was walking aimlessly through the fields that Eurydice realized... She wasn't upset. Shouldn't she be sadder? Wasn't it the greatest of tragedies for young lovers to be separated before their time? Weren't people afraid to die?

The first time that Eurydice died, she felt nothing.

She didn't know how much time had passed when she was summoned to an audience with Hades and Persephone. It had only been a few hours since her death, but it could've been days for all she knew. The *nothingness* of her afterlife existence consumed her. The last person that she expected to see attempting to bargain with the God of the Underworld was Orpheus.

He had been enamored with her—everyone had told her so —but this? Eurydice took his side and embraced her husband. She filled her head with love and desperate hope because she was supposed to, right? The bargain was struck, and Eurydice followed Orpheus out of the Underworld. She was comforted by the deal. Maybe she felt confused and empty because she wasn't supposed to have died. Her thoughts were determined as she followed dutifully behind Orpheus.

This will fix things. I'm only confused because I wasn't supposed to die. Orpheus loves me. Orpheus loves me. Orpheus loves me. I love...

The second time that Eurydice died, she felt everything.

For a brief moment, the warm rays of the sun kissed her face. She could smell the forest, her precious forest, and could hear the far-off sounds of her friends. She could've sworn that Pan's voice called out to her, overjoyed at her return. Then it was all over. Eurydice saw only a flash of Orpheus's eyes, and then all she saw was darkness. The clouds of Erebus obscured her vision and pulled her back into the Underworld. She didn't remember conversing with Makaria or Thanatos. When the smoke cleared, and her eyesight returned, Eurydice realized she was sitting right back in the Fields of Asphodel.

Eurydice was enraged. She was heartbroken. She was betrayed. There was nothing for her in the Underworld, only a stagnant sense of detachment. For a shining second, she had allowed herself to envision running in the woods again and swimming with her sisters. And Orpheus! They had loved one another on earth — she knew that — but now, she wasn't so sure. Everything had been taken from her, and he couldn't trust her long enough to walk in a straight line. There were no parties in the Underworld, no solstice nights under the full moon, with hours spent sipping wine and dancing with dryads.

Eurydice spent days walking in circles through the fields, running her fingers through the grass. Finally, Makaria — a goddess that Eurydice had never heard of when she was alive — took pity on her. Makaria ushered her through *all* of Asphodel, including its great forest. The sight of so many trees lifted Eurydice's spirits, and she disappeared amongst them without a second thought.

As time went on, things got better. Eurydice buried whatever she had felt for Orpheus, from love to hate. Pan even worked out a way to come visit her. No living soul could be in the Underworld, but since Pan was a lord of the forests, he argued with Hades that the forest in Asphodel counted. Eurydice wasn't sure how Pan managed that, but she assumed that Persephone had been in the room for that conversation. Eurydice accepted her fate.

Until she didn't.

Eurydice was lounging on a tree branch when she heard the news. Her lithe body was stretched out across the tree like an extension of it, the perfect picture of repose. Makaria appeared through the trees, her shining hair giving her away before she got too close.

"My friend," Eurydice said as a way of greeting. Makaria said nothing in response. Eurydice sat up straighter, frowning when she saw the empty expression on Makaria's face. "What is it?"

A beat of silence passed between them.

"Orpheus has died. He's on his way to the Underworld."

Eurydice felt everything, all at once.

———

ALSO BY MOLLY TULLIS

The Asphodel Series

Consort of Darkness

Don't miss the first story in the Asphodel series: the story of Nyx and Erebus.

Lost to Witchcraft

Hecate, Nyx's best friend, fights her heart's attempt to fall in love.

The Romanov Oracle

A fantasy stand-alone based on the story of Anastasia Romanova.

ABOUT THE AUTHOR

Molly Tullis would have picked the Phantom of the Opera over Raoul and named her French bulldog Jean Valjean. She only believes in black clothing, red lipstick, and never turns down an iced coffee or tequila. She enjoys writing fantasy, romance, or any genre with an opportunity to insert a dark-haired, morally grey man.

When not identifying as an author, she identifies as a woman with bangs, finger tattoos, and a nose ring, who can tell you what planets are making you sad.

Her DMs are always open on Instagram and Patreon (@thebibliophileblonde), and you can get information on all upcoming projects at www.thebibliophileblonde.com.

Printed in Great Britain
by Amazon